THE HEART OF THE HOUNDED

AN EDEN ACADEMY PREQUEL

GRACE MCGINTY

ALSO BY GRACE MCGINTY

Hell's Redemption Series

The Redeemable: The Complete Novel

The Unrepentant: The Complete Novel

The Fallen: The Complete Novel

The Azar Nazemi Trilogy

Smoke and Smolder

Burn and Blaze

Rage and Ruin

Dark River Days Series

Newly Undead In Dark River

Happily Undead In Dark River

Pleasantly Undead In Dark River

Eden Academy Series

The Lost and the Hunted (Prequel)

The Heart of the Hounded (Prequel)

Black Mountain Mates

Hunting Isla

For Lana,
Thank you for talking me off the ledge and making my
words better.
G x

THE HEART OF THE HOUNDED

PROLOGUE

Tonight, I cursed the human race, especially those with Y-chromosomes. Unfortunately, I wasn't a bad ass witch or voodoo queen, and I couldn't make the curse stick.

But if I could, I'd curse Pete Bukowski to a lifetime of shrivelled nuts. Maybe a micropenis too. Or maybe one of those really huge dicks that were good for nothing *and* tiny shrivelled nuts. Yeah, I liked that. No one would be able to look at him naked without laughing or running away.

I snarled into the night air. It was for Pete Bukowski that I'd ditched my natural cynicism towards teenage boys. Pete Bukowski, who'd asked me, Layla Lee, nerd and complete social pariah, out on a date and I'd been far too blind to second-guess his intentions.

Pete Bukowski, who'd thought I'd be so grateful to

spend even a minute in his popular, football jersey, beer bong breath presence, that I would gladly climb into the back of his overpriced, trash-filled SUV and do whatever the hell he asked.

Boy, was he wrong.

Just thinking about it made me angrier. Our evening picnic was really just a drive up to Hallaran Point, the local make-out spot. We'd scoffed down Wendy's, and kissed a little bit. Then he'd tried to go further and I'd said to stop. Spoiler alert, he hadn't.

What he didn't understand was that I had a lot of free time because of that pesky little no friends problem. Which meant I watched a lot of YouTube videos on how to maim a guy with three well aimed strikes.

I'd punched him in the balls and slammed out of the car in my indignation. I guess it really only took one well-aimed strike when it came down to it. I'd fully expected Pete to feel ashamed by his shitty behavior, maybe be a gentleman and drive me home. What actually occurred was Pete calling me some vile shit and roaring away too fast in a hail of mud, twigs and stones.

And so, I hated all men at this moment. Maybe I'd become a nun. Or like, a scientist so I could figure out a way to remove the need for men completely. What I would not do was cry. Instead I'd take all the anger, hurt and fear I felt right now and meld it into a ball of molten hot rage, then plot my revenge. It would be epic and probably get me thrown out of school, but by god it would be worth it.

The night noises made a deafening soundtrack to my shame, my own breathing nearly drowning out the owls and other nocturnal creatures. However, nothing drowned out the sound of the wolves in the mountains. Their chorus of howls was too loud, and adrenaline bounced along my nerves. As the howls sounded closer, my white ball of fury turned into a lead weight of fear in the pit of my stomach. I walked faster, well, as fast as my high heels would let me without breaking an ankle, and the crunching noise of my feet was a small comfort.

Until it wasn't.

With a sudden intake of breath, I halted but the crunching continued for a brief second. As much as I would have liked to dismiss it as my imagination, I knew that would be a stupid, and probably fatal, mistake. I continued walking, slowly now, my ears straining to hear the footfalls behind me. They were soft and light, obviously not human and they were coming from many directions. There was no doubt in my mind what forest creature was stalking me now.

Stopping again, I leaned down and removed my shoes. Wrapping their straps around my wrists, I shot off into the darkness towards the muted glow of the town lights and the safety they represented. Tears had started to stream from the corners of my eyes, creating cold rivers over my cheeks. They told us not to run from predators, but the other option was what? Lying down and being eaten? No fucking thank you!

A scream burst from my throat as a wolf leaped in front of me, appearing from the darkness like a vision from my nightmares. I skidded to a stop, forest debris spearing my foot. I was oddly aware of the warm pain radiating up my leg, the same way you are aware of pain when given a local anaesthetic. The wolf stood rigidly in my path, its heavy breath creating clouds of hot mist visible by the pale moonlight. I knew the rest of its pack had me surrounded, just as I knew with complete certainty that I was about to die. Frozen in fear, I couldn't cry or scream, I just stood there, staring into the eyes of the predator, listening to the rest of the pack closing in behind me.

Move your fucking ass, Layla! Despite the words I was shouting in my head, I remained as frozen as a deer.

Then the leader leaped for my throat.

Screaming, I twisted around as the animal attacked, its jaws missing its jugular target and landing the bite on the scoop of my shoulder. I swung my high heels at the animal's head, getting it in the eye with a lucky shot. The monster let me go with a yelp, but its pack mates were on me as soon as it released its jaws. A bite got me in the back of my leg, bringing me to my knees. I curled up in a defensive position, covering my head and neck as teeth tore at my bare legs. Every inch of flesh radiated pain now. More bites got my arms, my back, each tugging and tearing at my skin.

Then, almost as one, they stopped.

Lifting my head only slightly, I saw the wolves backing away from me, growling defensively. A deafening rumble reverberated through the woods and my heartbeat stopped. Was it a bear? What the hell would scare wolves that way?

My brain had compartmentalized the pain I was in, like it knew there was a greater threat that I had to run from now. Adrenaline, already heightened, made me struggle to my knees.

I looked in the direction of the rumbling growl, my gasp drowned out by the cacophony of whining wolves.

A monster stood in the clearing.

My brain struggled to comprehend what I was seeing. It looked almost wolf-shaped, I guessed. However, it didn't look like any wolf I'd ever laid eyes on, nothing like the animals attacking me. The massive creature stood on its hind legs, towering over seven feet high. Its coat was shining in the moonlight but I couldn't tell what color. Its head was slightly more rounded than a normal wolf's, but its cheekbones were high and its features pointed. Its ears were stiff and alert, and it had furred hands rather than paws, tipped in long claws.

The monster gripped an attacking wolf around the throat and hurled it into the nearest tree with bone-shattering force. I was grasping at my neck, trying to stem the flow of blood, struggling to my feet as I watched it grab another wolf by the head. One of its massive clawed hands slid into the wolf's mouth, gripping its lower jaw and snapping it off with a noise that echoed around my head.

The wounded cries of the jawless wolf seemed to stun the other pack members into stillness. The monster leaned down and snapped its neck, ending the injured wolf's misery. The rest of the pack eyed the creature warily before turning and running away with lightning swiftness.

I wobbled on my one good leg as the beast turned on me. I swayed unsteadily, clutching a rock that I didn't remember picking up, ready to fight. Unfortunately, the blackness had started to intrude on the edges of my vision, my swaying becoming more violent, until I collapsed to one side.

The jaws must have hit an artery, a distant voice in my head deduced. I was suffering blood loss. I was screwed, but it was still probably better than being torn apart by wolves. Or whatever fate this monster had in store for me.

I stiffened as the thing lurched toward me, its stride long and powerful.

Run, run, run, you stupid idiot. I really wished my legs would obey the screaming voice in my head.

Instead, I laid still as the monster came close enough to lean over me, sniffing my face and the wound on my neck. It knelt down, sniffing the wound on my arm and behind my knee as well. It plucked the stick out of my foot, the way you would pluck a pesky bone out of a piece of fish before you ate it. It stood back up to its full seven foot height and stared into my face. The thing had a hold of my arms, keeping me suspended upright so that the tips of my toes barely brushed the ground.

I closed my eyes, my breath coming in gasps as I prepared myself for the feel of its jaws on my throat. Its head lowered further towards mine, the monster's breath hot against my face.

Then it licked me.

Instead of the piercing ache I had expected, I felt the warm glide of its tongue over my wounded neck.

My eyes snapped open, but all I could see was the oddly fine hair on the side of its head. My senses started to restore themselves slowly, and I became aware of other things. There was a soft humming sound coming from the wolf-thing's throat, not quite a growl and not quite a murmur; almost like a purr. It didn't smell of mange or rotten meat like normal wolves or wild dogs. It smelled almost comforting, like the woods;

pine needles and damp leaves. However, it was its eyes that were the most startling, the moonlight making them shine inhumanly bright. They stared at me with a look of knowingness, as if he knew all my secrets and pitied me. They were like looking into human eyes.

The monster's mouth moved up to my ear. "You'll be ok now; I promise." Its deep voice tickled my face, its English perfect.

I stared at the creature, in horror and confusion, then passed the hell out.

1

F*ive years later*

I SIGHED, thinking that if I had to endure one more stare of pity then I might go fucking insane. A small, slightly hysterical voice in my head decided that it would be deliciously ironic, considering the pitying looks of my fellow townspeople were due to the death of my mother two weeks ago from a degenerative brain disease, which had gradually sent her crazy. In the end stages, she'd been barely coherent, screaming for hours in gibberish, or having moments of complete lucidity and calmly talking about conspiracy theories, my biological father, and, most painfully, about me.

She would follow these episodes with weeks of not speaking at all, just sitting there mutely staring out the window of the tiny cabin we shared in the mountains of Minnesota.

The tulle of my fluro pink tutu scraped at my forearms, and it bobbed slightly as I strode down the main street, the buckles on my biker boots clinking with each step. While I got the odd side-eye, I'd desensitized this town to my 'craziness' enough that no one even commented anymore.

I never enjoyed coming into town and tried to do so as little as possible, but when I did, I liked to live up to the reputation I had fostered. They already assumed I was crazy, due to my mother's mental illness, which had to be hereditary right? Uh, no Rita, you judgemental old heffer, not necessarily.

So, at some point in my life, I realized I had two choices. One, to watch everything I said and did, so the gossips wouldn't twist every word to fit their insane narrative. Or I could embrace it completely, becoming everything they thought I'd be and more. Honestly, it was kind of freeing to live in a way where you didn't give a single fuck about what people thought of you. Want to wear a ballgown to go grocery shopping? Do it. Want to lie on the grass in the middle of town for three hours so you can appreciate the sky? Hell yeah. Want to go out on Friday night, dressed like a Joan Jett wannabe and dance by yourself in the middle of the dancefloor like no one was watching? Fucking go for it.

But still, just being around these people was kind of hard work. This time I waited until I was eating canned beans for dinner before I resigned myself to a shopping trip into town.

It was worse this time, of course, because I was getting much more attention due to the fact that my mother's funeral had been the previous Friday, after which I had skipped the wake and headed straight out of town, ready to lick my wounds in private. The abandonment of proper funeral protocol had resulted in more than a few disapproving looks and clucking tongues from the older citizens of Roseau today, which was actually a refreshing break from the pity or condescending looks.

The line at the post office was way too long, and I held in a groan. Gloria was the only teller, and she had to get every person's life story for the gossip files before she could move on to the next customer.

The door behind me opened again, the cold autumn air chilling the back of my thighs. I probably should have doubled my tights.

A throat cleared, and Gregory Staynes from the bank stood behind me in the line. His eyes drifted up from where they were checking out my legs. Damn pervert. "Layla."

12

"Mornin' Mr. Staynes," I sing-songed in my best dazed and confused voice.

"You missed your mortgage payment. It was due last Friday." Yeah, last Friday, the day of my mother's funeral, you piece of poo paper.

I gave him a wide-eyed look. "Did I? My house elf usually takes care to remind me of those, and she said we were paid up til next month," I exclaimed in a slightly higher pitched voice, and Shit Staynes winced a little. "I'll be right over to pay it after here, Sir. And I'll have a good hard talk with Glinda. What's the point of having a house elf if she can't keep up with the mortgage payments, am I right?"

Gregory Staynes' lip curled in something between pity and disgust, like craziness could be contagious. What a fucking imbecile. Bet if I suggested that I'd have sex with him to pay off this month's mortgage payment, he wouldn't give a shit about how crazy I was, the predatory dick cheese.

I mentally rolled my eyes and stepped up to the counter.

"Morning Layla, how are you holding up?" Gloria, was fifty-something, and she'd been the post office teller here for thirty years. She knew everything about everyone. She schooled her aging features into a mask of concern, and I gritted my teeth and answered that exact question for the thirtieth time today.

"I'm fine, Gloria. Thank you for asking."

My tone was flat even to my own ears, but who cared? I honestly couldn't understand if the towns-people really thought I would lay my wounded soul bare to any person who thought to ask, or if they were just following social norms and saying what was expected.

Gloria rifled around behind the counter, retrieving my mail, and she came up holding a stack of envelopes, which all look like late reminders for bills.

I'd been hiding from that particular problem for the past month. Tanya, my mother, hadn't left behind any savings and the medical bills alone would have crippled the average person. I schooled my face into an expression of manic happiness, with a grin that stretched my face in an almost unpleasant way, as the way-too-interested Gloria tried to read me, maybe see if I was having financial problems that she could gossip about.

I leaned in close. "I'm going to have to fire Glinda the House Elf. Do you see this shit? Good help is hard to find, even with the fairies."

I pushed away from the counter, murmuring my goodbyes. There was time to consider my financial black hole when I wasn't surrounded by nosey townies.

I headed straight for my battered SUV, sighing in relief as it came into view. It had never let me down, and was the one constant in my life these days.

Striding faster towards it, I prayed that no one would stop me, but apparently, God had forsaken me today.

Police Chief Tony Hammond waved at me from down the street, his broad face turned up in a smile. He had a round face, pink cheeks and looked like a cross between Santa and every sitcom grandpa ever, so it was almost impossible not to smile back.

My face felt weird twisting into my first real smile in... hell, I didn't even know how long.

The police chief and I had a lot of history. Most of it was good. Some of it was a little more tragic. He'd found me all those years ago after the accident. I called it an 'accident' because the word attack always made me shudder uncontrollably and hyperventilate. Basically, the dictionary definition of a panic attack, but I'd never been to see a psych about what happened that night. Or what I thought had happened. There was always something there at the edge of my consciousness, something I'd well and truly blocked out, and that drove me just as crazy. It was always on the edge of my mind, like if I had a little more sanity, I could just reach out and grab it. Instead, I had recurring nightmares that I couldn't escape, always just a little bit different so I knew it was a dream and not a memory.

I'd healed quickly after the accident, at least physically. When Tony and his wife Sue had found me, my clothes had been torn and bloody and I had eight bite marks, a broken wrist and a huge bump on my head.

They'd called the hospital and the local doctor had come out to determine if it was safe to move me to the emergency room. They'd sedated me for most of the first two days, my weird ramblings and wild behavior nearly getting me thrown in a padded room, so most of my convalescence was a pleasant haze. My body healed, but the whole thing had turned me into the recluse I am today.

Then there were the rumors. They started in the hospital. I'd heard the nurses whispering as I was just coming out of my sedated slumber.

"Her neck, Tina, look at it." The voice had hissed. "She should have bled to death in minutes from those wounds, but they are already scabbed over and on their way to being scars. It's not right, not possible."

Tina, my primary nurse, had shooed the other nurse out of the room.

It ballooned from there of course, spreading like wildfire when I left the hospital. Most of the rumors were wild and unrealistic, like the one where, while bleeding to death, I had lit a fire and cauterized my own wounds with a rock from the fire. I had always laughed at that one.

Others were more malicious, the worst one was spread by the older citizens who accused my mother of child abuse. My nails dug into my palm. I always got angry thinking how much that rumor hurt her.

But teenagers? They were the worst. Teenagers

could manage to be cruel just by breathing, which was quite a feat if you think about it.

The nickname 'Chew Toy' didn't take long to catch on, and it was fuelled as much by my icy demeanour as it was by the large raw bite mark on my neck. High school was half the reason I hated coming into town now, and almost the entire reason that I wrapped myself protectively in a persona of insanity.

I caught up to Chief Tony, and he wrapped me in a bear hug.

"How are you doing, Layla?" For some reason, coming from him, the question didn't irritate me like the others had, and tears actually started to well in my eyes. I blinked them back and smiled wanly at him.

"I'm okay, Tony. It's been hard, but I'm doing alright."

He smiled back. "I bet you are getting sick of being asked that question, right? Look, Sue said that if I ever saw you in town I was to invite you to dinner. Actually, she said *insist* that you come to dinner."

Tony looked sheepish, and I could almost hear Sue's commanding tone. She could be quite compelling for a plump grandmother of eight. Sue and my mother had been best friends, before my mother's mental health had turned a corner and she'd stopped coming out of the house. Even still, Sue dropped off casseroles and meals a couple of times a week, and washed the linen for me once a month.

"I wish I could but..." I couldn't think of an adequate excuse so I just shrugged. Tony, as expected, just nodded his head and smiled sympathetically.

"I should be going now. Crime stops for no man."

"Also, the diner is only running its lunch specials for another fifteen minutes."

He let out a booming laugh, and I chuckled along. Crime in Roseau was nonexistent. It was hard to be a knife wielding axe murderer in a town where your neighbors knew what time you brushed your teeth at night.

As I waggled my fingers in a goodbye wave, I headed to my SUV and took in this tiny speck on the map that I called home.

It looked average. Small town America in a nutshell.

I got to my SUV, patting the rear passenger door as if it were a faithful horse. I would probably cry when it chugged its last breath, and that day was coming soon. It squeaked where it shouldn't squeak, and chugged when it shouldn't chug. Turning the key, it roared to life, the noise in the cabin almost deafening. It probably needed a new muffler too. I didn't mind though, the rough chug stopped me from thinking the inevitable bad thoughts.

As I sped away from town, it was comforting to know that I wouldn't have to make that journey again for another month. Hopefully that was enough time for the townspeople's memories to dim and for me to decide what to do with my life. With Mom gone, there was really nothing tying me to Roseau anymore.

I navigated the straight country roads on autopilot, my mind preoccupied with the pile of bills on the passenger seat. I knew I wanted to leave Roseau, but I couldn't. I'd planned to leave as soon as my mother died, but the time came and went and I couldn't drag myself away. It wasn't that I felt any real affection for the town of my tormented childhood. I knew I could go back to college and finish the nursing degree that I'd abandoned to care for Mom, then maybe start a nursing career at one of the major hospitals. However, the more firmly I made up my mind to go, the more I procrastinated about actually leaving.

Letting out a heavy sigh, I finally noticed the turn off to my place, the Double U Ranch. It wasn't actually a real ranch, more of a hobby farm. Its maintenance had provided an easy existence for two people, but I soon found out it was a lot of work for just one. I had a full run of chickens, two dairy cows, a horse called Monster and five acres of veggies and orchards.

I squeezed the bridge of my nose and opened the front door of the house. Fred, the Labrador, lifted his head off the rug in the living room, and gathering it was only me, promptly fell back to sleep. My cat, Pip, was more excited to see me. He was a feral kitten I'd rescued from the top of an apple tree before he was even three weeks old. That was just the kind of nature he had. Since then, he had been a mischievous little shithead who didn't take attitude from anyone, not even Monster the Horse.

After ten or so trips back and forth from the car to the house, the sun had disappeared behind the mountains and I was ready to collapse onto the couch. I had armed myself with a sandwich, a good book and the local radio station playing in the background. The snow had started up again, making the radio a little fuzzy. They were predicting a heavy snowfall, one of the first of the season, and I was glad that I hadn't procrastinated the trip to town until tomorrow.

The fire was crackling nicely, throwing off heat that was only partially blocked by Fred's position on the hearth. This was the only time of the day I ever achieved any kind of calm, where the pressures and the problems of the day disappeared with the daylight, and the dreams that interrupted my sleep were still safely tucked away.

A few hours later my legs were dead, and my eyes were beginning to droop. A scratching at the door interrupted my trek to bed, but it wasn't unusual before a snow storm. Animals knew when to seek shelter, and I had more than a few half-domesticated ones rolling around my yard. Still, I grabbed the shotgun from by the door just to be on the safe side. You never knew when you were going to get a grizzly instead of a raccoon on your front porch. Loading the shotgun, I peeked around the door, switching on the porch light to stun the animal.

At first, I didn't see anything but the inky blackness of night that lay beyond the reach of the porch light. However, the faintest noise whipped my gaze down to the welcome mat in front of the door.

I slowly lowered my gun because there, lying face down in a pool of rapidly spreading blood, was a man. A naked man.

2

A cold gust of wind broke through my shock. Leaning down, I checked his pulse, which was thready and slow, hopefully due to the cold and not due to blood loss. There was a small round wound on his shoulder, bubbling blood, which I recognized immediately from my training at college; a gunshot wound. I made a quick once-over of the rest of his body, checking for broken bones before I turned him over. The man didn't regain consciousness the whole time, not even when I began rolling him.

Once he was flat on his back, I gasped in horror at the huge puckered wound on his right shoulder, two inches too high to be fatal but it was awfully close. It was obvious that this was the exit wound to the matching entry wound on his back. He'd been shot running away.

I whipped off my sweatshirt and wrapped it around the wounds on both sides, tying it tight. Grabbing his arms, I apologized loudly for the pain he'd suffer as I dragged him inside.

"If I don't get you inside, you're going to die of exposure. I know this will probably tear your injury even more, which will definitely hurt, but you're unconscious now which I am... ugh, definitely thankful for," I grunted as I heaved him over the threshold.

He was a big man, and pulling his dead weight was nearly impossible, but I just needed to get him a few more inches to the hall rug. Once he was on that, I could drag him easily across the floorboards to the warmth of the fire in the living room.

His grunts of pain tore at my heart. The puddle of blood had created a red trail worthy of any cop show. I'd get him inside and call an ambulance. Or the cops. It would take an ambulance a good forty minutes to get out here in the snow and maybe Chief Tony would be faster.

Picking up the corners of the mat, I slid him over to the fire, nudging Fred from his spot. I unwound my sweatshirt from around his wounds, my concern turning to surprise when I realized the bleeding had all but stopped. I grabbed the first aid kit from the hall cupboard, pouring antiseptic over the wound and cleaning the blood away. My surprise turned to disbelief as the cleaned wound turned out to be no more than a quarter of an inch deep, which was normally not deep enough to cause that amount of blood loss. I bandaged up the front side, carefully examining him for other injuries, but averted my eyes quickly when my gaze accidentally travelled below the equator. Like decency mattered in times like these.

Not finding any other injuries, I rolled him gently over again and examined the wound on his back. I was positive it was a bullet wound. Maybe I had been wrong about the one on his front being an exit wound and the bullet was still lodged in his shoulder. I probed the wound with tweezers, but after a few tentative pokes, I found nothing.

What the actual hell?

I cleaned and bandaged this side, chewing my lip compulsively. There was something wrong here, and I didn't know whether I'd had a complete mental snap or if there was something... off about this guy.

One thing was for sure; there was no way I was calling an ambulance or the cops. What was I going to say? Oh, I dragged a naked guy inside because he'd been shot, but now he doesn't look like he's been shot, but he's still naked and unconscious on my floor?

Yeah, maybe not.

I grabbed a blanket and pillow off the couch. I rolled the man onto his back again, propping a pillow under his head and giving him a bit of modesty with the blanket, with only a quick peek at his family jewels because it was impossible not to. The guy was built. Golden skin, sleek muscles, one of those fun V things that made it impossible not to look lower. You know the ones.

Feeling my face flush red, I felt his pulse again, and it felt much stronger. I reached down to check his pupils, berating myself for not having checked earlier for a concussion or possible fatal head injuries. Some nurse I'd be.

I started to lift his eyelid when they jerked open of their own accord, his body shooting upright. I scrambled backwards, away from the savage expression on his face. When his eyes focused on me, his entire body relaxed with a relieved sigh.

"Layla."

The guy's eyes rolled and he fell back onto the pillow. I stood, unable to move.

How did he know my name?

I stared at his face for a glimmer of recognition, but nothing came. Covering him back up with the blanket, I sat back on the couch and just stared at the man in front of my fire.

His straight, dark eyebrows contrasted with the sandy-brown shade of his hair. His deep-set eyes were framed by thick eyelashes and he had a long straight nose. Sharp cheekbones and an incredible jawline made him look harder, stopping him from crossing that border into pretty.

He muttered something incoherent in his sleep, shifting uneasily. I checked his temperature, making sure he didn't have a fever and was just having a run of the mill nightmare. You know, the kind you had after being shot.

Slumping back onto the couch and stuffing the remaining cushion under my head, I watched my patient in case things took a turn for the worse. However, it wasn't long before my eyelids drooped and exhaustion dragged me off to sleep too.

I woke up to a cacophony of hissing and growling. My eyes flew open and I saw Pip standing on the arm of the couch, arched and fluffed, looking his most ferocious. Fred, however, appeared to be asleep next to the couch, not paying any attention to Pip's hysterics.

My eyes shot to the guy on my floor, and for a half a heartbeat, I wondered if the whole thing had been a bad dream, like the ones I had every night for the last five years. Instead, a pair of golden eyes watched me back.

"How do you feel?" I was breathing like I'd just run a marathon. His eyes never left my face, searching my features like I was a roadmap and he was lost in the worst part of town.

"I feel fine, thank you." His voice was a deep growl, and I imagined I could almost feel the vibration of it flowing through my body. Well, one particular part of my body. "Actually, I'm a little hungry," he admitted.

Yep. It was monsoon season in my pants. *Put up the shutters and anchor down the lawn furniture, Jim, because it's going to be a wet one.*

I bounded upright, my cheeks on fire.

"I'll get you something." A sandwich would have to do for now but later I'd make chicken soup, which healed all ills according to my mother. I wasn't sure it extended to gunshot wounds though. I was rambling even inside my own head now. I needed to calm my ass down.

Taking two deep breaths, I counted to ten slowly while I quickly made a bologna sandwich. When I got back, the guy was sitting up, the blankets pooling around his waist. He was stronger than I thought he'd be, considering he'd lost so much blood.

I had a million questions on my mind and I blurted out the first one as soon as I was back in the room. "How do you know my name?" His brows knitted together, his face all of a sudden stern.

"I don't know your name," he stated flatly. "What's with the tutu?"

I looked down at my blood spattered tutu and winced. Yeah, that wasn't ever coming out now that it had dried. Though, I kind of like the aesthetic it created; murder couture.

"You bled all over me last night when you turned up naked on my porch. If you don't know my name, why did you yell it out last night?"

"I'm sure I didn't."

I gave him an openly disbelieving look, but for the life of me, I had no idea why he would want to lie about such a thing. Unless he was psychic, or maybe a stalker, and he'd come here to make sure no one else could ever have me by organizing a murder suicide.

Yeah, no more nordic noir before bed for me.

Yet, neither of those possibilities explained the bullet wound. Besides, you couldn't stalk someone in a town as small as Roseau and as for being psychic, well, I wasn't sure I believed in that stuff.

Judging by the set of his jaw, this line of questioning was going to go nowhere fast.

"Fine, if that is the way you want to play it. What's your name, then? I figure if I've seen your dick, I should at least know your name."

That got a response. His bronze cheeks turned pink and he looked faintly embarrassed.

"Micah. My name is Micah. I should say thank you for patching me up, I guess." He gave me a ghost of a smile, and it made my heart thud weirdly in my chest. I ignored the sensation. It was probably too much deli meat on my sandwich. Yep. Let's go with that.

I should probably fake being crazy. People didn't

want to abduct crazy people. Too much like hard work. Pick up the easy, whimpering ones.

"You're welcome, I guess. How did you get shot anyway?" I asked as casually as I could, like I didn't give a shit about the answer, but I eyed his bandages suspiciously all the same. His gaze drifted towards his chest too and he shrugged his shoulder, wincing.

"Hunters confused me with a bear, maybe? I was out hiking and the next thing I know, I was shot. I barely remember dragging myself towards the light of your cabin."

I had to stop myself from scoffing out loud. "Hiking naked? Just before a snow storm? Bitch, I might be crazy, but I'm not an idiot."

I had seen his injuries. The gun that shot him was not a hunter's shotgun, of that I was sure. The whole thing set my teeth on edge. Micah knowing my name, the bullet wound that wasn't a bullet wound, the story about the hunters. The guy was lying through his teeth, and he needed to leave.

Micah was saved from another round of questioning by my dog barking at the door. I rushed to the window and saw the police cruiser pull up, Chief Hammond behind the wheel. I threw a quick look at Micah to see his reaction. He was completely still, but didn't seem overly anxious about the fact the law had just rolled down my driveway.

As if he knew my train of thought, he shook his

head softly. "I haven't done anything wrong. He's not here for me."

Yeah, we'd see. I shrugged on my jacket and stepped out onto the snow-covered porch to meet Tony.

"Morning, Layla. That's a fair blanket of snow we got last night."

I murmured my agreement and shut the door behind me. I wasn't sure why I didn't want the police chief seeing Micah, when by his own admission he had done nothing wrong, but I still distracted Tony anyway.

"Sure was, Tony. You just caught me on my way to feed the girls and Monster, you can come with me if you like? What brings you out here today, anyway? I can't imagine you hiking it all the way out here to talk about the weather."

Picking my way along the snow path I'd cleared the day before, I paid special attention to where I was putting my feet out of habit. One slip on a secluded farm like this and you'd bleed to death in minutes from a head wound, no one finding your body until wild animals had eaten off your face. I, for one, wanted to look pretty in my coffin.

"You're right. I just wanted to have a talk with you. You're out here by yourself these days." He broke off as he helped me ease open the barn door. The flurry of activity was comforting; chickens scratching in the straw, Gladys the dairy cow bawling her welcome over the stall door. Tony stopped my progression into the barn by putting his hand on my shoulder and turning me around to face him. His face was no longer congenial, he was in full police chief mode now.

"Layla, two people were murdered on the edge of town last night. I'm getting the Feds down here as soon as possible to lend a hand, but I'm still worried. They were found by hikers." He took a deep, fortifying breath. "Their heads cut clean off. I just wanted to tell you to be careful, okay? Sue would have my ass if anything happened to you. She's quite fond of you. Actually, I'm pretty sure she likes you better than me."

I was stunned into silence and I felt the blood drain from my face. Had Micah had anything to do with the murders? The holes in his story seemed a lot more ominous now. Regathering my wits, I smiled at Tony, even if the expression felt forced. I wanted to soothe his worries, at least about me.

"I appreciate your concern, I really do, but I'll be fine out here, Tony. However, if it will make you feel better, I'll make sure I'm in the house before dark and keep all the doors and windows locked. I'm also pretty handy with a gun, you know?" I grinned at him and waggled my eyebrows. Tony was from the new school, where women should be able to protect themselves in any way possible, so he'd taught me to fire a gun with deadly proficiency when I was still a teen.

Against my screaming better judgment, I still didn't

tell Tony about Micah and his arrival last night. Tony was looking back at the barn door again, probably anxious to get back to investigating the biggest case Roseau had ever seen.

"What would make both Sue and me feel better is if you moved into town for a bit." I was shaking my head before he'd even finished his sentence. I had too much to do out here to just leave it behind to become a townie. "I figured you'd just say no, but Sue wanted me to try. Just remember to be careful, okay?"

With that he shuffled out of the barn, looking every one of his sixty years. I made him all sorts of promises, swearing it every which way.

Then I made a liar of myself as soon as the cruiser was no more than a speck in the distance, racing inside to the man who may or may not be a murderer.

Milking the cows would have to wait. Getting the information I needed came first.

3

I marched into the house, wet boots and all, and stood in front of Micah, fixing him with my most angry stare.

"Who the hell are you? Cut the crap this time, I want to know if I'm harboring a murderer."

Micah just stared right back, the liquid gold of his eyes darkening to the color of whiskey.

"I told you, I didn't do anything wrong and I certainly didn't murder anyone."

But I wasn't having any of his vagueness this time. I leaned over to his bandages and grabbing a corner, tore it off. Even though I expected the result, I couldn't stifle my gasp of disbelief. There was no wound left, only a faint pink patch of new skin. I poked the spot and he winced in pain. *Good*, I thought with twisted satisfaction, *it still hurt*.

"How do you explain that then? What the hell are you, some kind of science experiment gone horribly wrong and being chased by the CIA?"

He chuckled low in his throat "That's the first thing you think of? You're one of a kind, Layla."

He'd unwittingly given me more ammunition. "Oh and that's another thing, how the hell do you know my name? Because I definitely never told you. You'd better start talking buddy, or I'm getting the cops back here."

He sighed, his shoulders tense. I needed to find him a shirt, or a shroud, or something. His muscles bunching was distracting me from the fact he could be a goddamn murderer.

"It was five years ago. You've probably blocked it out, but I haven't."

I registered his voice and it set off faint echoes in my mind that snowballed into an avalanche of memories.

"The accident? The... monster?" He was just looking at me and nodding slightly as if I'd made the right connection, but I was floundering and just as confused as ever.

A sad smile twisted his face. "I guess 'monster' is just as good of a description as anything else. Maybe too good." His face shuttered, and then he was perfectly neutral again. "I'm a supernatural. A Lycan-thrope to be exact. It's why I heal so well." Micah nodded towards his now healed shoulder.

I slumped back into the couch, feeling faint. "I don't understand."

I searched him for any other resemblance to the creature that haunted my dreams. He was big, but nowhere near that huge. He wasn't all that hairy either, though he had a smattering of curls across his chest and in a thin line down to his...

Yep. He needed pants and I needed to pull my mind out of my vagina ASAP. My eyes quickly darted back to his face, and he raised a perfect eyebrow. He looked nothing like the animal who had rescued me that night, but something inside me recognized him now. Maybe it was the eyes? Or the voice?

"How?" How did this man before me turn into a giant, hairy... thing?

"I can shapeshift into my semi-canine form whenever I like, however on full moons it is compulsory." He let me process that piece of information. "You caught me on one of my... compulsory nights. It was pretty lucky really, otherwise I would have been in Boston and you would have been dead."

I'd waited so long to have answers to what really happened that night, and here he sat, with all the knowledge I'd craved for so long, but my brain had stuttered to a stop.

Actually, there was one question though that had plagued me for five years, one question that had haunted my dreams even when I tried my hardest to block that night from my mind.

"What did you do to me that night, when you licked me? Was it because you were hungry, or was it something else?"

He huffed out a laugh. "I healed your wound slightly. I coagulated the blood to slow the bleeding long enough to get you to safety. It's a Lycan thing." He ran his hand over his forehead, pressing his fingers a little more firmly into his temple. He yawned and his eyes started to droop, but I wasn't finished yet. "Do you have any more questions?"

"How did you know my name? I don't think we got down to polite formalities while I was dying from blood loss."

He shrugged. "I stuck around for awhile. Made sure you weren't suffering any lasting effects from my healing. I learned your name in the process. Anything else?"

"Um, only the one I've asked a million times before; who was it that shot you?"

"Hunters, like I said. Actually, they're bounty hunters of a sort. They get paid hundreds of thousands for the life of one Lycan, more if you can get the pelt before we morph back." Micah's eyes narrowed in disgust. "As we get fewer, the reward on our heads gets higher." His explanation just bred more questions in my mind.

"What about the murdered people?" His beautiful eyes turned sad, his expression world weary, which seemed out of place on his youthful face.

"Maybe other supernaturals, or just genetically unlucky people with all the physical markers of a Lycanthrope. The height, the eyes, the immortal face, it wouldn't be the first time the hunters have made a mistake. The safest way to be sure a Lycan is a Lycan is to hunt them down on full moons. It's more dangerous though. They're more likely to end up dead in our jaws. No, bounty hunters are cowards who prefer to hunt us when we are in our weaker human form, which means innocent people die."

I breathed a sigh of relief that I wasn't harboring a cold-blooded killer. I'm pretty sure the 'he's not a murderer, he's a mythical creature' defense wouldn't really cut it when I was being tried for aiding and abetting a serial killer.

4

icah said it would be at least a week until he was at full strength again. So he puttered around my place helping with the chores, but only the manual labour. The barn animals went into hysterics whenever he went near them. When he tried to milk Gladys, she stepped on his foot, fracturing a bone. Micah assured me that it would heal fine in a day or two without being set. He also didn't seem to feel the cold, even in the middle of winter, chopping wood without his shirt on in the snow, his back muscles rippling as he swung the axe with absolutely no exertion.

Honestly, watching him do chores might have been the hottest thing I'd ever seen. Maybe I was changing my man-hating ways. I walked toward the barn to milk the cows, and wondered if this is what it would be like to get married and have a husband. Then I slapped myself on the forehead for being so damn pathetic.

"Hey Monster," I said to the horse, who chuffed back at me. "What do you think of him? Other than the whole, 'ooh he's a predator and could possibly do bad things to me' vibe you get? I mean, I get it too. Only I kind of want him to do bad things to me, and that's probably not right either."

I swear Monster rolled his eyes and I turned back to the cows. "Pfft, what would you know, you're a guy. The girls know what I mean. Sometimes you just see a guy, err bull, with a nice rump and all logical thought goes completely out of your brain."

I walked into Gladys' stall and she let out a plaintive moo. I looked over my shoulder at Monster. "See?"

Unfortunately for me, Micah was also standing there, his face stretched into a smile so wide it made my stomach do flip flops.

"I think both me and the horse see your point now."

My face flamed. Well, shit. "Uh, we were talking about, uh some other guy. From Roseau. Yeah. I better milk these cows. They aren't gonna milk themselves." I stared at Gladys' udder with so much intensity, it was a wonder the milk didn't turn to cheese.

Micah chuckled. "Layla."

I milked into the pail and pretended I couldn't hear him over the tinny clang. Slide, squeeze, slide, squeeze.

"Layla, come here. Otherwise I'm coming in there and Gladys will try to bite me again."

Yeah, Gladys wasn't Micah's biggest fan, despite her understanding the lure of a good rump.

I swallowed hard and stood, moving the bucket so Gladys didn't kick it over. For the first time, I kind of regretted pretending I was crazy. I didn't fall nearly high enough on the hot vs. crazy scale. Guys weren't willing to take a chance that I'd be fantastic in bed, if they were likely to wake up to me staring at them in their sleep. Which I never did.

Okay, maybe like once. But the guy had sleep apnea and I was honestly worried he was about to die.

I dragged my feet to where he was standing in the doorway. "Who's the guy?"

"What?"

"Who's the guy you were talking to the livestock about?"

Dammit. "Um, Brian? You wouldn't know him. He's, uh, an accountant."

No one asks questions when you say that you're an accountant.

He grabbed my wrist and pulled me closer. "Respectable job. Do you think he'll be able to provide for you?"

He'd leaned closer, and I'm pretty sure I forgot how to breathe. "Um, I think so."

Micah smoothed a piece of my hair behind my ear. "Do you think that he'll make you happy?"

I blinked rapidly. I was definitely having heart palpitations now. "Sure?"

He moved until his lips were barely an inch from mine. "Do you think he'll make your heart beat this fast? Or kiss you like this?"

Then his lips touched mine and it was... everything. The warm press of his mouth, the way his tongue snuck past mine when I gasped. His hands moved to my waist and he pulled me tight against his body.

My brain finally seemed to catch up and I kissed him back. I tried not to happy dance with my feet as I kissed him, the way you did a little dance when you tasted something yummy.

Micah was freaking delicious. My tongue tangled with his and my hands snuck up around his neck, threading into his hair and he groaned.

He gripped my ass and lifted me easily. I almost came on the spot. Isn't that every woman's fantasy? To be thrown around like a ragdoll as you're ravished by a sexy as hell man?

He pushed me against the exterior wall, and I wrapped my legs around his waist. The way the long line of his body was cradled by my soft curves was complete perfection. He kissed his way down my neck and then over the rough scar in the curve of my shoulder. It had been the only one of my wounds to scar, the rest of them had healed up like they'd never even existed. He sucked it into his mouth and I swear to god, it was like there was a golden cord from the pink flesh of that scar to my devil's doorbell. And Micah, he was ringing it like he was Quasi-fucking-modo.

I was living the dream and I didn't ever want it to stop

Then it stopped.

Dammit, I'd jinxed it.

Micah lowered me to the ground, his face looking all sorts of conflicted. "I should, uh, go back to chopping wood."

With that, he hightailed it out of there like his fluffy tail was on fire. I could sense his turmoil, his lust, his fear.

What was he scared of, and more importantly, how the hell could I feel his emotions at all?

5

I couldn't concentrate on anything else, but Micah and that kiss. I wanted him to do it again. I could feel the turmoil running through his head like a dull fog in the back of my mind. It was weird and I was pretty convinced that I'd finally lost it. Apologies to Rita, maybe mental illness was hereditary.

I took stock of how I felt. One, I was extremely attracted to him, that much was obvious, but there was something else. I had never felt much for boys or men growing up, especially not after the fiasco in the woods. I had only ever kissed two boys and been on a handful of dates. I mean, I'd gotten close with sleep apnea guy, but we'd never gotten past the Netflix part of Netflix and chill.

I'd thought that maybe I was a lesbian there for a

little while, but I didn't much like other girls either. Asexual maybe? I just didn't like people very much and had resigned myself to a lifetime of being a spinster with a thousand cats, and I'd eventually get my face pecked off by chickens when I had a heart attack in their coop. It was a real fear. They were tiny dinosaurs, after all.

Well, apparently I was really wrong because what I felt for Micah wasn't particularly non-sexual. Scratch that. It was red hot, grade A, prime membership to PornHub sexual. He made me feel things that went above attraction. I had almost spontaneously combusted when he kissed me. And I wanted more. A lot more.

My newfound psychosis told me that he was really into me as well. I poked at the weird spot in my head that I assumed was Micah. It was broody and just kind of *felt* like him.

I was trying to decide how to tell a wolf/man that I wanted him, and also that I knew he was horny for me too, as I walked through the front door of the house. I was prevented from saying anything by Micah's sudden appearance in my path.

"I'm so sorry, Layla. I had no right to do what I did."

I wasn't particularly sure why he was apologizing but I nodded in a forgiving way, unable to say anything that would even sound like I regretted one millisecond of that kiss. I felt his relief rush through my mind.

I gave him my biggest smile. "Micah, the only regret I have is that you didn't take off my pants and bang me into last century. It was the best two minutes of my life, and I'd very much like for you to do it again and again."

I felt his desire spike before he quickly squashed it. He turned and walked away from me, drawn to the roaring fire. His measured movements seemed so graceful and fluid that it was obvious he did not suffer from human frailties. He didn't have stiff muscles from all the manual labor, or a bad knee that was playing up in the snow from his glory days of highschool football.

I shrugged off my jacket and went into the living room too, moving towards the fire to melt the chill in my bones. I didn't push about our kiss. There was time for this attraction to percolate between us. I wasn't in a rush. He knew how I felt now, and I knew how he felt, even if he hadn't voiced the words.

That was a stalker statement if I've ever heard one.

I cleared my throat and changed the subject. "Tell me more about being a Lycanthrope. About you."

Micah looked over his shoulder at me, and he was so freaking beautiful that I had to clench my fists in order to stop myself from touching him.

"I was born in Persia, two hundred and fifteen years ago, give or take a few years. You stop counting your birthdays after the end of a natural lifetime. Being a Lycan is no different to being any other kind of supernatural. I guess we are most closely associated with shifters, except we can live forever. Unlike the shifters, I'm not two-natured. I'm me in either form, though I am a little more volatile as the monster."

Holy shit. I'm sure a couple of centuries wasn't an insurmountable age gap. Leaning closer to his body, I laid my head against his shoulder. He tensed, and I reached out to stroke his face. When he didn't pull away, I cupped his cheeks with both hands, pressing the tips of my fingers into the sides of his head. The shape of his high cheekbones molded into my palms, the stubble on his chin scraping my wrists. I stared so deeply into his yellow eyes that I lost my breath, finally understanding what drowning in someone's eyes actually meant.

"You're not a monster. I was wrong." I hesitated. "And I meant what I said. I want you to kiss me again, Micah." My voice faltered a little, barely a whisper. I leaned forward until my face was a breath away, waiting.

This time I would make the first move.

When his lips touched mine, they were so hot it almost burned. His hands buried themselves in my hair, pulling me closer and holding me away at the same time. I deepened the kiss, running my tongue along his lips and then darting it into his mouth before he had a chance to change his mind and pull away.

He groaned, his body shuddering against mine,

and I felt the moment he let go. He sank back onto the couch and dragged me onto his lap, his arms snaking around my waist. His hand slipped under my shirt and rubbed my lower back as he took control of the kiss. He sucked my bottom lip into his mouth, and I made a whimpering noise that seemed to snap him out of his reverie. He dumped me unceremoniously off his lap and back onto the couch.

"I need to go before the next full moon."

If I hadn't been able to sense his emotions, his lust and frustration, I would have been pissed. I shifted back towards him and wrapped my arms around his neck. I was being so brazen that I hardly knew myself.

"There are two more weeks until then. I'd rather spend two weeks completely with you then always wonder what being with you would have been like." My mouth made a trail of kisses up his neck, and he groaned and wrapped his arms around me again.

"This is a bad idea," he muttered before kissing me until my vision swirled. It was like someone had unshackled his hands because he kissed me like a dying man. He pulled me back onto his lap and onto the hard cock beneath his sweats. Or like, my sweats. We still hadn't been to town to pick him up new clothes. We weren't the same size, but luckily I had a few items of men's clothing lying around, because that shit was comfortable. There's a reason we steal guys hoodies.

I slid my hand beneath the waistband of the sweats. "Does this mean I'm getting into my own pants?" I panted against his lips.

He chuckled, shaking his head. "If you can still think random thoughts, I'm not doing my job properly," he growled and in one fluid movement, shifted us to the floor in front of the fireplace.

Fortunately, it wasn't being occupied by Fred the dog. He was in my bed under the blankets.

All thoughts of anything but the man between my thighs, rapidly flitted away when he pushed up my shirt. I was still sitting on his lap, and I raised my arms as he pulled the whole lot over my head, and my bra was quickly thrown in a pile right alongside the rest of my clothes.

Micah stared at my boobs like they were a gift. He lifted his hands, cupping their weight in his hands and I was a little worried he might lose an eye, because my nipples were achingly hard right now.

He leaned forward and sucked one of them into his mouth and I nearly leapt off his lap. Holy shit. This was... amazing.

I should probably tell him I was a virgin right?

Yeah, I definitely should. After he finished doing that swirly thing with his tongue.

He switched to the other nipple, and I rolled my hips against his hard dick. I wanted those sweats gone, preferably into the fire for good.

He laid me back onto the rug, and caught my lips again. His dick kept grinding into my core and I was pretty sure I was going to come from just dry humping. But then he was kissing his way down my body and catching the hem of my jeans and just tugging them down. Bless the person who thought putting elastane in denim was a good idea. I was going to send them an Edible Arrangement or a Christmas card or...

Holy fuck. His thumb slid across my clit and I nearly folded in half. His other hand pressed against my hip as his mouth traveled down my body to join his hand between my thighs. He gently pressed my knees further apart with his shoulders and I forgot to be shy because he licked my slit with one, long stroke.

Holy fucking shit damn. I mean, I'd thought about writing the manufacturer of my vibrator several times in my life and thanking them profusely, but now I realized it pales in comparison to the real thing. You couldn't fake the scrape of stubble of his cheek against my thighs, or the press of his fingertips on my hip. You definitely couldn't fake the gentle sucking on my clit.

"Oh my god!" My voice sounded way too high. Then he chuckled on my clit and slid his fingers inside me and I came.

It. Was. Fucking. Glorious.

I panted, but he wasn't done. His tongue moved down to my entrance, away from my swollen yet incredibly happy clit, and then he ate me like I was the last spoonful of berries in the bottom of the yogurt cup. And he'd just lost his spoon.

I threaded my fingers into his hair and gripped it for dear life. I was pretty sure I would take off, just float away, if I didn't hang on. I came again and he moaned in a sound that was the very definition of male satisfaction.

He sat back up between my knees and looked down at me. "Why'd you have to be so fucking beautiful?"

I didn't know how to answer that, but that was okay, because he was taking off his shirt and words weren't overly necessary. He pushed down his sweats, leaning over to kiss me as he kicked them down his legs. Kind of impressive if you ask me.

I could feel his cock nudge at my pussy, and his kiss deepened, doing that pornographic interpretation of what his dick was about to do. And I wanted that so bad, it was an actual ache.

I tore my mouth away. "Micah," I gasped.

He stilled completely, pulling back to look down at me, knitted brows replacing the lust that was there before. "Do you want to stop?"

I snorted, and it wasn't sexy at all. "God no. But I do have to tell you that I might be, no I mean there's no might about it, I definitely am, I mean it's a fake construct anyway and who cares-"

"Layla."

Ugh. Here we go. "So, I'm a virgin and it's no big deal."

He frowns slightly, his eyes staring into mine as if he could sense the lie. This was a big deal, it was only an emotional first. Physically? Goliath the Dildo had taken care of that years ago. A girl has needs, even if she wasn't interested in the current generation of dickholes.

"Okay." He rolled off me and my heart started to sink, but then he was pulling me on top of him. "It's all up to you. Go as fast or slow as you want, I got you."

See? Emotionally a big deal. I lifted myself up, but he stopped me. "Are you on contraception? I'm sorry that I, uh, didn't think to ask before now."

I nodded. "Yep, I'm on the pill, for medical reasons. You aren't going to be all weird?"

He raised an eyebrow. "Because a grown woman wants to lose her virginity? What is this? The nineteenth century?" He teased. "I'm clean. We aren't vulnerable to human STIs. But pregnancy is a possibility."

My face was definitely flushing pink now, and the quickest way I knew how to end this conversation was to grab Micah's dick, line it up with my entrance, and slide slowly down. And it was definitely a show stopper as he stretched me. I hissed a little, the feeling foreign, and Micah's hands moved up to hold my hips. I spread my hands on his chest and let him lower me down inch by inch.

"You okay?"

I nodded because I was pretty sure my vocal chords were broken. Finally, I just slammed myself down. Like ripping off a bandaid, right? Our collective groans echoed around the living room.

"Yes," I whispered.

Despite Micah's proclamation about me being in control, he shifted my hips a bit, so my clit ground against him. The sound I made was nearly feral. I began to move, and holy shit. I got it now. Like, I wasn't a stranger to an orgasm. But the things that Micah's dick was doing, the way our bodies were moving together, that was something else. Something greater than sex.

My body was so primed, that when Micah's hand moved to my clit, that was it. Wave after wave of pleasure ran across my body and I panted. He thrust up into me in short, sharp strokes as I rode out my orgasm.

I finally pried open my eyes and looked down at him. Fuck, he was so damn beautiful. And the way he was looking at me? That was something else. It made me feel exposed. Bared to the world.

"Fuck me, Micah."

He growled low in his throat and flipped us one more time. He shifted my leg up over his shoulder and then pulled out, slamming himself home again.

Oh shit.

My fingers gripped the rug as his body thrust into mine. He leaned forward, kissing me roughly.

"Are you going to come again for me?" His voice was so deep that it basically strummed my clit.

"Yes."

He moved down and took my nipple into his mouth, scraping it with his teeth, and I did exactly what he asked. I came again, and I didn't know how it was possible, but this one was even more earth shattering. Every single muscle in my body felt like it'd turned into a pretzel, and I locked my ankle around his waist, holding him inside me as my pussy milked him. His short shallow thrusts kept bumping my clit, and when he came on a groan, I swear I saw Nirvana behind my eyelids. The place, not Kurt Cobain. No offense, Kurt. That would be weird.

He collapsed onto his elbows, moving his teeth back to the scar on my throat, and pressed his teeth there like he did when we were in the barn. My body cradled him like it was made for it.

I panted in an effort to get enough oxygen back into my body, as he rolled off me and onto the floor. My skin glistened with sweat, and I swear, I got it now. I got the joy of sex. It wasn't just about the orgasms. It was about the connection.

A warm satisfaction pulsed in Micah's emotions

and I grinned. "Is this a bad time to tell you I think I'm a psychic, or an empath, or something?"

He chuckled, pulling me onto his chest. "Why's that?"

"Because I can tell how happy you are right now. And horny. How the hell could you possibly want to go again already?"

Micah's body went rigid under mine, and I worried that I'd said the wrong thing. Maybe we weren't at the joking stage of our sexual relationship yet.

"That's weird. When do you think this started?"

I shrugged. "Just today. Maybe your kiss reset my mojo or something. Though if people get superpowers by kissing you, there might be a line. We better get you a chapstick."

He laughed, but it sounded a little strained. "Sleep, Layla."

6

W e settled into a domestic routine that was both comforting and exciting. Two weeks after I first found Micah on my doorstep, I had to go into Roseau for supplies; my month worth of food depleted quickly with two mouths to feed. I took Micah with me, although it took a bit of convincing to get him to come, dressed only in my sweats. Eventually, I had to resort to guilt tripping him into it. I never said I was perfect.

"But Micah, the bounty hunters may still be in town. I can't go by myself." I batted my eyelids, and I could tell he didn't believe that I was scared.

"Please, you thought I was an axe murderer and you still didn't kick me out. You have a concerning lack of self preservation." But he'd relented.

Walking around town with Micah on my arm felt

right. Oh, I was still getting stares, doubly so. He was attracting way more attention than my outfit, and I'd gone all out with an ensemble of thigh high striped rainbow socks, high waisted shorts with two rows of shiny gold buttons, and a military cut jacket. I looked like I just escaped a carnival. When I'd walked outside this morning, Micah had just raised a single eyebrow, kissed me and told me I looked beautiful.

Our first stop had been the menswear store, where I'd gone in and bought a stack of jeans and tees, and then I'd had the pleasure of watching him try to wiggle into them in the car.

But nothing beat this moment right now, as I laid my proprietary claim to him when the head of the cheerleading squad in my high school year came up to me and talked to me for the first time since the ninth grade.

"Layla, how are you doing? I haven't seen you in so long! Sorry to hear about your mom. Who's this?" She all but purred that last part.

"Oh, this is Micah, Micah this is Sinky." Cindy went to correct me, but I gave her my crazy smile and just continued. The other thing about pretending to be crazy? You didn't have to follow social cues. "He's down from the city, to help me recover, you know?" I gave an exaggerated wink as if the innuendo wasn't as obvious as a slap in the face. Micah looked at me, his lips turned up slightly, but he wrapped his arm around my shoulders and pulled me close into his chest.

He kissed the top of my head and my blush was definitely real. "Nice to meet you, Sinky."

"It's Cindy," she said, rolling her C like her name was exotic and not the world's most basic white girl name on the planet.

Cindy's eyes narrowed, and her smile tightened. I could hear the cogs turning in her head, wondering how the 'Chew Toy' ended up with someone as hot as Micah.

I chuckled about the irony of it all; the Chew Toy ending up with the Wolf Man.

Not that I would end up with Micah, because he would be gone before the full moon in a week. I quickly finished off my conversation with Cindy, which hadn't got any less strained in the five or so years since graduation.

"Well, we really have to go, Cindy. I have to be home to put out the jelly sandwiches for the Babadook otherwise he'll possess my house for a month, and I have to tell you, the last time he did that he ran up my electric bill something terrible. Oh look, there's Chief Hammond! I promised him that Micah and I would go to his place for dinner tonight. It's been good catching up, we should do it again soon. I'll let the sprites cook. Those bitches make a mean margarita."

I'd rather stick hot pokers up my nostrils than hang

out with Cindy. The feeling was definitely mutual too. I could feel Micah's amusement in my head, even though his face was impassive.

Cindy turned to Micah, a frown marring her freshly botoxed face. Obviously she cheaped out and the surgeon missed a bit. "You realize she's fucking nuts, right?"

"Yeah," he sighed. "But she's not wrong about the sprites though. Their margaritas are delicious."

Cindy's mouth opened and closed like she was a fish, before she turned on her heel and walked away, shaking her head.

The part about dinner with Tony and Sue hadn't been a lie though. I had run into Tony and he did invite Micah and me to dinner, but I assumed it was more to grill Micah than for any other reason. As we walked back to the truck, Micah didn't take his arm from around me.

"Why do you do it?"

"Do what?"

"Act like you're nuts. Like you see things that aren't there."

I raised an eyebrow. "Aren't they, Mr You-Know-What?"

He chuckled and tipped his chin. "Touché. But I'm pretty sure the Babadook wasn't taking up residency in your spare bedroom, so the question still stands."

I shrugged, my eyes tracking the people who were

out and out staring at me. No one's mama told them it was rude to stare, apparently. "After the night with the wolves... No, it started before that. I first noticed it when I was a child and my mom still came to town. She would spout all this crazy shit about my father and the government, and people started avoiding her. They wouldn't let me come over to play with their kids, hell most of them wouldn't even let their children be friends with me, as if the craziness was catching. Then the accident happened, and I was all chewed up, and it was like it was proof. It didn't help that I was making outlandish claims about Pete Bukowski as well. I went from pariah to leper in a month."

I realized I'd stopped walking, and Micah had pulled me into his chest. "Anyway, I decided that if they were going to treat me like I was insane, then I was no longer going to give a damn. It was easier than defending myself at every turn. I mean, what was the worst that could happen? They already thought I was nuts. So, I guess, I kind of set myself free from society. I didn't go to church on Sundays like I was expected to do. I didn't wear the clothes I was expected to wear. I didn't enter parades, didn't try to get a date to prom, didn't say please or thank you or watched what I said. At first it was hard, but now it's kind of nice. I like watching people's faces; you can tell a lot about a person by the way they talk to a mentally ill person."

Micah just nodded and held the driver's door to the

SUV open to me. When I climbed in and was face height with him, he leaned in and kissed me. His kiss said a lot of things that I was probably not ready to hear, and I kissed him back with just as much passion. His hands slid up my socks until they scraped under my shorts. "I appreciate the socks. I appreciate the real Layla. And this fake you, this armor that you wear? I appreciate her too because she kept you protected. I promise one day, you won't need her anymore."

He kissed my nose and then strode around the front of the truck as I watched him with my mouth hanging open. He climbed in, and I just stared at him.

He grinned, and the expression was devastating to my ovaries. Hell, it would be devastating to ovaries everywhere. "We better get going or we'll be late."

"We don't have to go to dinner tonight, Micah, I can cancel and they'll understand." Then we could go home and I could hump him into next week. That was a way better plan.

Micah just shook his head. "No, it's okay. Maybe I can help misdirect the police chief away from getting himself killed on his current case. Those bounty hunters believe in collateral damage, and one backwater police chief will hardly be a blip on their radars. Besides, I know you want to show off your new boyfriend."

The teasing note in his voice made me turn the most pathetic shade of red, and I pretended I had no idea what he was talking about. Boyfriend. Who said anything about a boyfriend?

After running errands and picking up groceries, we headed to the edge of town where Tony and Sue lived. Their sprawling house looked like the front of a cookie tin and the warm glow from inside the house was enticing. Standing in front of their blue door, I looked up at Micah. And I meant up. The guy was like a big ass tree I wanted to climb.

"When you rescued me five years ago, did you know this house belonged to the police chief?"

He'd delivered me onto their back porch. That's how Tony and Sue had found me. Literally walked through the back door to take the dog out to pee and bam, broken Layla doll on their lawn.

"Yes."

He was saved from giving me anymore answers by the door swinging open, and the fact I was immediately pulled into the arms of the woman who'd been my surrogate mother for years.

"Oh Layla, darling, how have you been? I haven't seen you in so long, and with everything happening around here, I was so worried. Tony is working such long hours and unable to check on you..." She managed to sound gentle and disapproving all at once, and that was the real magic of Sue. She finally looked around my head and noticed Micah standing on the porch. "Well, maybe you had a reason to be hiding out there in the hills. Layla, introduce me to your young man."

Sue put her hands on her ample hips and beamed at Micah. I smiled and introduced him, sticking to the story that I had been spreading all day; Micah was my boyfriend from college, and we'd just reconnected. Sue raised an eyebrow, totally disbelieving, but she didn't call me out on my lie.

"Oofta, it's cold out here. Come inside where it's warm. Where are your pants, Layla Lee? You'll catch your death."

She ushered us into the hall, taking our scarves and coats, although Micah's were purely ornamental. Tony met us in the living room and hugged me just as hard as Sue had. He shook hands with Micah, and did that male posturing thing that guys sometimes did, where they maintained macho eye contact. Sue bustled around, getting beers for the boys and wine for us, before returning to the kitchen to finish dinner.

I threw a quick look at Tony and Micah, who had seemed to decide who got to be Alpha, and were talking about who was going to win the Super Bowl this year.

Excusing myself to go help Sue, I wandered along the familiar hallways to the warmth of the kitchen. Being in here always felt like wrapping myself in a blanket of love, even when I was a sullen teenager.

Sue smiled when I came in, fully expecting that I'd

follow so we could girl-talk. Apparently, I was predictable.

"Well now, he's handsome, isn't he? Big, strong muscles and those smoky eyes." She fanned herself and I laughed. "I only have to take one look at you to tell you're smitten."

"He's only here for a little while and then he'll go back to the city. His life isn't in Roseau, and it isn't with me. What we have is just for the here and now. So don't go getting excited and planning my wedding just yet, okay?"

Sure, I felt lust through that weird connection we had, and maybe even a little something that felt like way more. But I had no idea what love felt really like really. My mother hadn't had the capacity to love me. Sue and Tony were the closest I'd ever come. What it came down to, really, was that I didn't want to hope for too much.

I focused on our connection in that moment, and all I felt was burning hot anger. What the fuck?

I jumped to my feet, mumbling something about drinks to Sue as I all but sprinted to the living room, only slowing when I got near the doorway.

"It's not right Micah, you should have stayed away. All you're doing is putting her in danger, both emotionally and physically, especially if what you told me about the hunters is true. I love Layla, and if you think I'll just stand by and let you hurt her then you're not as wise as you think you are. You aren't right for her, and you never can be. You're not even of the same species, for God's sake!" The note of familiarity in Tony's voice didn't imply that he'd only just been told a centuries old secret. I moved closer so I could lean on the doorway casually, my eyebrow raised. Completely cool like I hadn't just realized that these two men weren't strangers at all.

"Well now, this looks cozy. Would someone please like to tell me what the hell is going on here? Because it sounded like you were deciding my future without me."

Micah was the first to recover, walking over from the fireplace to stand in front of me. He leaned down and kissed my forehead, a blatant act of defiance to Tony's earlier comments.

"Chief Hammond and I are old acquaintances."

"No fucking shit." Okay, so maybe I was a little mad now. I gestured for him to continue, but it was Tony who spoke.

"When I was a lot younger than I am now, I had just returned from the police academy in the city to join the station here at Roseau. Back then, I was fit and young, and I don't mind saying, one hell of a hunter. I used to go out on the weekends and hunt deer and other game. This was before I had met Sue and she started to occupy all my weekends with courtin'. Then in the summer of 1982, there were rumours flying around of a giant brown bear or Bigfoot roaming the woods. I got it into my head that I wanted to catch this thing myself, like an ode to my machismo. I packed for a week-long hunt, and tracked his prints for days." He shook his head. "All the tracking skills in the world wouldn't have helped me find him, but I stumbled on him by accident, morphing back into a man in a small clearing." Tony's eyes glazed over and he gently shook his head, as if he still couldn't believe it after nearly forty years.

"He screamed like a girl. Scared the hell out of me. I spun around and here was this grown man screaming at me, his gun pointed at my head." Micah grinned. "It took some serious talking to get him to put the gun down. Eventually, he got over his shock and we cut a deal. He would keep my secret and in exchange, I would help him find anyone lost in the woods, and stay well away from town. I've found about a dozen people in the last few decades. Lost hikers, kids who've run away from home, cattle rustlers." His grin turned into a bone-melting smile as he looked into my eyes and I had to blink several times to refocus. "And you."

"How long have you actually lived around here?" I was still processing the fact Tony knew all about Micah. It was hard to grasp, after believing I'd imagined him for the last five years, that someone else knew he existed.

"I've been visiting this area for nearly fifty years. I

like the woods around here and there are no other Lycans that I've happened across. I like the seclusion. I'm normally not much of a people person. But I didn't live here until a few years ago."

I might have imagined the '*until you*' that hung in the air. I tried not to read too much into his words even if they warmed me to the very tips of my toes. I had other questions but I'd leave them for when we were alone. I turned to Tony, pinning him with my stare.

"Why didn't you tell me that I was saved by a were-wolf, when I thought I was going crazy after the accident? Does Sue know? I can't believe she wouldn't have told me if she knew."

Tony had the good grace to look guilty, shrugging and mumbling about giving his word, and a man only being measured by the strength of his word. "Besides, he saved you. I owed him your life and my gratitude, and keeping my mouth shut seemed like a small price to pay for that." His eyes begged me for my forgiveness.

Damn him for pulling out the emotional big guns.

Sue's voice piped up from the dining room, informing us that dinner was ready and Tony was saved from any more guilt-tripping. I struggled through dinner, making pleasant conversation with Sue, until I was desperate to escape.

They'd put up with my 'quirkiness' for long enough that when I said we'd skip dessert, they didn't put up too much fuss, though Sue looked at me and waggled her eyebrows, like dessert was waiting at home and it came in the form of a huge ass man.

I held my questions the whole way home, but the silence in the car was a comfortable one, even given my peevishness at him for keeping his acquaintance with Tony a secret.

As soon as we entered the house, I threw my arms around his neck and kissed him. I had been dying to do it all day, and my desire for him had almost quashed my anger. Almost. I bit his lip hard and he let out a yelp.

"Why didn't you tell me about Tony?" I demanded.

He growled at me but I could sense his happiness. He scooped me up and carried me through the house to the bedroom.

"You don't need to know everything, Little Red. But I guess there is no point hiding it now. I didn't tell you because the less it's discussed, the better. People forget that the world has ears in every corner, especially in small towns. Besides, I figured if Tony wanted you to know about his involvement in my existence, he would have told you."

I nuzzled into his chest, and let him carry me to bed. "Little Red?"

He dropped me down onto my comforter. "Uh huh, and I'm the big bad wolf." He grinned, and his teeth flashed in the bedside light.

I groaned. That was cheesy as hell. "Are you going

to eat me?"

He crawled between my knees, gripping my shorts and peeling them down my thighs. "Uh huh, and I promise you, you're going to enjoy every second."

Cheesy he might be, but he was not wrong.

MUCH LATER, my body lying spooned in his, I approached the topic that made my chest feel too full. I snuggled closer to him so I could feel every groove of his body.

"It's almost the full moon." My voice was small, and it kind of hurt to even whisper the suggestion. Micah tightened his arm around my waist, stiffening.

"I was talking this over with Tony and we both agreed. With the bounty hunters in the area, I shouldn't delay leaving until the full moon. It's too dangerous for the town and especially too dangerous for you, so I have to go. I was going to tell you earlier tonight but I got... distracted. I'll leave tomorrow night, but I promise you Layla, it's not forever. I *will* come back for you."

It felt like someone had dropped a hot coal in the pit of my stomach, and I felt instantly sick.

"I'm glad you and Tony had a good discussion about what's best for me, but don't I get a say in my own wellbeing?"

"I didn't save you five years ago to cause your death

now. You cannot be with me on the full moon, bounty hunters or no bounty hunters. In my Lycan form, I'm a potential danger to you. My urges are different, my sense of right and wrong is skewed and I might decide you look tenderer than an elk and turn on you."

He was trying to scare me but I wasn't so easily deterred. "If your Lycan, or you, or whatever, wanted to eat me, I was a lot more tender and infinitely less bitter five years ago." Micah didn't even crack a smile, and I sighed. "You're right, of course, they could track you here and I wouldn't be safe."

His eyes narrowed in suspicion, but I just waved a hand dismissively. "No, no, I really do agree, from what you've told me, these bounty hunters are ruthless mercenaries who will stop at nothing to get you. I mean, even if you're gone, they may torture me for information. I mean, that's if the rewards are as big as you say they are and they are as dismissive of human life as you suggest."

Check and mate.

Micah looked pained and there were waves of annoyance flowing through the spot he occupied constantly in my mind. But buried underneath all that annoyance at being manoeuvred into a corner, was a genuine feeling of fear. That fear took the shine off my victory.

"I'll have to take you to Eden with me. You better go and pack. We leave in the morning."

7

W e'd driven for hours. Despite Micah's grand declaration that we'd ride at dawn, we didn't leave until just before midday. I'd arranged someone to look after most of the animals, and the neighbors had taken in Monster the Horse and the dairy cows.

We'd stopped a couple of times, grabbed some lunch in Minneapolis and then stretched our legs again in Madison. Apparently good sex and a little life upheaval was exhausting though, because I slept from Madison to Boston.

I woke to Micah scooping me out of the passenger seat. "We're here."

I snuggled into his chest and closed my eyes again, unwilling to wake up just yet.

He sighed and kissed the top of my head. "Fine, I'll

carry you up the stairs but then you have to go in on your own steam or they'll think I've lost my mind and brought home a snack."

I laughed as he heaved me up the stairs of an average looking apartment building. There was no elevator, but he strolled up five flights of steps like my added weight meant nothing. He wasn't even out of breath. I'm pretty sure I was more exhausted just watching him.

When we stopped outside an apartment with a deep red door, he set me on my feet, kissing me softly.

Then he rapped on the door like he was the Feds or something. "Do you want to yell 'FBI' while you're at it?" I teased, but I was straightening my clothes.

I was wearing a hoodie that had unicorn horn and ears, and yoga pants that had kittens wrapped up in burritos printed all over them. These were my normalish clothes. I had the choice to pack work clothes that still smelled a little like Gladys, or my crazy clothes, and obviously kitten in burrito pants had won.

"You look fine. They'll love you," Micah whispered, before the door was opened by a stunningly gorgeous man with white blonde hair and amber eyes the same shade as Micah's. He looked like a Swedish masseuse, or a Rolex model, or something. He had thick rimmed glasses and mussed hair. In short, he was steal-your-breath hot.

"You guys have finally made it. Come on in."

He waved to the inside of the apartment, his smile wide and his eyes sparkling.

The apartment seemed to be one large open plan, with a couple of doors off to the sides. The pretty guy pointed to the couch. "Please, have a seat. I'm Alistair. You must be Layla. I've heard a lot about you." He thrust out his hand and I met it with mine. It was strong and soft, his fingers long enough that I had wildly inappropriate thoughts considering Micah, my brand new lover, was standing beside me. At the same time, his touch was comforting. I frowned at the dichotomy of the situation. Could you simultaneously want to hump and hug a person?

A woman with the same white blond hair as Alistair came through the front door, a huge welcoming smile on her face. Was this Alistair's girlfriend? She didn't seem to have a key, but that didn't mean much.

"We never lock the doors. Eden owns all of this building, and everyone here is family. You are so welcome here, Layla. Also, I'm his niece. Alistair is single." She slow-winked and I died of mortification.

I didn't realize I'd voiced my question out loud. She turned towards Micah, her smile getting wider if that was possible. "Micah! It has been too long, my friend." She embraced him in such a fierce hug, I started to feel slightly jealous. I looked between Alistair and the woman. They were similar enough in appearance to be siblings, except her eyes were a brown so dark they were almost black and his were the same gold as Micah's. She had a faint accent that I couldn't quite place. She focused those black eyes on me again.

"My heritage is South African."

My mouth swung open in surprise. This time I knew I hadn't voiced the question out loud. Alistair gave the woman a stern look.

"Penelope, you shouldn't read people without their permission. It's rude."

Micah was nodding his head in agreement, attempting to look solemn but barely able to suppress a smile.

Penelope screwed up her nose. "I'm sorry. Sometimes I confuse what people say out loud with what they're thinking and find myself commenting on their thoughts or not answering verbal questions. I am Penelope, telepath and shape shifter. Lesbian. You're cute. I'm also single." My eyes felt too wide, and I looked between them all, blinking rapidly.

"You're a mind reader? What the hell is this place? A halfway house for hot people who turn into things that aren't human?"

Penelope burst out laughing and Alistair smiled at me, shrugging. "I guess as you are here now, you may as well know and it will save you getting a shock when you meet the other... housemates. I don't know how much Micah told you."

"Uh, he told me nothing. He's basically Fort Knox with a penis."

Penelope snorted.

Alistair cleared his throat, but he bit his lip like he was trying to remain serious. I think I might want to do that too. Bite his lip, I mean, not mine.

Argh, no. Bad Layla. Give the girl a little bit of D and she turns into a ho. You have Micah, and he is more than enough for one woman, you greedy snatch, I chastised my vagina.

Now Penelope was laughing so hard that I thought she was going to pee herself. Dammit. Mind reader. Think blank thoughts. Or of Micah's giant, hard di-

"Uh, ew!" Penelope made a gagging noise and I smirked to myself.

Alistair cleared his throat and gave Penelope a stern look. "As I was saying, we are an organization for the supernatural and preternatural. Micah and I started the organization in 1924 as a safe haven for Lycans with the intention of creating a new pack. However, we were soon convinced to extend it to other immortals when Locke came along. You'll meet Locke later, I'm sure. Then, Penelope turned up and convinced us to extend it to preternaturals who would only live mortal years. As she said, she's my niece, a few generations removed." He looked at her indulgently, even though they looked like brother and sister, not niece and however many times removed great uncle. "She can be persuasive when she wants to be, always pre-empting my arguments by reading my thoughts. Micah and Locke agreed with Penelope on the subject and Eden was born."

I wondered what Penelope's other form was.

"An owl. Oops, I'm sorry. I'll stay out now, I promise." She smiled warmly, a hint of apology in her eyes. Micah grabbed my hand, twining his fingers with mine.

"You know why I brought Layla here. The bounty hunters are getting more blasé about human collateral every day. They killed two normals in Roseau while they were looking for me. This needs to end, they grow more mercenary with every day." Both Penelope and Alistair looked solemn. "All I know is that I can't take Layla home until no trace of my trail is left."

I was fully aware of his hunted existence and I couldn't even begin to understand what it would be like for him, for all of them. I had never faced the bounty hunters, never had to run for my life from people to whom my only value in this world was my skin.

But if it wasn't for the hunters, I would never have reconnected with Micah. Talk about an emotional quandary.

"Every dark cloud has a silver lining, no?" Penelope's voice lilted into my reverie.

I frowned, not liking the invasion of my thoughts again.

She merely shrugged apologetically. "Whoops."

After a few minutes of silence, it was Alistair who spoke up. "We'll call an emergency meeting. I'll even try to call in the people who are integrating in the world. We can put it to a vote. I'll not order people to fight, even if I thought they would listen to me."

"Fight?" I squeaked, but Micah merely nodded and tugged on my hand.

"I'm going to take Layla to my quarters now, if they're still available?"

"Your apartment is your own, you earned it. We would never use it, except in the direst of circumstances. Most members don't even know there is a sixth level to the building," Penelope said softly.

Micah nodded and gave her a tight smile as he guided me toward the door. I got the impression he wanted to heft me back up into his arms and drag me to his apartment like a caveman.

Alistair waved. "My door is always open if you have any questions, Layla." He paused, and then a dazzling smile stretched his face. "Plus, I love your pants."

Penelope laughed, but I could hear her yelling, "Me too!" even as Micah dragged me to a door at the end of the hall. He opened it onto a room no bigger than a supply closet. I looked around and raised an eyebrow. "Think you got the short end of the deal, Micah."

He snorted and pointed to the stairs in the middle of the space. "Up we go."

I climbed a set of spiral stairs, and wondered how the hell anyone got any furniture up here.

When we reached the landing, Micah slapped his hand around, looking for the lightswitch.

"Sorry. It's been awhile since I've been back here."

He finally hit the lights.

I sucked in a breath as my eyeballs bounced around, trying to take in everything at once. "Woah."

The room was gigantic, stretching right across the building, the pitched ceilings tapering in sharply so I knew we must have been in the loft. It was not cramped at all, and even Micah in his morphed state could have stood comfortably in the room. Floor to ceiling, wall-to-wall glass-brick windows were at either end of the space and polished floorboards stretched between them.

My eyes snagged on the biggest feature of the room, and I couldn't look away. There, in the corner, was the largest four-poster bed I had ever seen. It was like a small football field. It could have slept six people and even then they would barely be touching. The bedspread was made from a dark bronze silk, and it had jewelled silk pillows in deep reds, greens and purples. Emerald green curtains wrapped around the bedposts, ready to be pulled down to give privacy to the occupants. I stood there and gaped like a cod.

"My Persian roots came through with the bed. Make yourself comfortable, I'll go down and get your things." With that, he went back down the hidden staircase.

I wandered around the room, heading first toward the bed like a moth to a flame. I reached down and touched the silk bedspread. It was soft and sensual and had to be custom made. I ran my hands over the intricately carved bed posts, hooking my fingers through the decorative brass rings.

Was that for bondage or decoration? My face flamed at the thought. Maybe I could get him to tie me up on this island of hedonistic pleasure.

I headed towards the only other room in the apartment, which I assumed was the bathroom. I stepped into the room and was greeted by a large spa bath. It had a beautiful view out the window of the city, and I was going to beg to use it tonight.

I decided to stop nosing around and went to lie on the couch. I was exhausted. The last few weeks had felt like a tornado, but like the good kind, where I ended up in Oz, with the Lollipop Guild and a bitching pair of glitter heels.

I heard the door close and the sound of Micah's boots trudging up the stairs. I'd brought everything I thought I'd need and the things I knew I couldn't live without. Unfortunately for all involved, that included Pip and Fred, who I decided I couldn't just leave alone out there on their own, when they had never been alone a day in their lives. Fred raced in ahead of Micah, apparently happy not to be in the car any longer. He walked around sniffing everything. Pip looked extremely grumpy in his pet carrier, though he'd probably only just woken up from the tranquilizers. I placed his litter box in the bathroom and opened the cage door. I'd let him out gradually over the next couple of days.

I walked over to where Micah was placing my suitcase on the trunk at the end of the bed. Fred weaved between his legs, huffing excitedly.

Micah sighed. His apartment was beginning to look more like my farm and less like a bachelor pad. "Thanks again for letting me bring them."

He hugged me back, resting his chin on the top of my head. "I just thank god you didn't want to bring Gladys the cow. Besides, the organization will enjoy having pets in the vicinity, especially the shapeshifters. I know Penelope especially loves cats." He kissed me, sucking my bottom lip into my mouth until I made an embarrassing moan. "Now that we are all unloaded, how about you let me show you the view from our bathtub." I was naked before I even reached the bathroom door.

. . .

I woke the next morning in a panic. Gasping, I looked around the unfamiliar space. Where the hell was I?

I took a quick, calming breath as things started to come back to me. Alistair and Penelope, Eden, and Micah in all his beautiful glory as he made love to me in his giant bath. I reached over and patted the lump in the blankets next to me.

Lying back down, I wrapped myself around his back, my hand running over his smooth skin. I kissed the back of his nape and he made a sleepy 'mmm' noise in the back of his throat that I swear went straight to my core.

"Good morning, Little Red." He rolled over, kissing my forehead before he moved down to my cheek-bones, and then further down to my lips. He gave me soft, sipping kisses that managed to be tender and full of heat all at once. I didn't even worry about having morning breath.

He pulled away and stared down at me. His yellow eyes were still hooded with sleep, and it made him look like pure sex. "Stay in bed. I'll make you breakfast."

Not going to lie, a girl could get used to this really quickly. He pushed back the blankets and was out of bed, stretching tall in his full naked glory. Honestly, he was beautiful. So were Alistair and Penelope.

Maybe they only accepted beautiful people into the group?

"Are all the organization's members as beautiful as you guys?"

He pulled on his clothes and I pouted. Sure, it was a little chilly, but were clothes really necessary? I mean, I was all for body warmth and saving on laundry.

"Most of the immortals are, I guess. We are like all non-living things, as time passes we become smoother and more refined, our rough edges just sanded away. But no, Eden isn't filled with models or anything. We are as varied as mortals. But the supernatural world doesn't judge one another on looks like normal society. We tend to judge each other by our perceived power, which is far more dangerous then if someone finds you aesthetically pleasing to the eye."

While I was happy that I wasn't going to be surrounded by beautiful people all the time, because let's face it, my inadequacy issues ran deep, I was still a little freaked out by the idea of being the only human in a building filled with people who were *other*.

Micah made me bacon and eggs, and delivered it to me in bed on a tray like we were in a romance novel, and my heart did a weird little somersault in my chest. He sat beside my legs, his big hand wrapping around my thigh. "I have to go see some people today, and I can't take you with me. Will you be okay?"

I nodded, stuffing some toast in my mouth because food made by someone else just tasted better. And it had been a long, long time since someone had made me breakfast in bed. "I'll leave you a key in case you need to take the dog outside. There's a library and common room on the third floor; if you like you can meet some of the other members. Penelope also spends most of her time there mentoring. But you are more than welcome to stick around here if you want, I know you aren't a huge fan of crowds."

I was honestly curious to meet the 'members' of Eden, and besides that fact, my aversion to people and crowds always stemmed from being a freak in a perfect world, so maybe here I would find my kindred spirits?

My tongue darted out to lick some bacon grease from my lip, and he watched the movement with hungry eyes. "You make me want to climb back into bed and feast."

I didn't think he was talking about sharing my bacon. So I ran the tip of my tongue over my bottom lip one more time, just for good measure.

He groaned, leaning forward to kiss me. "Tease. I'll be back later and then you'll pay for that." He gave me one last kiss and then tore himself away.

For the first time in a long time, I just lazed around. Eventually, I climbed out of bed and had an amazingly long shower under the pissed off gaze of Pip. "Don't worry, baby. Today I'll let you come out of here. Baby steps, hmm?" He growled at me, turning and showing me his butthole. Yep. He was cranky.

True to my word, I let the cat out and pottered around the apartment, putting my stuff into the drawers Micah had cleared out for me, and keeping an eye on Fred and Pip. When I was done, and Fred had begun to whine a little that he had to pee, I put on my armor of a poodle skirt printed with skulls and a knitted sweater in bright pink.

I left Pip asleep on top of a bookcase and took Fred downstairs to do his business on the sidewalk. I was going to take him to the library with me. I needed all the support I could get.

Standing on the cold sidewalk, I remembered that I forgot to ask Micah what part of Boston we were in. We were in a middle class area I assumed, because there were a lot of SUV's, newer than mine of course, surrounded by apartment buildings and every now and then, a row of townhouses. We appeared to be inner city, because there were a few people striding down the sidewalk purposefully, and I could see the very tip of skyscrapers above the tops of the apartment buildings. Other than that though, I was still as lost as ever.

Walking back inside out of the chill, I climbed the three flights of stairs to the library. The apartment building was filled with people. Most of them were young, well they looked it anyway, and every single one turned to stare at me and Fred when we walked by.

Their expressions varied. Some seemed suspicious, some seemed open and friendly.

When I got to the library, there were even more people outside in the halls. They reminded me of my college days, everyone waiting outside the lecture halls to take their seats. Suddenly, Penelope appeared in front of me, her warm smile closely followed by an even warmer hug.

"Layla, how did you sleep? Micah said you might come down here to say hello. He also said that you brought some of the farm with you; his words not mine." She flashed her teeth in a smile before kneeling in front of Fred, making cooing baby talk and scratching his ears. Like they were waiting for someone else to make the first move, a few others came over to do the same, and Fred lapped up the attention, his golden tail wagging happily.

A cute boy, probably a little younger than me with short dreadlocks and a wide smile, was the first to come over.

"Hi, I'm Terrance. Shapeshifter."

I was a little shocked that he just put that out there. "Hey, I'm Layla, I'm a human?" Terrance laughed so loud that it startled me. "Nice to meet you. Sorry, bad habit. We tend to tack on our species onto introductions to cut out the guessing and posturing about power. But I can't believe you're just a human, because why would you be here? Normals don't usually get past the front door. Can't hold their tongues, you know?" He winked like he was telling a well-worn joke, and my cheeks flushed.

Penelope stood up, addressing Terrance loud enough that it could be heard by everyone. "Layla is our special guest. Micah's special guest."

Terrance's eyes widened at the mention of Micah. His gaze flicked back to me, a new appreciation in his expression. I noticed that Penelope didn't say anything about me being a 'normal' though.

"Also, she has a brilliant track record of silence." The finality in her voice informed everyone that was the end of that. She turned to indicate two girls standing at her side. "Layla, I'd like you to meet Caroline and Lorelei. I will let them tell you their extra abilities if they wish."

The two girls in front of me were fairly ordinary looking teens, about eighteen or nineteen at the most, mouse coloured brown hair and plain features, but wide friendly faces. The most unusual thing about them was that they were identical twins. Well that and the fact that one looked like she was straight out of a Norman Rockwell painting in a beautiful floral tea dress, and the other one looked like she was straight out of a metalcore club, her face heavily made up with dark eyeliner and black lipstick. I murmured something about them being identical, the normal mundane stuff you say when presented with twins.

"We aren't really identical. Our powers differ but I guess you would call them complementary. My ability is that I can confuse people, muddle their thoughts to varying degrees, from something as simple as not knowing why they were standing at the fridge to more extreme conditions like not understanding who or what they are." I was guessing that the girl speaking was Caroline. I looked at Penelope and she confirmed my guess. Penelope being able to read my mind was handy sometimes, I guess.

Lorelei looked bored with the whole conversation. "I can compel people to do anything I want. You would be amazed how quickly confused people will latch onto any coherent suggestion, no matter what it is. Of course, I can do it to people who aren't confused; it's just a little more of an effort. Would you like to see?" She gave me a grin that was probably designed to be creepy, and man, she pulled it off well. I was going to tuck that expression away in my memory for the next time I was in Roseau.

I shook my head quickly, politely declining. I'd be more scared if I hadn't lived through being attacked by a pack of wolves and saved by a monster at their age. Your standard of scary changes after an event like that.

Though god knows, teenage girls are terrifying, regardless if they were supernatural or human.

Gently touching my elbow, Penelope directed me through a door that said 'Library'.

"Do you like to read, Layla? We have a great collection here, from old classics in latin to some modern paperbacks. Loads of young adult novels as you can imagine, but we have fiction and non-fiction. Feel free to take whatever you like back to your room or, if you feel comfortable, you're welcome to stay and read here." She looked across the room, where Fred had managed to corner a group of people, and was laying on his back like a hussy, getting all the belly rubs. "I know the members would like to spend more time with Fred. Most miss having pets, being in the city, especially the shapeshifters. We have a special affinity with animals, as you can imagine."

The library was huge, but by now, I had grown accustomed to whole apartments being turned into single rooms. What was spectacular was the floor to ceiling bookcases, packed to capacity with books. It had a brass rail around the room, a sliding ladder running along it to help access the books at the very top. It was a bibliophile's wet dream. I wondered if Micah would be mad if I got a sleeping bag and just lived in this room. Penelope laughed, reading my thoughts. I got mischievous and mentally pictured Micah and I in the spa last night and I heard her suck in her breath.

"Sorry, sorry! The line between what is verbal and what is mental gets blurred, like I explained last night. I do try, I promise, but I have to be constantly vigilant in such close proximity." I shook my head and smirked at her blushing cheeks that managed to turn her whole face bright pink.

"It's okay," I said softly. And it was. I was kind of getting used to her being able to read my thoughts now that the initial shock had worn off.

The space between the bookshelves contained a long study table and different sized couches, all in dark brown leather.

"Would you like to browse now or would you like to see the common room first?"

I bit my lip. "I'd like to see the common room first, I think. I'll come back to the library, because if I settle in now, I might never leave."

She laughed and led me back into the hall and through the next door. The noise hit me as soon as I entered. Everyone had gathered around the massive TV that was hanging on the wall, the crowd of people three deep and cheering. I quickly surveyed the room, bookshelves on one wall and computers on the other.

Penelope began weaving her way through the crowd, looking interested. I followed, crowd anxiety be damned.

All of a sudden, the group let out a cheer, and I registered the images on the screen as the videogame Mortal Kombat, with one avatar on the ground in a pool of blood and the other looking victorious.

Just then, the largest man I'd ever seen stood up,

leaning down to shake the hand of his unseen opponent. The crowd was laughing and teasing both the
players, and the guy joked along with them. He was
freaking beautiful. Taller and wider than Micah, he
had golden hair and was so... just beautiful, that I
forgot to breathe.

What the hell was wrong with me? No, scratch that,
what the hell was wrong with this place? It didn't have
any right to house this many attractive men. It should
be registered or something.

Finally noticing Penelope and me, the golden god
moved toward us through the crowd and people naturally got the hell out of the way. If a linebacker and a
basketball player had a baby giant, it would be this
man. Penelope snickered just as he reached us.

"What's so funny, Pea?" He winked at me and I
died. I was deceased. Wrap me in furs and push me out
onto the ocean, because I was done. "Hi, I'm Locke. You
must be Layla." He thrust out his giant hand to shake,
my whole hand small enough to fit in his palm. Micah
had said that Locke was another immortal, but his
ageless face gave that away. He could have been 25 or
450 equally. I mumbled something in return and he
smiled at me, his perfectly straight teeth winking at me
in the light.

"You're so pretty," I breathed, and then slapped a
hand over my mouth. "So, uh, pretty good at Mortal
Kombat. That's what I meant."

Locke threw back his head and laughed, and I felt it all the way down to my lady parts. My clit was doing the Macarena and my nipples wanted to join the conga line. "I see why Micah found you so irresistible now. You're cute as hell. I thought Micah was nuts to go back after he rescued you in his morphed form. I mean, it was bad enough that the local police chief knew, let alone a teenage girl, but he just felt compelled to keep going back and back until it made no sense for him to keep commuting." He finally noticed Penelope's scowl. "Whoops, was I running my mouth again?"

What did Locke mean?

Penelope huffed, and crossed her arms over her chest. "I was going to leave you to show Layla around but if you are going to insist on telling secrets that aren't yours, I'll ask one of the juniors to do it. At least most of them have learned the art of discretion." Penelope's voice was stern but Locke didn't look even remotely chastised, just grinning back.

She let out a theatrical sigh and turned back to me. "If you think you'll be okay, I have to leave you now. I have a class to teach and then errands to run. This place doesn't organize itself and unfortunately, some people are no help," she directed a look at Locke but it was affectionate.

Before I knew it, I was being crushed into the concrete wall that was Locke's chest.

"Don't worry about us. I'm sure we'll be great

friends." His playful confidence was catching and I rolled my eyes at Penelope, who rolled her eyes back and then left. Locke led me to the table and then held out a chair for me.

"So Layla, what do you think of Eden so far? I bet you've met more freaky people today then you've ever even read about. Speaking of which..." He looked around the room. "Ramer!"

Locke's opponent in Mortal Kombat jumped up from the couch and I could not stop my jaw from dropping.

"Ramer here is our most visually impressive member," Locke whispered.

"I heard that, Locke," Ramer growled and punched the big man in the arm, which must have hurt like a bitch. The guy's hand, not Locke's arm. I'd felt his chest. Pretty sure he was made out of titanium.

Locke hadn't been wrong though. Standing in front of me was the hairiest man I had ever seen. Thin hair grew all over his face, longer where his beard would have been, and soft and flowing on the top of his head. I knew he wasn't a Lycan, he wasn't tall or broad, and his face wasn't canine at all.

"Hi, I'm Ramer. I know you're a friend of Micah's so I'll clear up the fact that no, I am not a Lycan, or even a shapeshifter. Actually, what Locke said was right, I am visually impressive, but not all that impressive on a preternatural scale."

I didn't know what the correct response was right now. So when all else fails, go with self-deprecating humor. "Oh? You think that's impressive? You should see my legs when I haven't shaved all winter."

Locke let out his booming laugh again, and even Ramer smiled.

"Well, it's not just hair I grow. It's a hard power to describe, but I make all biological organisms grow faster; plants, flesh and bones, hair on my own body and anything else that has a biological lifespan. Half the time I think that's why Locke is so big." It was a well rehearsed speech, as if he had repeated it a million times. He smirked at Locke but I saw the sadness flash in his eyes for a brief second.

Locke scoffed. "I was this big when you were still a hairy little grub."

Ramer, who was only of medium height and size, launched himself at Locke, laughing. "Who are you calling a grub?"

They did that weird dude wrestling thing, and I took a quick step back. Locke was big but Ramer was quick. Not quick enough though. Locke got him by the ankle, flipping him upside down and shaking him like he was trying to divest him of his lunch money. Holding a swinging Ramer away from his body, Locke turned to me.

"So, other than the library and the common room, there's not much else to show you. How about Ramer goes and shaves his face and we show you the city instead?"

I watched Ramer's body go still. "No thanks, Locke. I'm all out of razors, plus I told Pea that I'd do some mentoring this afternoon."

I realized they all called Penelope 'Pea'. The cute name suited the bubbly blond.

Locke looked down at his friend sadly, though Ramer couldn't see it from his upside down position.

I bent until I was upside down as well, so I was face to face with Ramer. "Could I ask you a favor then? Could you please take care of Fred for the afternoon? He's old and will probably just sleep but he likes the company and he won't be a problem, I promise!"

Ramer hesitated for a long time but then nodded reluctantly, which I thought was extremely strange. I was about to release him from his agreement when Locke flipped him the right way up. Setting him back on his feet, he squeezed the guy in a man hug. Then he grabbed my elbow and was directing me towards the door.

"Grab a coat and we'll go. I'll meet you at the entrance." He smiled and descended the stairs. Not going to lie, I watched his ass as he walked away. Then I felt guilty because I had feelings for Micah. Feelings that were new and exciting and I shouldn't be looking at giant, golden men like I wanted to eat them.

Decision made, I smiled at Ramer and gave him

Fred's lead and then raced upstairs to get my coat. I could be platonic friends with Locke. I needed friends more than I needed potential love interests.

Decision made, I hurried back downstairs to meet my new platonic friend.

When I reached the bottom of the stairs and he smiled at me like I was the most exciting person he'd ever met, I told myself to breathe and chanted, *platonic, platonic, platonic* in my head over and over.

Maybe it would stick.

8
———

He unfolded from where he was sitting on the stairs, and rose to his full height. I don't know what they fed them at Eden, but they were all huge. Maybe there was some truth to Ramer's theory. He held the door open for me, and I stepped out into the cutting winter chill. It blew my skirt up full Marilyn Munroe style, and I squealed. Yep, skirt probably wasn't a good option.

Locke laughed and pulled me a little closer. "I'll act as a windbreak. There are some benefits to being this big."

The people walking down the street in the opposite direction naturally moved out of the way of Locke's towering bulk, and he tucked my hand into the crook of his elbow.

"Ever been to Boston before?" I shook my head. I

didn't want to tell him I hadn't even been out of Minnesota before. I went to college in Minneapolis and that was about the furthest I'd been from home.

Locke led me around something gross on the sidewalk. "I thought I might take you to Franklin Park today. They have a zoo and a nature park there, with a truly amazing pop-up butterfly exhibit at the moment. No one likes to go with me, the shapeshifters don't like to see anything caged, which I totally get." He turned me down a side street. "I just like being among the normals for a bit. Such short lives but they find so much joy."

I knew Micah was old, but the way Locke spoke hinted that he was even older. I couldn't put my finger on why, it was like he had an odd lilt or something.

It definitely would be impolite to ask.

"Just how old are you?" Dammit. I was too damn curious to hold my tongue. My mother had always told me it was rude to ask a person their age, but this time I had to make an exception to mama's rule.

"Hmm, about five hundred?" My feet stilled, but he pulled me along easily.

Five hundred. He was five hundred years old. Holy shit. When we approached the station, he led us up to the ticket counter. He pulled out a fifty, slid it beneath the plastic safety screen, indicating that the station attendant should keep the change. The man looked totally jaded, shrugging as he slid the two tickets back under the screen.

The platform was crowded, and I pushed down my anxiety. Luckily, here in Boston, no one gave me or my outfit a second glance. Still, I stood a little closer to Locke and he seemed to encompass me without even touching me.

I had to raise my voice a little to be heard. "So, what are you exactly? A vampire? I know you're not a were-wolf, because you don't have the yellow eyes." He laughed at the suggestion, shaking his head.

"I'm neither, thank fuck. No offence to them, but having to turn hairy once a month, or chase my food and drink its blood, sounds miserable to me. As far as I know, I am one of a kind. In some senses, I am truly immortal, more so than either Lycan or vampire; there are methods to killing them both if you know how." His face turned grim, his shining blue eyes losing their mischievousness. "Nothing I've found has killed me yet, and trust me, I tried. Bullets to the brain, stakes to the heart, poison, trains, severing my own head in 1781. That last one was painful, never going to try that one again. With the help of an old lover, I tried severing parts of my body and burning them, but as long as there was one tiny specimen of my DNA, I grew back. It took decades but I grew back. The journals Mari-anne kept are quite fascinating, if you'd like to read them."

I just stared at him. This big, larger than life, smiling man was suicidal? The thought made my heart constrict. I couldn't imagine living so long, being so done with life that he would torture himself in such brutal ways just to end it all.

For the first time since I met Micah, I appreciated my mortality. It would be awful watching the people you loved die time and again. I hadn't realized I'd spoken out loud until Locke answered.

"It's soul destroying." The train arrived, cutting off the conversation, and I wasn't disappointed. His smiling face masked such a terrible sadness and it made my heart ache.

As the doors slid open, I was honestly surprised that Locke fit through. He had to stoop low just to avoid bumping his head. We sat down on ratty brown seats, next to windows covered in scratched graffiti.

"Did I upset Ramer earlier? Doesn't he like dogs? If I'd known I wouldn't have asked, I promise." That was so like me, to make people uncomfortable by just existing.

Locke grinned, reaching up to pet my head like an errant puppy with his giant mitts. "You really are special, Layla. Micah couldn't have been more right." He shook his head, but the way he looked at me made my chest flutter. "It was nothing you did that made Ramer sad. Unfortunately, Ramer's ability can sometimes be more of an affliction than blessing. He's exiled himself from the normal world and doesn't leave the house if he can help it."

I was still confused. "Is it because he's so hairy? Because I know this hair removal cream that will burn those suckers right off for at least a day or two." Locke let out a belly laugh and several people turned around to stare. I should clarify, several men turned around. The women were already staring and I didn't blame them one bit.

"No, it isn't because he is hairy. Ramer doesn't like to touch people, and walking through the streets of the city is almost painful for him, in an emotional way, I mean. Really, I shouldn't be telling you this, it's his story and I've already gotten in trouble once today for blabbing secrets."

I could respect that, despite how much my curiosity burned. We finished the trip in a comfortable silence, each deep in our own thoughts.

Coming to Eden had been... not what I was expecting. Not because of all the preternaturals, as Alistair had called them. I was surprisingly fine with the idea that there were people out there who weren't like me.

No, my real problem was sitting right next to me. Up until a month ago, I'd had zero attraction to men. If someone had asked me to put myself in a box, I would have said I was asexual.

Boy, was I wrong. Maybe.

I looked around the train car, and spotted a good

looking guy in a business suit. He was fit, definitely worked out, had dark eyes fringed with thick lashes and just the right amount of stubble. He was GQ handsome.

And he did absolutely nothing for me. He could be standing in front of me naked, doing his best impression of a Chippendale, and I wouldn't want to go to bed with him.

But the man next to me?

When he shifted and his thigh brushed mine, I was acutely aware of it. I wanted to squeeze his thigh muscle like a stress ball.

Where did that leave me and Micah? I had feelings for him, feelings that were quickly spiralling away from lust and toward something scarier. I showed all the signs; the fullness in my chest that felt like an ever-inflating balloon when I saw him and the hollowness in its place when he was gone. Then there was the overwhelming happiness when I woke in the mornings and realized he wasn't a dream. The contentment I felt when I fell asleep at night curled in his arms.

I was glad Penelope wasn't here at the moment because she would probably be inclined to puke at my sickly, lovestruck thoughts.

Locke nudged my knee with his. "This is our stop."

I stood, almost toppling to the side as the train hit the brakes, and Locke had to put a steadying hand on my waist. I convinced myself it was the motion of the train coming to a standstill that caused my temporary vertigo and not the thoughts of Locke making me go weak in the knees.

A short cab ride from the station, we arrived at a huge park, bustling with people despite the cold weather. As we walked up to the entrance of the zoo, Locke pulled out his money wad again.

"I guess that's one of the perks of living so long, you'd get shitloads of money. And knowledge, of course."

Way to sound like a gold digger, Layla.

He smiled that golden boy grin at me again. He was the exact opposite of Micah's bad boy pensiveness. "Unfortunately, I spend it as quickly as I gain it. Eden takes a lot of money to run, and holding down a job where I just never age is hard now. Social security numbers, accidentally injuring myself at work, the fact that my employee ID photo never dates, you get the idea," he teased.

Well, that made sense. Immortal and poor it was then.

Wrapping my arm in his again, we strolled into the zoo. "So Layla, now it's my turn to ask questions. Are you feeling overwhelmed by Eden and its members?"

I contemplated how I felt about my reality being turned upside down. All the things I thought were fairy tales were really true, to a degree. I'd also fallen in love with the villain of most fairy tales instead of

Prince Charming, although in Micah's case, I wasn't sure if they weren't one and the same.

"I'm doing okay, I think. It's an entirely different world, and I'm still kind of an outsider, being human and all. It's taking some adjustment but Alistair is very nice." And hot. I didn't say that bit out loud though. "So is Penelope. I think it'll take some getting used to, the fact that there are so many more variations to life than just human and animal. So many shades of grey in between." I wondered if I should bring up the brain meld thing that Micah and I had.

"Hey, have you ever heard of a person being able to feel the emotions of another person?"

He raised an eyebrow. "Like an empath?"

I shook my head. "No, I mean I can only feel the emotions of one particular person."

Now both of Locke's eyebrows were raised so high that they nearly touched the wispy blonde curl on his forehead. "Micah?"

I nodded. "Uh huh. If I concentrate hard, I can tell what he's feeling, like inside my mind. It's like there is a little fenced off section in my brain and his emotions are beamed there for me to see. Like right now, I can tell that he is frustrated and angry wherever he is, but underneath that, I can feel his longing to be home. Like, how can I even tell what that feeling is? It doesn't make any sense." I stopped walking and looked at him. "Do you know what it is? I asked

Micah but he either doesn't know or is unwilling to tell me."

"It could be a lot of things? Maybe you aren't as normal as you think, or maybe it's a Lycan thing, I can't be sure. Why don't you ask Alistair?"

I eyed him, and had a feeling this was one of those palm-off situations, like I'd just asked where babies come from and he was like 'I don't know, why don't you go ask your dad'. Except Alistair wasn't my father. Wouldn't mind calling him Daddy, though.

I resisted the urge to face-palm myself.

I'd unconsciously come to a stop outside the wolf enclosure. As I stared at the shaggy animals in front of me. Tomorrow night would be the full moon. I remembered only brief flashes of how Micah looked in his other form all those years ago. I tried to concentrate, recalling his hands and his eyes but not much else. The wolves and Micah had looked similar in the same way humans and chimpanzees looked similar. You can tell they were from the same anthropological family but that was it.

I turned towards the big cat enclosure and Locke told me that Terrance shapeshifted into a puma. I looked at the puma now, lazing on its back, its belly warming in the brief glimpses of sun. It was a truly majestic creature but one born to be a predator. Was it the same for shapeshifters and Lycans too?

I suddenly wanted to leave, to run away from the

disturbing thought that Micah could ever be a threat to me, despite what he said. Locke picked up on my mood, suggesting we move to the butterfly tent.

"You know, I was once a lion tamer in a traveling circus back in the early 20th century. The golden era of circuses before the world caught on to how cruel the practice was. I met a lot of other lion tamers in the profession and lived long enough to see how they all died. The trainers who treated the lions as animals, using fear and pain to train them because they feared the creatures themselves, well, nine times out of ten ended up getting mauled to death in the ring. Those who respected the animals and really loved them, who knew of their rightful place as an apex predator, as a king, well, they lived well into their old age. I guess what I am trying to say is that if you only see the bad in something, then you will always lose in the end."

I was disconcerted that Locke had picked up the direction of my thoughts so easily. I would never have aired the thought out loud, but I appreciated the advice.

We'd reached the butterfly tent, and as we entered, dozens of brightly coloured wings floated around a tropical paradise. The humidity in the room made sweat break out on my brow as my body adjusted from the winter chill of Boston to the tropical heat of a rainforest. Locke went over to the pretty auburn haired keeper, who was smiling and swishing her hair around, and he was talking animatedly back, directing a charming smile in her direction. I turned away as I saw her write something on a piece of paper and slide it into his pocket.

As he walked back towards me, I conceded that Locke was beautiful, so I couldn't blame the keeper. He could have been chiselled from stone by a master artisan. He had a wide unlined forehead and his features were perfectly symmetrical, right down to the dimples in his cheeks. His hair was a dirty blonde color, trimmed shortish around the sides and the top was slightly longer, finger combed in a way that made him look a little roguish.

And his body. Damn. It was the thing that wet dreams were made of. He had shoulders that tapered down into a narrow waist, strong thighs and muscular calves. He looked like the typical 1940's leading man.

Locke's voice broke into my perusal of his body and I instantly blushed.

"Take your jacket off, Layla."

My eyes shot to his face as his big hands reached over and slid my jacket off my shoulders. He reached down and pulled my sweater over my head too. When I was standing there in just a holey Black Sabbath tee, he nodded. His eyes darted down my body, a lot more subtle in his perusal of my body than I'd been a moment ago.

He cleared his throat and his cheeks flushed. It was probably the tropical heat. Yeah. Let's go with that.

"Now close your eyes." My eyes snapped shut of their own accord and I wondered if he had compulsion like the twin, Lorelei. A beat passed, and then something warm and wet slid along the bare skin of my arm like a lover's tongue. My eyes shot open, but Locke's smiling face was the only thing in my vision.

"Closed," he chastised gently.

I reluctantly shut them again. I stood there, absolutely still, for only a dozen or so seconds, not sure what I was expecting but my heart was thudding a million miles an hour. His hands took hold of mine, and he lifted my arms up so they were straight out in front of my body.

"You can open them now." His voice was a rumbling purr and I couldn't help the shiver of pleasure that ran over my skin. I slowly opened my eyes one at a time.

My arms were two long strips of fluttering color. Dozens of butterflies had landed on my arms, drinking from whatever Locke had smeared on them. I felt the smile stretching my face as I stared at the delicate rainbow of colors in awe.

"Locke, they're so beautiful. Why are they so attracted to me?"

Locke laughed at my excited expression. "Maybe you are just attractive to all creatures, great and small?"

He laughed as I rolled my eyes. Yeah sure, that's what it was. My animal magnetism. "Or maybe it's the fructose mix I rubbed on your skin."

We stood in silence for a moment, just letting the butterflies have their fill until they started to fly away one by one.

"I miss new experiences, you know, that joy and excitement of the unknown. When you're as old as I am, you feel like you've seen and done everything. But it's just as magical watching you experience them."

Just then, a Queen Alexandra butterfly landed on my finger, its large blue and black wings gliding together majestically. I watched it with a fascination, appreciating the delicate beauty, but when I looked up, Locke was watching me, his face pensive.

He met my eyes, and then quickly looked away. He cleared his throat, and the charming smile was back on his face. "I better get you home before Micah thinks I'm trying to steal his girl." The look in his eyes made it clear that it was a definite possibility.

Yes. I should get back home to Micah, before I caught the dreaded feels for this handsome, charismatic man.

The crowd was even more congested on the trip home, people hustling on their way back from work. It didn't matter. I talked with Locke like he was an old friend. We talked about Minnesota, and the fact I was studying nursing before my Mom got ill. He told me about all the jobs he'd had in his life. He had a whole lifetime of funny stories and I was rolling around on the train laughing, completely distracted from the crowd.

Locke stopped me just inside the front door to the Eden apartment building. He stood close, looking down at me with those sky blue eyes. "I had a good time today. You're really something special."

"Yes, she is," a voice growled from the shadows of the stairs and Micah stalked out. His face was unreadable but I could feel his jealousy. I smiled even though I knew I shouldn't but I was so happy to see him and a little chuffed that he cared enough to be jealous.

"Micah! I missed you today." I launched myself at him, wrapping my body around him and hugging him close. I felt his jealousy turn to something softer as he nuzzled his face into the curve of my neck. I didn't want to let him go, but I peeled myself off. His jealousy flared up again as he stared at Locke menacingly, but Locke just smiled good-naturedly, an eyebrow raised a fraction.

"You're lucky. Don't forget it either, because some of us won't." His tone was teasing but his eyes were serious. With that, he shrugged and moved on like Micah wasn't glaring at him. "I'd ask how the meeting went but Layla informs me that it was extremely frustrating. Handy trick she has there." There was something in Locke's voice, some kind of warning, but it was drowned out by the low rumble in Micah's chest. Was he growling? I knew he could morph any time, but now, over this? He heaved a large breath, to calm himself.

"Works both ways, you know? I've felt everything she has today. I mean everything." Yep, that was definitely a warning growl, and Locke smirked. I should get out of the way. Micah was definitely going to shift and start a fight.

Wait. Since when could he feel my emotions too?

I drew back, trying to look up into his eyes, and I felt Micah tense under my hands. He quickly changed the subject. "Alistair would like to talk to you. We're having a conference the day after the full moon. We contacted most of the members through Annabeth, and Penelope will contact the rest. Layla, would you like to go up to our apartment now? You look tired." He gave me a primal look and I nodded immediately. That look promised all the pleasure I could handle, if only just to claim me like some caveman.

On the flipside, I didn't like being maneuvered overly much, so I turned to Locke.

"I had a nice day too. Thanks for taking me to the park. I enjoyed myself. Maybe next time we can convince Ramer to come too." I paused, remembering something. "You never answered my question. Why didn't Ramer want to take care of Fred?"

Micah looked slightly alarmed and my body went tense.

"You know how he accelerates the growth of things? Well, that includes cells. He can age a person by touch. He was probably scared Fred would die while you were out. He's an old dog and even two or three pats from Ramer could mean death from old age."

I couldn't believe that the possibility hadn't occurred to me. A cold sweat spread across my body as panic set in. I know it was silly, he was an old dog, but he was the one constant in my life.

I raced up the stairs to the third floor, ignoring Micah's calls, and rushed into the library. I saw Fred, lying unmoving on the ground. *No, no, no.* I ran to him, kneeling down, grabbing his head in my hands.

Fred jumped to his feet, startled from a deep sleep, a dazed look on his old face. I breathed a loud sigh of relief, and someone cleared their throat behind me. I looked up to see Ramer, the forlorn look on his face making me feel like complete and utter shit.

"I made sure I didn't touch him. I could tell how much you love him, and I didn't want you to be angry at me."

I felt like an utter asshole. I was so concerned for Fred that I'd completely disregarded Ramer's feelings.

"Fuck, I'm so sorry if I offended you. I was being completely inconsiderate." I crossed the room and hugged him. He was stiff in my arms but I didn't release him. "I know this will decrease my lifespan, Locke explained, but everyone needs touch. If I can give you even a little human contact, then the few hours it detracts from my life will be well worth it. I'm sorry."

The hair on Ramer's face tickled my cheeks as he softened in my arms. I heard him swallow hard as he pushed me away and rushed out the door, his head hung low. I saw Micah in the doorway, his face soft.

"Did I make it worse?"

He motioned me over and wrapped his arm around my shoulders, kissing my temple. "No Little Red, you're the sweetest person I've ever met. He only left in such a hurry because he didn't want anyone to see him cry. Come on, let's go home." I snuggled into his shoulder

"Why didn't you tell me you could feel my emotions too?"

He shrugged and led me toward the stairs. Ah, sweet Micah, I'm not that easily distracted.

9

Apparently, I was that easily distracted. Last night, Micah made love to me until I forgot my own name, let alone that line of questioning. I was kind of mad that I'd let myself be bamboozled by the D.

D-azzled, if you will.

The streaks of morning light landed on the breadth of Micah's back as he slept, making his skin look delicious. It was D-Day, not dick but doom, in our relationship. The moon would be full tonight and the inevitable would happen; Micah would transform into a Lycanthrope. We hadn't discussed it and Micah had shut down the conversation each time it arose.

"I'll be far away from here." That was the end of the discussion as far as he was concerned. Penelope had hinted that he would go with Alistair, but where or when hadn't been mentioned.

I snuck quietly out of bed, pulling on jeans that were more tears than fabric and a sweater with a dachshund on the front, before sneaking out of the apartment while Micah still slept. I was going to see Alistair and get some information about the Lycan-thropes once and for all. I was tired of waiting for Micah to tell me in his own good time. Descending the flight of stairs one floor, I hesitated outside their door. What if he was still asleep? My hand poised to knock, I let it drop. I'd find a way to see Alistair without Micah knowing later.

"Come in, Layla," Penelope's voice lilted through the door.

Oops, psychic-busted. Opening the big blue door, I saw her making coffee in the centralized kitchen. "Alistair's just in his bedroom. He'll be out soon. Would you like coffee?" I murmured my agreement and sat at their breakfast bar. Penelope set a steaming mug of coffee in front of me.

"Alistair, Locke and I usually eat breakfast with some of the members in the common room, especially the visiting ones. You are welcome to join us if you wish."

I shook my head. "Not today, but I'll definitely take you up on that tomorrow. I just want to talk to Alistair, if I could?"

Alistair appeared as if I'd summoned him with my request, his blonde hair combed back to perfection. This place was a smorgasbord of good-looking men, and I had to keep telling myself that I was seeing where things were going with Micah. I needed to keep my perverted eyeballs to myself.

Penelope snickered. "Why choose?"

I blinked at her rapidly, my brain trying to formulate a good argument why one hot, sweet guy was better than three. She looked over at Alistair. "I heard Micah and Locke nearly came to blows for Layla's affections yesterday and then she made Ramer cry." She looked back at me, her face soft despite her teasing words. "I'd say you are having a profound effect on *all* the men of this organization. Even Terrance told everyone that he thinks Micah's new girlfriend is hot."

This time I blushed hard. "He's a baby!"

Penelope just laughed, coming over to give me a quick hug. "I'll leave you two to talk. I'll see you downstairs, Alistair. Be good, you two." She winked and my mortification hit critical levels.

I was blushing furiously, repeating over and over in my head that I wasn't interested in Alistair. This made her laugh harder as she left, and I heard her still chuckling down the hall. Alistair turned back towards me, his smile charming.

"She is such a tease, don't pay any attention." He sat down at the breakfast bar beside me. "Unfortunately, I can't read your mind so you'll have to tell me how I can help you today?" I shifted uncomfortably in my chair, having one hundred questions but not sure which I should ask first, so I just barreled in.

"As you obviously know, tonight is a full moon. However, Micah won't tell me anything about what will happen or really anything about being a Lycanthrope. It's like he thinks that he can ignore it, shelter me from it, and it won't affect our relationship. That's why I wanted to talk with you; not only because you are a Lycanthrope, but because you're a scientist. You should be able to understand my desire to know the how's and why's, right?"

He reached to the end of the bench, dragging a bundle of leather bound books toward me. "These are my journals. Everything I learned about our kind, I first wrote in here. But remember that Micah and I differ in self perception, due to the way we've lived. Micah's life before Eden was filled with death and destruction. It is because of this that Micah thinks that being a Lycan automatically makes him a monster."

"And the fact I can read his emotions?"

Alistair looked uncomfortable. "Locke mentioned that you have recently... acquired the ability to read Micah's emotions. That is definitely a discussion you need to have with Micah, however."

I huffed, taking a gulp of my coffee. I needed the

caffeine. "I'm so new to this, I don't know what's normal."

He chuckled. "There is no normal in Eden. No one expects you to be an expert on our society in a day."

I flushed. "I meant men and relationships. You guys are harder to understand than people who turn into pumas."

Alistair raised an eyebrow, shifting on the stool. "Micah is your first relationship?"

I nodded, my cheeks turning from pink to bright red. "I didn't have much interest in guys until Micah came along. Then it was like my soul breathed a sigh of relief. And I was happy, you know? I was okay with that. I thought I was done. And then I came here…"

"And?" he breathed, and I turned to look at him, his eyebrows were drawn down over his shining golden eyes.

"I wondered if the feeling was really such a one off, or maybe it was just that I was broken and now I'm fixed."

Alistair took a deep breath and gave me a reassuring smile. "Some things are just magic, Layla. They aren't meant to be explained away. Fate hands you what you need, but you have to decide whether it's something you want. No one will judge you for taking what you desire, especially not here in Eden."

I looked at him, like really stared, in the hopes that it would help me comprehend what he was trying to tell me. Instead, what stared back at me looked an awful lot like desire. He leaned closer, and I held my breath.

Holy shit. Holy shit. Was I catnip for supernaturals? If so, I think I was okay with this.

Alistair stood abruptly, taking his cup to the sink and pouring it down. His shoulders were stiff, and I noticed the muscles that rippled underneath his shirt. When he turned back around, he had his smile back in place. "Apologies. This close to the full moon, my restraint gets a little taxed."

I frowned, because I was confused as fuck. I thought he was going to kiss me. Was he going to kiss me? Did I want him to kiss me?

The answer to that one was easy. Yes. What the hell was going on with me?

I pasted on a perfectly pleasant smile too. "I understand." I slid from the stool and stood. "Thank you for the journals. I'm sure they will be very helpful."

He guided me out the door and to the entrance of Micah's apartment, holding the stack of journals. "I've put post-it notes on all the pertinent sections that might help answer some of your questions but if not, I'm more than happy to answer them." He leaned down, passing me the journals, and then inhaled deeply. He kissed me on the cheek and I tried not to blush. "You make a nice coffee companion." I looked up into his Lycan gold eyes, which contrasted with the white-blond shade of his hair. It should have clashed but somehow he made it work.

"I like your coffee too. I mean drinking coffee with you," I mumbled and mentally slapped my forehead.

He gave me a brilliant smile, his teeth so white I was momentarily blinded. Oh Grandma, what bright teeth you have.

He waved and I watched him disappear down the stairs. What was with these three? Micah I was irresistibly drawn to, but Locke and Alistair made my hussy of a heart beat faster.

10

I sat down on the winding stairs that lead to Micah's quarters and opened one of the large notebooks. I hoped one of these books was 'Lycanthropes for Dummies', otherwise this was going to be hard reading. Flicking to the first of the post- it notes, I began to read.

"THE FOLKLORE that surrounds the Melenchola Canina or Daemonium Lupum, more commonly known as a Lycanthrope or Werewolf, has been largely falsified, given a menacing edge due to the resemblance to the typical wolf, often regarded as the biggest natural threat to outlying villages in Europe. As with most folklore surrounding anything considered mythical, many traits supposedly attributed to the metamorphism or destruction of werewolves has been vastly blown out of proportion.

However, one characteristic that, in essence, has maintained its accuracy is the effect of the full moon on the Lycanthrope. Although they possess the ability to morph at any time, during the full moon phase of the lunar cycle, it is inevitable that the Lycanthrope will morph into its non-human form, regardless of its individual will.

The metamorphous itself is a lot less painful than fiction would have us believe. Although there is a slight ache as the muscles and bones elongate in the order to accommodate the increase in height, there is little pain involved after the very first shapeshifting. The body becomes accustomed to this transformation very quickly. During metamorphosis, the bones above the knee are erected and stiffened into position by the contracting of surrounding muscles. This adds, on average, nine inches in height to the Lycanthrope. The second transformation occurs in the spine, with the muscles encasing the spine also elongate, before contracting around the spine..."

THE MECHANICS of the whole process made it seem completely un-magical. I stood up and walked quietly to the top of the stairs, peeking around the corner to see if Micah was still asleep. He'd rolled over, exposing his torso but still snoring softly. I crept toward the couch, my butt numb from sitting on the steps. I stuffed the three other books underneath, hiding them from Micah before I continued to read.

"IT SHOULD BE NOTED that not only the physical elements of the Lycanthrope change. The emotional changes in the subject are far more erratic than in the human form i.e. quicker to anger and sadness. However, they do not lose complete control or turn animalistic due to transformation, as stated in many ancient accounts. It is not unlike normal society, normal stimuli can result in sometimes extreme reactions."

I SMIRKED. I found it, the evidence I need to shut down Micah's objections.

"What are you reading?"

Involuntarily, I snapped the book shut at the sound of Micah's voice next to my ear, immediately looking guilty.

"Uh, nothing? Just something I picked up from the library. I didn't want to wake you up, and you look so cute when you sleep."

I jumped up and threw the book on the couch like

it was diseased. Micah gave me a sardonic look and reached around me to pick it up.

"Lycanthropes: a self study. Alistair's research is hardly light reading, Layla." I could feel his annoyance and frustration through our bond. The whole thing was tainted with the beginnings of anger.

"It was easier for you to just ignore the fact that tonight you were going to change. Instead of showing me the other side of the man I'm growing to love, you decided to hide away like you're some kind of leper."

I could do anger as well.

"I'm not responsible for your *feelings*," he snarled, saying it like the word was a curse. That hurt but I wasn't going to take it lying down. "You can't hide from me, you giant furry dick. I know everything you feel."

Micah turned from me. I couldn't understand his anger, didn't comprehend why he wouldn't let me into his life completely. It was like he thought I was too fickle to be able to handle his differences. He whipped around to face me.

"You want to see me morph, Layla? Well you don't need to wait for tonight, I can do it any time." He was getting taller as he spoke, the muscles in his face popping like a million bugs crawling under his skin. Hair spread down his body like a wildfire, springing like straw from his shoulders and softer on his front. "This isn't a fairytale!"

He was shouting now, the decibel of his voice

almost ear splitting. His tone was lower, but it was unmistakably his voice. "Little Red Riding Hood didn't fall for the big bad wolf. He ate her in the end. I am a monster in this form, something that has been feared since the Dark Ages."

He had reached his full height now and loomed an easy two and a half feet over me. He had backed me up against the windows and all I could feel from him was anger and misery.

"I read the book Micah, you aren't an animal, and you don't lose control in this form any more than you would in your human form." His eyes narrowed, the exact eyes he had as a human.

"You read the book and think you know everything, do you? You know nothing about me, Layla. I have killed hundreds of people. Humans and supes alike. And I *enjoyed* it." The spot in my head where Micah's emotions lived went blank. I felt nothing there except coldness. For the first time, I was scared.

I mentally yelled for help, hoping Penelope could hear me. I didn't fear Micah, but I did fear that blankness. That haze over his emotions.

I tried not to shake, and I knew that he was trying to scare me into running away. It wouldn't work. I wasn't the same scared little girl I was five years ago. "We both know that is not who you are anymore. A killer wouldn't have rescued me in the woods from real predators. A killer wouldn't have started a refuge for people like themselves. A killer wouldn't smile at me the way you do every morning." I was trying to reason with him but he refused to hear.

"A wolfish smile. It can't be trusted. Why won't you understand that I'm doing what's best for you!" I winced as his roar hurt my ears, but I refused to cover them.

"Because I'm doing what's best for us," I screamed back.

He advanced on me, and that terrible blankness disappeared as the red hot heat of anger was back. "There is no us."

I lifted my lip in my best impression of a snarl. "Coward."

Just then, Penelope, Locke and Alistair burst through the door and Penelope let out a gasp.

"Micah, what are you doing?"

She strode into the room completely fearlessly, standing beside me. I didn't take my eyes from Micah, and he stared straight back. Then Locke was there, blocking me from his view.

Alistair walked over to Micah, murmuring something too low for me to hear. Micah turned away and slammed into the bathroom, and the pots and pans rattled where they hung in the kitchen.

Alistair turned toward me, his posture stiff. He'd been ready for a fight. "Are you okay?"

He placed his hands on my shoulders, and my

body shuddered with relief. Something about Alistair was calm and safe. "I'm fine."

"It'll be okay," he whispered, and I watched his fingers flex as if he wanted to reach out and hug me. I wanted to believe him, but it didn't feel particularly okay at that moment.

Locke turned and hauled me into his arms. He wrapped me up against the safety of his chest, and it didn't even occur to me to protest. "I'm taking Layla back to my apartment. Micah can have her back when he appreciates what he has," he yelled at the bathroom, and marched out of the apartment. I could hear the sound of something smashing as we walked down the stairs.

I kind of wanted to protest about being dragged around, but if I was honest with myself, I didn't really want to be in my apartment anyway. Locke was muttering as he carried me easily, like I weighed absolutely nothing.

"What a damn idiot. So determined to be a martyr that he can't see what he has right in front of him."

He squeezed me a little tighter, and then let go, placing me on my feet. He still reached out and grabbed my hand, gently guiding me down the hall to the stairs. "My apartment is on the first floor. We can go there and I'll have a drink. You can have one too, if you want. I have a nice single malt." He cleared his throat. "Or you can sit in the library, or maybe go and see Ramer, he won't disturb you."

I knew I should say take me to the library, but I didn't want to be there, under everyone's scrutiny. More than that, I kind of wanted to be with the safe haven that was Locke.

Why was this shit so tumultuous? Why couldn't I have gotten a normal boyfriend who didn't turn furry once a month?

I concentrated on the warmth of Locke's hand encasing mine. He pushed open his door and I stepped into a typical guy apartment. Except for the huge artworks on the wall. Every available wall surface was covered in art. Oil paintings vied for space with black and white photographs. Small watercolor scenes were scattered around giant abstracts. It was like a gallery.

"Holy crap, Locke. This is amazing," I gasped, walking toward one of the walls. I noticed that it wasn't as random as it seemed, instead there was a theme running through each wall. One wall it was shades of blue, and another wall it was variations of cloud art, which seemed like a strange choice until I realized they all depicted storms and down the bottom was a small acrylic canvas of a boy on a beach by himself. It looked like the very heavens were about to open up and rain down on him. It was forlorn and made me feel so incredibly sad.

Locke came up beside me. "That tiny canvas cost

the most of all the art in this room. Not because it was painted by someone famous, but because it made me feel so much that I gave the street artist my beach house for it. Seemed justified at the time. I was a tortured, yet romantic soul back then. Obsessed with my own pain."

I looked over my shoulder at him. "And now?"

"Now I have no more beach houses to give away," he said softly.

I swallowed hard and stared at the art again. It reflected my turmoil. A glass of amber liquid appeared in front of me and I took it. Locke was behind me, and the warmth of his body was reassuring.

"Do you want to talk about it?"

I shook my head. "No."

"Is there anything I can do?"

I paused. I knew the timing was bad. I was hurt and angry, but I didn't care. "Would you kiss me?"

I felt Locke stiffen behind me. "Why?"

Well, that wasn't a no. I didn't really know why, I just blurted the first thing that popped into my brain. "Because I want you to. Because I'm attracted to you even though I shouldn't be. Because I'm sad and confused and I don't know what the hell I'm doing here. At least in Roseau I knew who I was, even if I was fucking miserable."

Locke let out a shuddering breath and spun me around to face him. "You are who you've always been.

Strong. Amazing. Caring." He let out a shuddering breath. "Beautiful." Then he pulled me into his chest and held me tightly. I melted into his body and let him become my cocoon. "I'm not going to kiss you, Layla."

Embarrassment hit me like a wave, and I tried to pull out of his arms, but he held on. "Not because I don't want to. God, do I want to. Not because Micah is my best friend either." He squeezed me tighter. "When I kiss you, I want it to be because you can't think about anything else but kissing me. I want you to be happy and know that you belong right here in my arms. Until then, I'm just going to hold you and lend you a little of my strength, okay, Butterfly?"

I nodded and my whole body shuddered. And that was when I realized I was crying. I was crying because of Micah, but it was more than that. I was crying because I had no one left but these strangers. My whole family was gone and just when I thought I was making a new one, it was all ripped away.

So for the first time in a month, I let myself mourn my mother.

And Locke just held me close through it all, like he understood my pain even better than I did.

11

L ocke held my feet on his lap and we watched game shows as I ate chocolate. I'm not saying it's a cure to the world's problems but lets just say there'd probably be less world wars if everyone just had a foot rub and a box of Godivas.

There was a knock at the door and I jumped. Locke gave me a reassuring smile and then stood. He opened the door, and I could hear Micah's voice on the other side. Locke stepped outside with him, shutting the door behind him.

I crept over to the door. I was pretty sure he was tearing him a new one, but I still wanted to hear. I pressed my ear to the door.

"It's not just you, Micah. I won't let you chase her away because you've got some unresolved fucking self-loathing thing happening. You'll treat her with respect, or I'll beat the respect into you, understand?"

I couldn't hear Micah's reply, but I stepped back as Locke pushed the door open again. He raised an eyebrow. "There's someone here to see you."

Locke squeezed my hand on the way past, and I stepped out into the hallway.

Micah looked like shit. Good. "I'm sorry, Layla."

I crossed my arms over my chest because I wasn't going to be that girl. I was going to have lady balls. "We haven't been dating for nearly long enough for you to pull that intimidation bullshit."

It would help if I couldn't feel the depth of his remorse. Totally cheating.

"I know. I won't do it again. I'm just struggling. Struggling to understand how anybody could love this?" He pointed to himself, though I knew he wasn't referring to human Micah. "I can't protect you from myself. What if Alistair hadn't turned up today? How far would I have gone to prove that you deserve better than the love of a predator? How far would I have gone to prove that I'm a monster?"

I sighed, wishing he would just pay attention to the matching space in his head that contained my feelings and would accept what he felt there wasn't an illusion. "This wouldn't be a problem if you would get it through your thick head that I'm kinda in love with you. In this fairytale, Little Red sees past the wolf's sharp teeth and they live happily ever after. At least they will, if the big bad wolf pulls his head out of his ass."

He let out a low chuckle. "Is there more than one big bad wolf in this story, because I know how you felt the other day when you were out with Locke. I know what you felt just now when you looked up at Alistair like he was your knight in shining armor."

I froze, like my body had hit the pause button while trying to work out if it should fight or flee.

Welcome to the game, old fight or flight response. Could have used you a couple of hours ago.

He shook his head, but didn't push it. "You're right Layla. I love you too much to live without you, no matter how selfish it is. I've loved you since you were seventeen and trying to fight wolves with a stiletto. From that moment, I've felt empty if I was more than two miles from where you were. I watched you return home from the hospital, battered and bruised, but with your head held high. I was so close that I heard you cry yourself to sleep at night, when you thought no one was around. Even when you were at college, I would follow you to classes and wait until you walked out of the doors again."

I snorted. "I'm pretty sure that's not romantic, just plain fucking creepy, Micah. You have to work on your grand declarations game. Little more *The Notebook*, little less *Fatal Attraction*, okay?"

He lifted his hand and pressed his finger against my lips, silencing me. "I lived in the woods for years, almost in exile, seeing and speaking to no one just to be close to you. Because you're my mate. It's why we have this connection. When I cleaned the wound on your shoulder five years ago, I linked you to me forever. It's why it never healed. It's why you can sense my emotions."

Mate. I wondered if that meant what I thought it did. Penguins mate for life. Beavers too. Does this mean my beaver won't ever want to see other people? Should I feel the attraction to Alistair and Locke that I do, if Micah and I are mates?

I didn't have the heart to tell him that I already knew that he'd hung around in the woods outside my town for years, that Locke had let it slip the day before. My brain was shying away from his words and latching onto trivial shit.

There was an incredible amount of love flowing through my mind in that moment, through our bond, like he was trying to convince me.

I felt... turmoil.

"Are Lycans like beavers?"

Micah blinked. "Excuse me?"

"Are they monogamous and mate for life? Like, are you meant to have only one mate and that is your only mate forever?"

That chuckle was back again. "I sense your

emotions, remember? You don't have to hint. But to answer your question, there aren't many groups in the supernatural world that push for monogamy. Lycanthropes definitely aren't one of them. We are... different from human society in that way. There are less women, less reproduction, which keeps our numbers low. So we often create groups." He let that hang in the air, letting me turn it over in my brain. I was going to have to turn this conversation over in my brain so much, it might turn into a cement mixer up there.

He leaned forward and kissed me tentatively, then looked at his watch with a sigh. "I need to go, Alistair is waiting for me. Is everything okay between us now?"

"Everything will be fine."

I just had to cross my fingers and hope I wasn't lying, because I had a feeling we weren't out of the woods just yet.

12

After Micah left, I was left alone with Locke, and somehow, I think I almost got permission to pursue something with the giant immortal man.

So I freaked the hell out and ran back to my apartment. Because I barely knew how to have a relationship with one man, let alone two. Locke had let me go with a wink and a kiss on the cheek that I felt all the way to my toes, and now I was restless as hell.

Pip was still hiding out on top of the bookcase after Micah's shift, and I could understand his wariness of a giant dog-man. Fred had defected already, basically spending all his time in the common room, where he was guaranteed food scraps and ear scratches all day. One of the apartment's inhabitants would deliver him back to the apartment each night, and I swear he was beginning to waddle.

Maybe, I'd go check on him. Yeah, that was an idea. My own company was driving me crazy, and Locke's company was just as confusing and let's face it, sexually frustrating.

I wandered into the common room and spied Fred sitting at the foot of an armchair, a pretty red haired girl scratching his head. He opened his eyes, wagged his tail once at my arrival, and then went back to his blissful sleep. Traitor.

The common room was in its usual state of chaos, people yelling at a video game on the big screen, others drinking coffee and chatting loudly. I decided that the library better suited my mood and barely stepped through the door when I walked straight into Ramer.

"I'm so sorry, I didn't see you there Ramer," I said, a little flustered.

I still hadn't forgiven myself for being such an inconsiderate asshole yesterday. Ramer mumbled something in return and launched himself at the door. I grabbed his hand before he could fully make his escape. I didn't want him to feel as if he had to avoid me for the remainder of my stay, which meant we had to talk sooner or later. To my surprise, Ramer spoke first.

"I really wish you wouldn't touch me, Layla. Please."

I frowned, but I let go. "I understand the risks in touching you and I don't appreciate you undermining the decisions I make as an adult. I want us to be friends, and I can't do that if you are terrified to even brush my arm. Now, will you please sit down, so I can get to know you and peer pressure you into getting to know me too?"

He took in my outfit of fluffy purple pants, suspenders and a t-shirt with a monster face on it and huffed out a laugh before sinking into the closest couch. "Okay. I kinda want to know what's going on with your wardrobe anyway."

I sat down next to him, careful not to invade his space. I didn't want him to avoid me out of fear, but I wasn't going to force him either.

"First, I'd like to clear the air. I apologize for yesterday's debacle. How about we forget about it completely and start again." I put out my hand. "Hi, my name is Layla. I am Micah's girlfriend and have no real special abilities of note." I smiled encouragingly.

He raised an eyebrow, and I only knew it was his eyebrow because it was slightly darker than the other hair on his face. "Uh, my name is Ramer and I make things grow so fast that they die prematurely of old age." He didn't shake my hand but I didn't take it personally.

Obviously, he was going to sulk about this, but he was underestimating my stubbornness and my ability to corral people to my way of thinking; it was one of my mother's primary gripes about me. I ignored the negativity in his statement.

"Grow faster, you say? I hear you have a green-house for an apartment, I would like to see it some-time, if I may?" Something sparkled in his eyes and I could tell he had a genuine passion for his plants.

"Wow, a bit forward, inviting yourself to my apart-ment already. You haven't even taken me to dinner yet."

I gaped and then gave him a mock outraged look. "Sir, what kind of hussy do you take me for? My inten-tions are completely platonic."

The sparkle in his eyes dimmed a little, before he pasted the smile back on his face. "That's okay. You don't have all the parts I like in my partners anyway," he said with a wink. "Would you like to see them now? My plants. Not my parts."

My laugh was too loud in the library, and I slapped my hand over my mouth to stifle the noise. "That sounds great. Lead the way." He led me out of the library and down one flight of stairs.

He unlocked his door, apparently not everyone adhered to Alistair and Locke's open door policy, and then turned to me. "You should close your eyes."

I don't know what it was about these guys and the

sense of sight, but they seemed to like to keep me in the dark. Still, I obediently shut my eyes.

"Okay, two steps inside. To the left. No, your other left." He huffed and held my elbow. Score one for Layla. He guided me into the room, barely touching me before he dropped his hand. "Open your eyes."

I blinked several times as my eyes adjusted to the vision of nature in front of me. I was surrounded by a blanket of green foliage, spotted by roses of every imaginable color. I could see violets, sunflowers, gerberas and lilies, and they were just the species I could name. The entire color spectrum was represented, from the whitest lily, to the reddest tulips, to a black rose that had veins of red running to the tips of its delicate petals.

"Ramer, this is spectacular! I've never seen so many flowers growing at once. It's amazing." It reminded me again of the butterfly exhibit that Locke took me to yesterday, except the smell in Ramer's room was intoxicating.

"I grew them all from seeds. They'll grow in any season with my help, so I have this many all year around." I walked from plant to plant, smelling the different perfumes, each as varying as the colors.

"Remind me to get you to plant my mother's vegetable garden next year."

With everything that had happened, my mother's death seemed like it had happened ages ago, but the pain was still a raw wound buried just below the surface, as evidenced by my breakdown in Locke's arms. Ramer must have guessed the cause of my sudden change in mood, because his face turned sad as well.

"How long ago did she die?" I was shocked that he had guessed the exact cause of my heartache, but then I assumed he had become an expert in bereavement.

"One month and two days ago. I wish you'd been there then too, Ramer. You would have liked her, when she was healthy anyway, and you could have shortened her suffering. She had a brain tumor that was completely inoperable. It was a very painful way to go." Ramer looked downcast, his gaze distant and deep in thought. "My parents have been dead for decades now. My mother was forty-one when she died but she looked like an eighty-year-old woman; I was nine. My father didn't come anywhere near me after her death but he still died at fifty-three of senile decay."

I couldn't even begin to understand his pain. He would have been so small, and completely oblivious to the fact that his affection was killing his parents until it was far too late. Anyone could see he carried the guilt over their deaths. I would have liked to dismiss it as irrational but I carried the guilt over my own mother's death, no matter how logically I knew it wasn't my fault.

"I'm sorry. I'm sure your mother loved you and had

she known, she wouldn't have changed a thing. But it wasn't your fault, you were a child, you couldn't have known." I was sure his father's abandonment hadn't helped.

I probably should change the subject. I didn't want to start our friendship on such a painful topic, bonding over our mutual orphan status.

"How long have you been with Eden for?" I sat down on one of the cane chairs that seemed to emerge from beneath the foliage. I noted he didn't have a TV, but classical music played softly in the background. His bed was surrounded by ferns, hanging from the roof and spilling over their pots on his bedside tables. There were bonsai plants on his table, and herbs on his kitchen windowsill.

"I was the 'Wolf Boy' in a circus when I was eleven, and Locke was the lion tamer. When he realised the exact nature of my power, before I even knew the true nature of it, he took me away from the circus and the public. Eden was small then, barely more than Alistair and Penelope, and Micah, of course. That would have been fifty years ago now. Locke spent a lot of time around fairs and circuses back then, it's where the paranormals tended to turn when they realized they weren't normal. That was before word of Eden got around. Now they end up here instead of being exploited for Normals."

Now I understood why they called the organization

Eden. It was an idyllic safe haven to those who had nowhere to turn.

"You don't look a day over twenty. Talk about a baby face."

He laughed, grabbing secateurs and gliding from plant to plant, cutting blooms from every plant. Soon he had the biggest bouquet of varying blooms I'd ever seen, but it hadn't even made a dent in the amount of flowers in the room.

"Take these. They'll brighten up Micah's rooms. I always wanted him to have more greenery up there but he refused. He was never home enough to care for it; he was always in the woods waiting for you." He snapped his mouth shut on what was supposed to be a secret. For an organization based on secrecy, they were pretty crappy at it. I patted his shoulder and for once, he didn't tense or shy away from my touch. Score two for Layla.

"Don't worry about it, Locke let that one slip the other day and Micah told me as much as well." I sniffed my blooms. "I might find a vase to put these in and then read some more. The library here is the stuff that dreams are made of."

I hesitated, knowing what I wanted to say but not knowing how to put it into words. "I'd like to be your friend, if I could. And that means I'll hug you when you need a hug, and punch you in the arm when you're being a dumbass, and not worry about every little touch. We'll be careful, but I want you to feel as comfortable around me as you do around Locke. Do you think we can do that?"

He screwed up his nose. "I don't know, Layla. Your friendship sounds kinda violent."

As if to prove his point, I reached over and punched him in the bicep.

Then I leaned in and kissed his cheek, and when he didn't pull away, I mentally gave a shout of victory.

13

Eden's members had begun arriving the previous day, but the true influx happened the following morning. I had met with the mysterious Annabeth, who had somehow gathered all the members in one afternoon. When I asked her how she did it, she spoke to me without moving her mouth, her voice sounding directly into my head.

"I can talk to people in their minds, like a voice in their head. It's quite easy actually, and I can talk to any person I've ever used my power on, no matter how far away they are. It's kind of like I have all their consciousness on speed dial in my mind, and all I have to do is focus on their essence and their consciousness is open to me. It comes in handy for group messages like this." She was a very nice older lady, and I instantly wanted to be her friend. Actually, everyone seemed nice in Eden; I wasn't sure if this was due to screening or if everyone was so glad to have a safe place in the world that it just made them thankful.

With all the people arriving, there came a variety of special abilities that I had never even contemplated. There was a man who could actually turn things into gold, who they'd nicknamed Midas. At least, I assumed it was a nickname and he wasn't the original King Midas. Micah had just laughed when I asked. Shapeshifters of every form, including one woman who literally became a fly on the wall.

There were people who got premonitions, those who could teleport, heal or change their human features to look like other people. The latter was actually a very funny man, who changed himself into Brad Pitt and threatened to steal me away from Micah. There was a woman who could control the temperature and a man who could lift a bus like a soda can. There were those who could turn invisible or walk through walls and one man who could generate electricity through his index fingers. All in all, it was a melting pot of amazing talents.

However, the most exciting, and terrifying arrivals would be the vampires. They were here as guests, and apparently that was where Micah had been the other day when Locke had taken me to the zoo. The vampires had their own society with its own power structure and rules, but everyone operated in the larger supernatural community. Micah and Alistair had gone to request aid, and a representative would be arriving soon to give their answer.

When I asked why they didn't just call, Micah had laughed. "They're show ponies. They like to stand center stage and pretend like they are saving us."

In preparation of their arrival, Eden members were organized by Alistair into defensive and neutral abilities, so that those who did not contain defensive talents could be protected from the vampires by those who could use their abilities to attack, who in turn would be protected by the immortals. When I asked Penelope why we were taking so many precautions if they were coming here as emissaries, she pointed to her neck.

"In a room full of heartbeats, sometimes it becomes hard for them to control themselves. It's just a contingency plan. I don't think anything will go wrong."

Lights were dimmed, windows covered by heavy drapes, and someone was dispatched to steal some O Negative from a local blood bank, all to ensure the comfort of the esteemed guests.

However, nothing prepared me for the actual arrival of the vampires. A wave of murmurs heralded them as the pair glided into the room while not visibly taking a single step.

It really was like the arrival of royalty, everyone holding their respective breaths as they walked past on their way to greet Micah and Alistair in the library.

Micah had placed me next to Locke, refusing to allow me to be by his side, arguing that if I was an elixir for him, I would be far too tempting even for the oldest, most restrained vampires. I leaned over to Locke.

"It's like they're rockstars. They're beautiful. It's like they are made of glass or something. And the woman has the most beautiful cape. I want a cape."

"A red one? So you can truly be the Red Riding Hood that Micah teases you about?" he teased.

I grinned, because that sounded fucking badass. I dare any person, grown or not, to wear a cape and not feel like a badass.

My eyes drifted back to the vampires. They were exquisite examples of beauty. The male was tall, his glossy hair hanging smoothly to his shoulders, which were slight in width but perfectly proportioned with the rest of his body. He was clad in an immaculately tailored black suit, the cut screaming big money. He had low brows and almost black eyes that had the faintest ring of deep blue around the edges. If he was extremely attractive, the woman was breathtaking. She reminded me of a glass angel atop a Christmas tree. She had perfect blonde hair that fell in ringlets down her back. Her lithe body was as graceful as a dancer's and her heart shaped face contained delicate features above perfect cupid's bow lips. Adding to her angel image, apart from the pearly luminescent skin, was that she was clothed in a white velvet dress that stopped just above her knees, trimmed with white fur, and long sleeves that looped over her middle fingers. Between that and the red velvet cape, she looked ethereal, like something that would step out of a teenage boy's wet dream.

As the door closed behind them, the chatter hit a fevered pitch and I turned back to Locke.

"Come on, they'll be in there for awhile." He grabbed my hand and led me from the room and down two flights of stairs to his apartment. He pushed open his door, and stepped through, and I followed him in.

"Layla?"

I moved to the couch, but he caught my hand again. I looked at him and frowned. "Yeah?"

"Can I kiss you now?"

I froze again. Shit. It was like I got stuck in a record scratch every time someone said they wanted to kiss me. I tried to think my way through it.

Pro: I really, really wanted to kiss him.

Con: Micah is my mate.

Pro: Micah seemed okay with the idea of me having multiple lovers. Hooray.

Con:???

"Um, I'd like that?"

He pulled me into his arms and then he kissed me. And I mean, really, really kissed me. It wasn't tentative or gentle. He kissed me like he wanted to own me and there was something about a kiss like that. It made you want to be possessed. I kissed him back, wrapping my arms around his neck. He slid his hands under my ass and picked me up, pressing me back against his door, then tearing his mouth away.

He was panting, his pupils completely blown out with lust. "That is better than I ever imagined. And I've imagined it every night since you stood in front of me in the butterfly exhibit, your lip trapped between your teeth and your eyes closed." He kissed me quick and hard, like he couldn't help himself. "Say you want this, Butterfly. Say it, and I promise I'll give you as much pleasure as your body can contain. I'll make you scream my name until your voice is hoarse and your legs shake."

His words went right to my core. My pussy clenched, wanting what he was promising. "But Micah is my mate."

"I know. He told me. He also told me that he was okay with me pursuing you, but if I made you feel even a little uncomfortable, he was going to rewrite new ways to make me die." Locke grinned, and I shook my head. This was too crazy. Too much to hope for. "What do you say, Layla. Do you want this? Want me?"

I slid my hand up into his hair and gripped it tight. "Yes. I want this."

He let out a shuddering sigh of relief, and then his lips were on mine again. He ground the hard length of his cock against the seemingly non-existent barrier of my underwear. "I saw you in that skirt today, and it was like it just short circuited my brain."

I was wearing a skater skirt printed with kawaii sushi, which doesn't scream seduction to me but hell, I'd take it. His hands slid up my thighs to my ass and he squeezed and groaned at the same time.

I rolled my hips against his cock again and the noise he made was almost pained. "We are taking this slow," he said, sliding my skirt up to my waist and not going all that slow despite his words. Not that I was complaining, especially when he lowered me to my feet and then dropped to his knees.

There was something about this larger-than-life man on his knees in front of me that made me hot all over. He pushed up my skirt and gripped my under-wear, sliding them down my legs. He groaned again, kissing the inside of my thighs.

"One day soon, I am going to run my tongue over every inch of you to find all the places that make your body sing. But right now, I'm going to do it the easy way."

Before I could get my mouth to move enough to ask what the easy way was, he was showing me. He gripped my leg and put it over his shoulder, nipping the sensitive flesh of my inner thigh, then he grabbed my other leg and he lifted me up until both my knees were over his shoulders and his hands were gripping my upper thighs and holding me pinned to the wall like a butterfly to a board.

I gripped his hair like a lifeline, and I didn't have time to feel awkward about having my crotch that close to someone's face because he was running his tongue up my slit and moaning like I was his favorite flavor. He lifted me higher, burying his face between my thighs and I lost all conscious thought except how talented he was with his mouth. I guess five hundred years gave you a lot of time to practice.

"Locke," I moaned and he doubled his efforts, scraping my clit with his teeth, which made me clench my thighs around his head. I was glad he was immortal, because I could have done some serious spinal damage when he thrust his tongue inside my core, his nose nudging my clit and doing this unbelievable roll with his tongue. He squeezed my thighs, spearing me with his tongue, before moving upwards and sucking on my clit.

It was too much.

I pulled him closer with my feet as my orgasm steamrolled me, coming all over his face. I panted, and when he loosened his grip, my legs wobbled until I collapsed to my knees too. He looked down at me, with my flushed cheeks and rubber legs and smiled. His face was glossy with my cum and he grinned before lifting his shirt and wiping it away. Then he kissed me again.

"I could do that every hour of the day for the rest of eternity," he moaned against my lips.

I wrapped my arms around his waist, pressing my face into his chest. "I think I'd like that." But reality was setting back in.

Shit. Micah would have felt all that. Should I be worried? Would he be mad?

Locke must have felt me tense, because he kissed the top of my head and held me close. "It'll be okay, Layla. We all just want whatever it is that makes you happy."

In this room, in this moment, in Locke's arms? I couldn't think of anything that would make me happier.

Except maybe an orgy.

14

T he chairs quickly filled, two at the front saved for the esteemed guests and two for Micah and Alistair. Micah walked out of the library and into the room, his hand resting on the female vampire's arm. Jealousy flared up inside me and I stared daggers at them both. He felt happy, damn him. I huffed and Ramer raised an eyebrow. I was squished between him and Locke, even though Locke rightfully should have been up in the immortals section too. Micah must have felt my gaze, because he turned and raised an eyebrow. Shit. He knew what I'd been up to while he was in his meeting. My cheeks flushed and I tried to tell if he was mad or jealous or cool with the whole thing. Unfortunately, he had his emotions locked down tight.

Alistair's voice rose above the noise.

"Members, I am pleased to introduce you to Alexi and Anastasia, representatives of the Vampire Council."

The two nodded their greeting before they sat at the front of the crowd. They didn't look like they were about to spring up and start a massacre of members, but everyone was on high alert anyway. Even Ramer was stiff, sitting as close to me as possible without touching me. He took his secondhand responsibility for my safety very seriously.

Alistair continued. "We've all gathered here due to a mutual threat to all preternatural beings. The bounty hunters that hunt us for profit have been a great threat over the years, however in recent months, an ancient organization has reared its head for a new era. The Hounds of God are as old as memory. Originally a militant offshoot of a renegade Vatican, their sole purpose was to find and hunt preternaturals, or demons and the possessed as they refer to us. Their goal was never to capture, but to eradicate." There was a fearful swell of noise, and Alistair lifted his hands to hush everyone. "In years past, The Hounds have believed in the sanctity of *human* life, which was why they hunted us with such ferocity. However, it has become apparent that the The Hounds have become more careless with their human collateral damage. The relative safety of the city is no longer a barrier. We are vulnerable here in our home like never before."

I looked around the room at all the pale faces. Locke's body all but vibrated with frustrated anger, and I slid my hand into his to center him. He looked down at me, his blue eyes softening, as he gripped my tiny hand in his.

Alistair waited until everyone calmed a little more. "I'm suggesting that we consider an offensive action to neutralize the threat before it walks through our front door."

There was a buzz around the room, some whispered and others outright shocked. A woman somewhere in the middle piped up.

"We don't know anything about them, they could outnumber us ten to one. We could be laying our heads on the chopping block for them."

Micah stepped forward, taking Alistair's position at the front of the room. "We have a myriad of powers that will even out the playing field no matter the numbers. Even the non-offensive powers can be invaluable. We are not helpless. From what I've seen, The Hounds are mostly human zealots, strong and deadly for sure, but still human. It's also not true that we don't know anything about them; we know their beginnings and their history. We know what they want, and I swear we will not give it to them without a fight."

Micah sat back down, leaning close to the female vampire, Anastasia, as he whispered something in her ear. Finally, he nodded and helped her from her chair.

I didn't understand why she needed so much support, she had supernatural abilities. She could probably jump from the street to the roof of this apartment building without even breaking a sweat. Anastasia turned to address the conference.

"I am Anastasia. I have been sent by the Vampire Council to speak on their behalf. The Council has given much thought to the situation that was presented before us three days ago by your brethren Alistair Cannon and Micah Ari. We were unanimous in our agreement that The Hounds are a parasite that needs to be eradicated." There was a small, hopeful chatter around the room, but Anastasia wasn't finished. "However, after much debate amongst the Council, we have decided not to pursue this war with you. Although we ourselves have suffered the very occasional fatality at the hands of The Hounds, we do not believe that they are a great enough threat to our survival to warrant involving ourselves in a full-scale war. It is believed that such a war will kill more of our numbers than The Hounds could kill in many centuries. We are not as physically vulnerable as your kind. The Council wishes you every success in this endeavor, however we officially decline your request for an alliance."

There was a roar of protests from the formerly meek members around the room, all fear of the vampires lost in their indignation. I could feel Micah's anger rising up, his rage muddling with mine until I wanted to tear someone's throat out with my teeth. Alistair stood up, trying to regain some semblance of order.

"All things considered, I suggest we take a break and continue this conference tomorrow, if our esteemed guests are willing to return." Alexi nodded his assent. "Thank you. A lot of things must be considered before we make our decision."

There was a great exodus from the room into the hall and I lost sight of Micah. He reappeared directly in front of me, his face stormy with barely controlled anger. His eyes lingered a little too long on where my hand was still twined with Locke's. I didn't know what to do. If I dropped it like I was doing something wrong, it would hurt Locke's feelings. If I didn't, I wasn't convinced that Micah wouldn't tear it off and beat Locke with it.

Micah took a deep breath, getting himself under control. "Let's go."

I threw an apologetic look at Locke and Ramer, and then doubletimed it to keep up with Micah. Weaving our way around the crowd, we were almost to the door when we were forced to stop by Anastasia blocking our path. Micah tucked me behind his body protectively.

"Micah, I really am sorry, but it was the will of the Council. In my personal defence, I was arguing for joining your forces. I believe the Council is being incredibly short sighted in their decision. I thought their injured pride over losing even one of our brethren to The Hounds would be enough to get them to agree to your proposal, but I was wrong. However, they are our governing body and their word is law."

Micah fixed her with a dead stare, and I very briefly felt sorry for her. "They're cowards."

We swept out of the rooms and up the stairs to Micah's apartments. He had barely walked through the doors before I noticed him growing larger and hair spreading across his body. He growled low and long. I didn't know if I should call for help again, but I decided to put my money where my mouth was. I trusted Micah.

"I couldn't do this down there without being perceived as a threat to the vampires," he growled low. "How could they just abandon us to die?" His voice had descended in pitch until it was a low rumble echoing around the room. I walked over and raised my hand to his stomach, gently stroking his fur, trying to comfort him. I hadn't gotten to touch him in this form with his anger so hot. The fur on his stomach was soft and a lighter shade to the coarse hair that ran over his spine. He was huge and I barely came up to his chest.

But he was amazing, and I still couldn't believe that this beast and Micah were the same person.

He made a low purr as I stroked my nails across his chest. "I know we were relying on their help, but we'll just have to adapt. Our plan can no longer be an offen-

sive one. We have to think of moving everyone somewhere safer. What about Roseau? My farm is yours to
turn into any kind of high security sanctuary you think
is necessary. We'll just tell the townspeople it's a
convent or a monastery or something. We'll figure it
out, Micah. We'll do it together."

His big eyes looked down at me, and his expression
was soft. "You smell like Locke."

Well, this is awkward. And probably not the time to
have this conversation but…

"I'm your mate, right?" Micah nodded his shaggy
head. "Does that mean I shouldn't feel things for other
people? It's not a one and done, for life kind of deal,
right?"

He shook his head, morphing back down to man.
He strode to the dresser and pulled on a worn pair of
jeans, sans underwear. "Monogamy is a human
concept. Many shifters, and a lot of other supernatural
creatures, believe in polyamorous family groups.
Sometimes it's a male with a group of females, but
more often it's one female and a handful of males.
Females are more scarce in our world."

I swallowed hard. He'd said as much before, but I
wanted to make sure. I felt like my heart was going to
explode in my chest. "Is that something you'd be open
to? You don't seem like the sharing is caring type, no
offense."

He was silent for a long time, but he seemed to

consider it. I wished he'd say one way or another because I was about to pass out, holding my damn breath.

"I think with certain people, I would be okay with it." He nodded decisively. "Locke is one of those people."

I wrapped my arms and legs around his body until I was cradled against his chest. "I got kind of lucky with you, you know that right?"

He snorted. "Half of Eden would disagree with you. But I love you, and I want you to be happy. I know I'm a moody bastard, and around the full moon I get..."

"Raging PMS?" I suggested, and he laughed.

"Basically. So if Locke can ease the burden of that time of the month..." He had to stop because I snorted so loud. That time of the month. He leaned forward and bit my lip. "Then I'm happy if you're happy."

He kissed me and I hummed contentedly as I kissed him back. I was lucky. I had a feeling that my relationship with Micah was always going to be a rollercoaster, but this feeling of giddy joy, of love, would always be there too.

"We need to establish an alternative plan before tomorrow so it can be presented to the conference. Tell me what you were thinking."

"For possible mates?" I squeaked out.

He laughed. "For a possible Plan B to save Eden."

He wrapped his arms around me as we discussed ideas, my head resting on his chest as he spoke.

I thought that any plan that involved Micah standing beside me was a good one, no matter the outcome.

15

We had a plan to protect those who needed protecting.

Micah eventually decided that he needed to discuss the plan with Alistair and Locke at around two in the morning and left me in bed. By about three, I got sick of tossing and turning, and headed down to the library. I found it eerily empty.

I moved to the common room, but halted at the door at the sound of voices and a woman's laughing voice.

"Really Ramer, we are millennia old creatures, you seriously think that our aversion to sunlight isn't the first thing we worked on overcoming? Some specially formulated barrier cream and a commitment to remaining covered from the sun's rays while outside pretty much cured that problem early on. Besides, our vulnerability to the sun has been vastly overstated, it's more like third degree burns then turning to a pile of smoldering ash. It hurts the eyes of the young ones for the first fifteen years though."

Ducking my head around the door, I saw Ramer leaning close to Anastasia as he replied. She gave a throaty laugh that was pure sex. Her head jerked up as she sensed my presence and she looked at me, a small smile tilting the corners of her mouth.

"Hello, Layla." Her voice sounded breathy. Jesus.

I'm straight, I'm straight, I'm straight, I chanted to myself. But honestly, she could make me switch sides if she tried.

Ramer smiled over at me, looking more at ease than I'd ever seen him. "Layla! Have you been personally introduced to Anastasia? Anastasia, this is Layla. She is Micah's mate." Ramer summed it up so nicely that I had to stop myself feeling a catty sense of satisfaction. At least she now knew to whom Micah belonged. Anastasia put her hand on mine. Her hands were cold but her grip was strong. She smiled, which reminded me of a crocodile, but her eyes held genuine delight.

"Layla and I haven't met officially, no. It's a pleasure to meet you, the woman who has Micah's heart. And not just Micah's, if I'm correct. But I can see why, you do smell unique, almost sweet."

I rapidly went from feeling vindicated that she had

acknowledged my superior claim to Micah and Locke, to being a bit uncomfortable. I imagined this was how lobsters felt in the tanks at restaurants. Ramer cleared his throat and she glanced his way.

"Apologies. I promise I'm not about to make her a snack." She looked back at Ramer and gave him a smile that was pure invitation. Her tone suggested that Ramer might not be so lucky and that he'd definitely enjoy it. Ramer just grinned back goofily.

Boy, he was smitten. Though, I thought Ramer was gay when he mentioned I didn't have the right parts the other day?

I mentally slapped my head. Vampires were undead, right? Well, Ramer definitely couldn't speed up her life cycle, because she was already at the end of it, biologically anyway. He could, uh, touch all he liked.

I shifted from foot to foot, trying to work out how to escape this situation without becoming a snack or causing offence. Anastasia must have noticed my uncomfortable mood, because she gave me that mysterious little smile again.

"You have nothing to worry about from me. I am over four hundred years old. I've learned a little restraint, no matter how delectable you smell. But I was being serious about your scent. I don't think I've smelled anyone with undertones quite the same as yours."

She squinted slightly as she sniffed the air, like

humans would when they walked outside and smelled someone cooking a barbeque, and it undermined the reassuring nature of her statements.

I forced a smile. "It's a mystery. I really should head back to bed. It was nice to meet you. Ramer? I'll see you in the morning. Um, don't do anything I wouldn't do?"

"Then I guess Locke and Micah are safe for the night," he laughed.

I stuck my tongue out at him and hot footed it back up to the apartments. The corridors were eerily quiet this late at night, even though I doubted anyone was getting much sleep after the day's revelations.

Turning on all the lights in Micah's apartment, I slid under the blankets like they could save me from the things that went bump in the night. Pip settled on my back, ensuring I was pinned to the spot, acting as sentinel even as I acted as cat bed. Then I finally fell asleep dreaming of fangs and threesomes.

The second conference was a much more subdued affair. The excitement over the vampires had dimmed, and our vulnerability to The Hounds had become a pressing problem.

The vampires sat up front again, Alexi's face set like marble. He obviously wasn't very happy about Micah's little shit fit. The ranks of defence employed in yesterday's meeting were abandoned in an act of good faith, however on closer inspection, it still occurred fairly naturally with the more vulnerable members sitting as far away from potential predators as possible. I sat next to Micah, with Alistair on my other side. I slid my hand into Alistair's, and he looked over at me, a frown on his face as he looked between my face and our joined hands. Then he squeezed it gently, and I finally breathed.

Alistair leaned over to whisper in my ear, and I shivered as his lips accidentally brushed the sensitive skin. "It's not too late to back out of this madness, you know." I pulled away and frowned, and though he was smiling, his eyes were serious.

"My mate bond would say otherwise."

He shrugged. "There are ways. But I think I'd miss you if you left." He winked, leaving me to wonder what the hell he meant as he stood and addressed the room. "Could I have your attention please? As you all know, in light of the decision of the Vampire Council to not render aid, the plan of an offensive attack on The Hounds is no longer viable. I will not risk even a single life to a plan doomed to failure."

There was a murmur around the room, and the tension in the air ratcheted up a notch.

"We now have to look to plans of defence, because The Hounds will not just disappear. The idea of disbanding Eden has been raised and needs to be considered by this conference. By dispersing members out into the world, we will not create such a concentrated target for The Hounds. However, this would leave every member vulnerable, especially those with neutral abilities. It would mean again hiding our abilities in the world of Normals, which in itself can cause distress to some of the members. I know this is not an ideal plan, however as I mentioned, disbandment must be considered."

There were some weak cries of horror, but mostly people just looked stunned. I was fairly sure that Alistair was not the only person who looked at Eden as if it were a family, the only people in the whole world who understood and accepted them as who they were, not who they pretended to be. Alistair continued.

"However, an alternative to disbandment has been presented to us by our newest member, Layla. In history, a well-constructed fort could keep out even the most malicious armies. We intend to recreate a modern version of an impenetrable fort. The suggestion has been made that a sanctuary be built, fortified as much as possible, and able to house all our members safely. It was also suggested by Penelope, that perhaps it could be utilized as an Academy for Preternaturals, both those who live with us on campus by necessity, and other Preternaturals in North America. This would help us create better relationships with the greater supernatural community, something that up until this time has been difficult."

I gaped. An Academy? I looked around the room,

and noticed that a lot of the inhabitants were young, many in their teens. Vulnerable and in need of a safe haven, but also an education. I knew Penelope did what she could, but as an Academy, maybe they would have the opportunity to be more. I liked it.

Alistair waited for the group to quiet down. "The use of it as an Academy might quell the general suspicion of us opening up a large facility in a probably isolated area. Rich humans do these kinds of things all the time. Adults who depend on our facilities will work as staff, guaranteeing them a wage and a livelihood, as well as a safe haven. I hope you all like children." There were groans and mutters from the crowd, as was expected. "We have discussed other probable covers, including a monastery and a mental institution, but given the general backgrounds of most of our members, and the vindictiveness of the Church, we think an Academy would work best. Any questions?"

A woman with flaming red hair put up her hand. "Where are we going to have this Academy, and what will stop The Hounds from just attacking us there?"

"That is a good question, Sarah. We hope that a remote location and state of the art security will help us get ahead of any attacks. We are open to ideas for locations, if anyone has any suggestions."

Anastasia cleared her throat. "I may have a potential location for you. In Canada. We will speak of it afterwards." Alexi whipped toward her, his face pulled down in a frown.

Alistair raised an eyebrow at her, and nodded.

More questions were asked, like would they accept Normals into the Academy? Would they be able to shift? Where would we get the money to build the Academy they were pitching?

That last one stung. Alistair just gave the man who asked a megawatt smile. "Don't worry about the money. Eden will take care of it." I knew that Eden didn't have that kind of money after my outing with Locke. That was going to be a problem, but I trusted Alistair. We'd do whatever it took.

Finally, all the questions had been asked and I heaved a sigh of relief. To me, it was the only solution, but the members deserved to air their concerns. I only wished the seats were more comfortable. It was time for the vote, the vampires excluded, of course.

"All in favor of disbanding Eden, raise your hand?" A couple of hands were raised, but I didn't recognize them. Members who lived outside Eden's compound then. This decision wouldn't affect them too greatly.

Alistair continued. "Disbanding failed. All those in favour of building an Academy?" This time the majority of hands went up and I let out the breath I hadn't even realized I was holding. They'd made the right choice. "The move to create an Academy has passed."

I doubt anyone missed the relief on Alistair's face. "I'd like to thank every one of you for returning when we needed you. I'd also like to thank Anastasia and Alexi for their participation. Anastasia has agreed to stay and help fortify Eden until we have relocated. If you intend to move with us, I suggest you start making preparations now. Conference closed."

16

There was something mesmerizing about watching the vampires drink blood from crystal goblets in Alistair's sitting room. The light caught it and it looked impossibly ruby in color.

Alexi pouted in the corner, his arms crossed over his chest and a bored expression on his face. Anastasia sat on the long couch, Ramer beside her but not too close. I kind of wondered what they got up to last night, but I wasn't about to ask. But judging by Ramer's goofy expression, it had been a good night.

"So, in Canada, there is a town."

Alexi snorted, giving his opinion on this town. Anastasia gave him an annoyed look but continued. "It is a colony of vampires who live by different morals than the rest of vampirekind. They have pledged not to take blood directly from humans, instead relying on bagged blood."

I couldn't help my surprised squeak. Alistair frowned. "That seems odd, for a vampire."

Alexi made another rude noise. "Insanity. Why torture yourself by resisting our very way of life? They can't possibly be satisfied sitting inside their tiny shithole town pretending to be human."

Anastasia spoke harshly to Alexi in another language, and the vampire went back to being sullen. "Their leader is very old. One of our ancients. He founded the town and according to our reports, it has been reasonably successful. There has been a little upset with their town doctor almost alerting the Canadian authorities to our existence, but generally they have kept to themselves."

Locke dragged me across the couch and into his lap. Alistair looked at us, his face alight with surprise. Guess no one had filled him in on our new relationship. "No offence, Anastasia, but setting up school next to a vampire colony doesn't seem overly... safe. Present company excluded, preternaturals and vampires haven't always had the most harmonious of relationships."

"He means you used to eat us," Locke added.

Alexi grinned. "Other supernaturals are delicious too. Just harder to catch."

My head whipped toward him, and Anastasia looked a second away from thumping him. "You're correct, Locke. But I believe that these vampires are different and will be sympathetic to your plight. They have a very strong relationship with a neighboring colony of shapeshifters, the Alpha of which is also the Alpha of the combined North Western Packs. That is definitely someone you could appeal to for aid." Anastasia looked directly at me, though I don't know why. I had absolutely no sway. "If you can get the land between them, garner their support and word to provide aid in case of an attack, I believe that you could not possibly possess a safer location."

Well, I was sold. Alistair looked pensive and I could all but see his brain working overtime.

"Thank you for the suggestion. And the offer of aid. We appreciate that it might put you in a difficult position."

Alexi opened his mouth to say something, and Anastasia flashed her fangs in a snarl. She went from beautiful to terrifying in a flash. I got it now, how someone so beautiful could be the deadliest of us all.

She turned back to Alistair and she was all smiles again. "We should go and brief the Council on the events of today. I'll return at nightfall," she said, and I saw the way her eyes slid to Ramer. Oh. Booty calls and philanthropy all in one. That was smart.

There were a few more pleasantries, and then the

vampires left. Alistair finally slumped onto the couch and raked a hand over his face. "What a mess."

I wanted to hug him, but I wasn't sure we were there yet.

Baby steps, Layla. You don't have to go from virgin to a dick in each hole in less than a month. Talk about over-achieving.

Still, the stress on Alistair tugged at my chest. I wanted to help bear some of his burden. I gave him a soft smile. "It's a good option."

Locke rumbled his agreement. "I'm with Layla on this one. I doubt there's many options like that in the rest of the world. It can't hurt to ask, right?"

Penelope poured two glasses of wine and handed me one. I was a bit of a lightweight when it came to alcohol. Day drinking with your dog is pretty frowned upon, even by other hermits. "What about the money? We can't ask it of the members, they're all as poor as we are. This place costs a small fortune to run, as well as ensuring the members in the world have emergency funds should they need to run. We could dip into that reserve, but it would leave them vulnerable. And it still wouldn't be enough. With the kind of security tech we'd need? Not to mention construction costs?"

She downed her glass of wine, and then picked up the bottle and swigged straight from it. "We need a benefactor. Someone from the supernatural community with large pockets and too much bleeding heart."

"Know anyone?" Micah piped up, and Penelope shrugged.

"Not off the top of my head, but I can ask around. Use my wiles on some rich old dude until he gives me cash."

Ramer snorted. "What wiles?"

Penelope picked up a pillow and threw it at his head. "I have wiles, butthead. Though the idea of saggy dick kind of makes me want to vomit."

Locke huffed out a laugh and it tickled my ear. "The idea of any dick makes you want to vomit."

Penelope took another swig of wine. "The man has a point." She sighed and handed me the bottle, even though my glass was still full. "So we try for a bunch of small benefactors. I'll move some money around, see if we can't make it stretch. We just need enough for land and housing. The Academy can come later when we aren't running for our lives."

We all agreed and they started making a list of possible donors. I was useless in this. I had no money, just debt. I stood to leave, but Micah hooked an arm around my waist and pulled me into his lap instead.

I spent the night being snuggled, passed back and forth between Locke and Micah. I added what I could, worked on timelines and the things I knew from being human. Anything I didn't know, I googled, including how to be a sugar baby at Pea's request.

It was a long night of going in circles.

"Actually, I've known a couple of shifters in my time, and more than a few of Eden's members are shifters. Maybe we can appeal to the Convocation Reps themselves?" Locke suggested. I didn't know what the Convocation was but there was a general hum of approval around the room. "Actually, I have the business card of a lion shifter I met once... Hang on, I'll go and find it," Locke said, dumping me into Alistair's lap and racing out the door.

Both Alistair and I froze, looking at each other. His arms had wrapped around my waist to steady me by instinct, but he hadn't dropped them yet either.

"Uh, hi?" I said, going to wiggle off his lap but he sucked in a breath and held me tighter. That's when I realized the hard thing under my ass wasn't his cellphone. It was his dick. Had he been this hard all night? Over what? Me?

"Hey," he said softly. "Do you want to move?" It was a hesitant question, and my instinctive answer was no. I looked at Micah, and although he raised his eyebrow, he didn't stop the conversation he was having with Ramer and Pea.

I looked back at Alistair. "Is it weird if I say no?" I wiggled to get more comfortable. Yeah, let's go with that. Alistair hissed out a breath, but shook his head.

"Not weird. Have you read those journals I've given you yet?"

I shook my head. "Only a little bit about the full

moon. There hasn't been time." He nodded and I didn't miss him inhaling deeply. Was he sniffing me?

We were both still sitting stiffly, and I let myself relax into his body. He leaned back, bundling me to his chest and he sighed deeply. I looked up into his golden eyes. "Are you okay?"

His fingertips played with the ends of my hair. "Mmm, I'm fine. It's just been a long time since I've held a woman in my arms. It's nice." There was something on his face I couldn't quite grasp, but still, I raised a brow.

"I find that hard to believe." It was true. Alistair was gorgeous.

I shifted my ass a little and he groaned. "Layla, you have to stop moving."

"Am I hurting you?"

He tightened his arms. "God no. Well, torturing me yes, but it's a good kind of torture. If you don't stop moving, one of two things will happen. I will succumb to the hard-on I've had all night watching your creamy thighs spread all over Locke and Micah and come in my pants like a teen. Or I'll slide my hand under your skirt, move your panties to the side, and let you ride me until the ache goes away," he whispered in my ear and I stilled. Well, ninety percent of me stilled. My core was clenching like it could detach from my body and make all our dreams come true. His body tensed under mine too. "Too much?"

I leaned in, until my lips brushed his ear. "Not enough."

I felt his body shudder. Locke burst back through the door, holding a gilded card above his head. "Found it."

His eyes took in me and Alistair. His grin was broad and he winked, but then strode back through the room completely nonchalantly. "Axel down in Chatsville. Fucking lion Alphas are nasty bastards, but Axel was alright." He sat back down beside us, and Alistair reluctantly passed me back to him. I frowned, as did Locke.

Alistair just smiled tightly. "Read the journals. I need a cold shower," he murmured softly. He looked at the rest of the group. "Let's pick this up tomorrow."

Then he left the room, the door to the bathroom closing quietly.

Locke had a surprised look on his face, his eyebrows nearly to his hairline. "Oh."

Yeah, Locke definitely knew something I didn't. "What?"

He grinned, setting me on my feet and swatting my ass with his hand. "The Professor gave you homework. Better get to it."

17

U*nlike most shifters, Lycanthropes can scent their mates. However, a mate bond can only be cemented by the transference of blood and the act of coitus.*

I read that part over and over again, trying to decide what that meant for me.

It meant that Micah had known I was his mate that night when he'd healed my wounds. It had meant he'd known that it would cement our mate bond when we'd had sex. I didn't know if I was mad or not.

I remembered his hesitation, how conflicted he was. The fact I'd basically jumped him. But on the flip-side, I would have liked a choice in whether I was attached to a man forever through a mate bond before it happened.

If he had told me, would I still have made love with

him? Yes. It wouldn't have changed anything. But I was still going to make him grovel for forgiveness.

The other thing that played on my mind was why Alistair had been hellbent on me reading this section. Was it even this section that he wanted me to read? There was a red post-it note on this page, which made it seem important, but was he just giving me information about mine and Micah's mate bond, or was it something else?

Something more personal.

Ugh, guys were confusing and the fact they turned into giant furry monsters didn't change that.

Micah was pouring over maps of the US and Canada, and I watched his strong shoulders bunch and flex. I kind of wanted him to fuck me on those maps.

"Did you know I was your mate when you saved me?"

He looked up, his golden eyes pinning me to the spot. "Yes. But you were too young for me to pursue."

Hmmph. I guess that was a half decent answer.

"So you smelled me and thought, yeah, I wouldn't mind a piece of that for all of eternity?"

He gave me a crooked grin. "Something like that." Then he went back to poring over the maps.

Maybe I smelled good? I know Alistair seemed to like... Holy shit.

"Micah!"

He vaulted over the island counter, and I'm not going to lie, it was hot as fuck. "What? Are you okay?"

He looked panicked and I held back the grin that wanted to split my face. Yeah, I kinda loved him, even if he was an asshole. Maybe I was crazy.

"Alistair is my mate." I said it casually like it didn't mean anything.

Micah huffed and pulled me into his arms. "Is that all? Christ, I thought something was wrong with you." He looked down at me, his eyes narrowing. "The jury is still out on whether that's still a possibility."

I elbowed him in the ribs. "What do you mean, 'is that all'?" I growled out the last words in a gruff mimic. "Don't you have anything else to say about it?"

"One, I don't sound like that. And two, I already knew that Alistair scented you as his mate."

Well, now I was pissed. "Excuse me?" I stepped back a little and looked up at his stupid face. "Are you telling me that you've known the entire time that I was his mate and you didn't think to say anything?"

Micah had the audacity to shrug. "What was I going to say? Oh hey Layla, I know you're still acclimatising to being with one furry asshole, but see that complete stranger over there? Well, you're the one person he's been waiting on for his whole life." He reached out and grabbed my wrist, tugging me back into his body. "How would that have gone?"

Gah. Damn reasonable bastard. I think I preferred

his hairy time of the month. He gripped my chin. "How would that have gone?"

"Probably not great," I grumbled.

He kissed the top of my head, and I rested my cheek over his heart. "He's waited this long, you don't need to rush anything. You aren't bound to be his mate. The choice is always yours."

I wrapped my arms around his waist, making sure he knew he was mine, whether he liked it or not really. "Would he find another mate if I didn't bond with him?" The idea of him having another mate made me more uncomfortable than I'd like to admit.

"He might find another. It's possible." His tone told me that while it was possible, it was freaking unlikely. Didn't really matter, because I liked Alistair before I knew we were possibly, maybe, mates.

Micah must have misconstrued my silence. "He'll understand, Layla. He's a nice guy and he'd hate if you felt obligated to be with him out of guilt."

Oh, I'd spent way too long not giving a fuck to be with someone out of guilt. No, I wanted to be with Alistair out of pure, unadulterated lust. I just wasn't sure that was better.

Let's just say that when we reconvened the next day, I was a weird combination of awkward and lustful. Which was basically me all the time these days, but today that weird mojo was laser focused on Alistair. I put on my favorite bright gold velvet dress, and I realized it matched both Alistair and Micah's eyes. I wondered if I'd subconsciously known when I bought it that Micah was my mate?

Locke had snagged me in the hallway, and Micah had huffed, giving me a quick kiss before leaving us alone.

Locke didn't waste any time, kissing me like he was starving for it. I kissed him back, the freedom of doing it without worrying that Micah would be mad was kind of liberating. I bit his bottom lip and he moaned into my mouth. "I want to fuck you through this wall right now."

He picked me up and I squealed like I was a giddy teenage girl. It was gross. But then he pressed me against the wall and I felt the hard line of his dick. So. Fucking. Big. Maybe he did intend to fuck me through the wall and I was here for it.

Instead, he kissed his way down my neck, sucking on my pulse. "I spent the entire night as hard as a rock. What am I going to do with you?"

I gripped his blond hair and dragged his face back so I could suck his lip. "Well, I have a few ideas."

He chuckled low in his throat. "Unfortunately, we have to go to a meeting and every person on the other side of that wall has supernatural hearing."

"Yeah, we really fucking do. Hurry up, Romeo!" Pea shouted and my cheeks flushed.

Locke grinned and slid me down his body. It was delicious, and I wanted to climb him so I could do it one more time.

"Did you do the Professor's homework?" he asked, wrapping his arm around my waist.

I scowled. "You knew too?"

Locke kissed my frown lines. "Not until yesterday, when he told you to read his journals while he had a beautiful woman on his lap and a boner like a steel bar."

He said that last bit way too loud as he pushed open the door. I felt mussed and every person in this room knew what I'd been up to in that hall.

My cheeks were so red now, I looked like borscht. Micah looked amused, and Ramer and Pea looked a little grossed out.

Alistair was staring at me and there was such lust in his eyes that it threatened to scorch me. Then he caught me staring back and shuttered his expression, giving me a warm smile. But I could spot the strain around his eyes now and there was no going back.

He cleared his throat. "Locke contacted his lion Alpha friend last night, who in turn gave us the phone number for the shapeshifter Alpha in Canada. I gave him a call this morning, and he's willing to meet with us. I pressed for as soon as possible, as time is of the essence, so a couple of us will have to go to Canada, to the village of Nîso, to meet with their Alpha and the Pack Elders. He said he would get a representative from the town Anastasia mentioned, this Dark River, to come up as well to help expedite things." He sighed, and looked me directly in the eyes. He looked beaten down. Stressed. "He seemed nice?"

I decided to go with my gut, stepping out of Locke's arms and walking over to Alistair. I wrapped my arms around his waist and just hugged him close. Still, it looked a little like a baby possum hanging off its mama, but I felt his body shudder under mine and I knew that he needed me. Needed this comfort, this touch. I couldn't imagine what it would be like to know that my mate was right there, but I had to watch others touch her how I wanted to touch her. Love her how I wanted to love her.

So I wasn't surprised when he curled his arms around my shoulders and held me tightly. "You're doing a good job, Alistair. We've got your back." I swallowed hard. "I've got your back."

He hummed low in his throat. "You read the journals," he said softly, and I was acutely aware we were having this moment in front of an audience. But it didn't matter. It wasn't a secret obviously and I wasn't ashamed. I nodded.

"You should have told me."

He gripped me a little tighter. "I didn't want you to

feel obligated. I don't want you to feel obligated now either. We can take this as slow as you need, get to know each other, and if you decide that I'm not right for you, then that is fine as well. We can be friends."

The idea of just being friends with Alistair made my chest feel hollow. But instead of saying that, I just whispered, "Okay." I paused. "I don't think I want to be just friends though. But slow is nice."

He smiled down at me and it was radiant. I wondered if some part of my human hindbrain recognized him as a mate too, because that smile did things to me.

Penelope cleared her throat. "Not too interrupt your moment, but if you guys continue to be so fucking sweet, I might vomit up my Cheerios."

Alistair frowned, then leaned down, kissing my forehead before letting me go. I looked over my shoulder at Micah and Locke, and both of them were giving me soft expressions, not a hint of jealousy between them.

Could I be this lucky?

"I vote that Alistair, Locke and Micah go to this Nîso place," Pea said, and she was looking mischievous as hell. "You might have to take Layla with you." She waggled her eyebrows and I flushed.

Alistair shook his head. "We can't all go. It would leave this place too unprotected."

Locke waved a hand. "I'll stay. Anastasia is still here

and she'll help if anything bad happens. I'd say we could leave Micah behind, but he and the pretty vampire clash a lot and his temper would make him a vampire chew toy in three seconds."

Micah scowled at Locke, kind of proving his point.

Alistair looked between us all, and then back down to me. I smiled and shrugged. I'd never been to Canada.

"Let's go on a road trip."

18

Apparently, it was safer for us to drive than to fly. Airports were like fishermen's nets for all bounty hunters, not just The Hounds. They waited in the baggage collection areas and then when someone came along with one of the traits of a supernatural, boom, they swooped in and grabbed them.

I didn't mind. I hadn't ever flown before, and I wasn't sure I was ready to start now.

I'd created myself a nest, curled up in the backseat of Alistiar's luxury SUV reading his journals and napping.

When I saw the turnoff that would take me back to Roseau, I bit my lip. I didn't want to go back. I didn't feel homesick for the town that had tortured me my whole life. But I did miss Sue and the Chief. I had to do something about the house, and the animals. Though if I could get them to hold onto them for a little longer, maybe I could take them with me to the Academy. Surely they'd want some kind of agricultural program?

We were driving straight through, the guys taking turns behind the wheel, and whoever wasn't driving was napping in the backseat with me. Right now, I was lying against Micah, who wasn't belted in but he still insisted that I was.

Just thinking about it made me roll my eyes.

He nipped my earlobe. "What was that look for?"

"Double standards of immortals."

He just snorted and closed his eyes, going back to napping. "How long have you guys been friends?" I asked. "You and Alistair, I mean."

Micah squeezed me closer. "Too long."

I saw Alistair roll his eyes. "Just over a century, give or take a few years."

Ah, now I knew who the talkative one was, if there was ever any doubt. "And how did you meet?"

This time, it was Micah who answered. "I punched him in the face during a bar fight."

"Pfft, I approached you about forming a pack, and you started a bar fight to cover the fact you wanted to kick my ass. At least don't rewrite history."

Micah shifted so his back was against the car door. Then he unclipped my seat belt and pulled me back between his thighs so I could lean back against his chest. "I was working in a mine, and in came this poncy, sparkling Brit, telling me that as we were the last of our kind, we should form a Pack. I didn't ever want to join another pack. My first one...They were animals." He shuddered. "Anyway, Mr. Shiny over there insisted, stating that we had almost no choice but to preserve the bloodlines of the Lycanthrope. That made me a little angry."

Alistair made a rude noise. "A little."

"I told him that I couldn't wait for the Lycanthrope bloodlines to die, and that I was happy to start with him. Let's just say, it escalated."

I looked over at Alistair, and he was smiling. "We're well matched, and it didn't end comfortably for either of us. We went away, healed, licked our wounds, and then I found him again. It took me a decade to convince him that joining up with me was best for us. But it took Pea and Locke arriving for him to really commit to our Pack, as such. He has a white knight complex he hides under all that gruff brutality."

Micah gave him the finger and I laughed.

A shiver raced over my skin as his fingers scraped up the insides of my thighs. "What else would you like to know, Little Red? It's not often you have the big bad wolves at your mercy."

I had the sneaking suspicion that I was the one at his mercy right now, especially when his fingers climbed higher. "Uh, are there no female Lycans?" I squeaked.

Micah grabbed my thigh and hooked it over his own, spreading me wider. "Alistair can answer that one better." Micah slipped his fingers beneath my underwear, sliding them along my slit and I sucked in a breath. I met Alistair's eyes in the rear view mirror, and saw his gaze go down to where Micah had his hand between my thighs.

Alistair made a pained noise. "Uh, no. There aren't any left. They got hunted to extinction. Quickest way to endanger a species."

Micah's fingers slid inside my pussy and I moaned. Alistiar's gaze flicked rapidly between my face, Micah's hand and the road. Micah slid up my skirt until it rested across my hips, and the wetness coating my thighs cooled quickly. Alistair sucked in a deep breath and his bright golden eyes got impossibly brighter.

Micah kissed down my neck. "You have any other questions, Sweetheart?"

He slid another finger inside me, and his thumb rubbed my clit and I could barely remember my name let alone think of questions about Lycans.

Except maybe...

"Do Lycans like to share mates?"

Alistair frowned. "I thought Micah told you that we were polyamorous?"

"No. I mean, do they like to *share* mates."

Alistair made a pained noise and slammed on the brakes, sliding us onto the shoulder of the road. I would have flung forward except for Micah's tight hold on me.

He chuckled, a sexy as fuck sound. "Now you've done it." He double tapped my clit and I bucked against his hand. Alistair was wrenching on the emergency brake and bursting out of the car door before we'd even fully stopped. He slammed open the back door and stood there, looking at me with wild eyes and a heaving chest.

"Layla, do you give me permission to make you come at least six times in the next thirty minutes? I promise not to bond with you."

I was helpless to resist the pure lust that poured from him. "Yes," I breathed. Seriously, when a hot guy asks you that question, who says no?

He looked over me to Micah. "Give her to me."

Micah laughed. "Oh, is that how we're going to play it, *Alpha*?" The way he said Alpha made my skin feel too tight and my breath too scarce in my lungs. Still, Micah sat me up and Alistair climbed into the car, tugging me onto his lap. Then he kissed me.

It wasn't soft and gentle like the man himself. It was demanding, purely sexual in a way that had me moaning against his lips and grinding on his dick. I was vaguely aware of Micah fiddling with the car seats, shifting luggage out of the way. I don't know what he did, but suddenly he was reclining almost all the way back, his arms tucked behind his head like he was watching his favorite show.

Alistair recaught my attention by tearing off my panties. Like ripping them clean off. I don't know why destroying my undergarments was so freaking hot, but I moaned loudly and ground harder on his dick.

He groaned, holding my hips. "Oh love, you keep that up and I am going to embarrass myself." I noticed his British accent was stronger now that he was so turned on.

He lifted me off his lap and passed me back to Micah. I would have pouted but he was sinking into the footwell of the car and kissing the inside of my knees. Honestly, I'd been lied to my whole life. I thought men hated giving oral? Is this how much head normal women got?

I was beginning to think there was some truth to my 'catnip for hot immortals' theory.

He ran his tongue up my inner thigh in one long stroke, looking up at me from under my skirt as I gripped his flaxen hair. He grinned back at me, looking so fucking devilish I wondered how I didn't see it before.

"You are so gorgeous. Worth waiting for," he murmured, and I wasn't even sure he was talking to me. He looked over my shoulder at Micah. "Flip her over and kiss your mate. I'll kiss somewhere lower."

Apparently Micah was now a good little minion because he flipped me like I weighed nothing so I was back to straddling his lap. He caught my lips and kissed me possessively. "Looks like you riled the good professor right up, Sweetheart."

He leaned back further and I chased his lips like they were a drug. My ass was in the air and my knees either side of his hips, and I wanted to climb on his cock more than King Kong wanted to climb the Empire State building. And then I felt Alistair's hands running up over the backs of my thighs and the globes of my ass. He pushed my skirt up around my waist and I could feel his warm breath on my wet core.

"Holy hell," I whispered against Micah's lips.

Alistair ran his tongue up my slit, from my clit to my entrance. His hands gripped my ass cheeks and he buried his tongue inside me.

"Oh my god," I squealed and pushed back against his face. Micah's hand snaked between us and his finger rolled my clit. Oh hell, oh shit, oh fuck.

I came all over Alistair's face, and his tongue lapped up my juices.

I looked over my shoulder, my eyes too wide from the shock of coming so damn fast.

His smile was pure smug male satisfaction. "That's one. Five more to go, Love."

I wasn't sure my heart or my clit could take it, but dammit, I wasn't raised a quitter .

19

I was exhausted. I didn't do any driving but a full day trapped in a car was hard. We stopped at a couple of places to eat and stretch, but the guys just traded off driving and sleeping, and I spent my entire time sleeping on one or the other.

When we made it to the next largest town over from Nîso, Alistair booked us into a hotel, all three of us in the one room.

The concierge had blinked at me, then at the guys, who both had proprietary hands on me, and then back at me. Granted, I'd changed into a pair of tights with tentacles all over them and an oversized hockey jersey in honor of being in Canada, so I didn't really look like the kind of person who could pull two of the hottest guys that had ever walked into this cheap motel.

So I just winked and grinned like I had a chinese

finger trap for a vagina, and followed along behind Micah with a little extra sway in my step. Small towns were small towns, no matter where you went. They all had that one thing in common. Anything that didn't fit into the mold was to be ridiculed or shunned.

Alistair huffed out a small laugh behind me, stepping close until I was pressed between their bodies as we got on the elevator.

"What do you think she'd say if I made love to you against the wall of this elevator?"

I swallowed hard, my body flushing with his words. "She'd probably think you were a deviant and I was a whore. And she'd be terribly jealous of us both."

Micah snorted. "She'd probably pity her considering we're only going up three floors and if you can fuck her that quick, I'd be sad for you both."

Alistair laughed, flipping him the finger, while leaning in to nip my lips. I tried to remember what Alistair said about going slow, but my traitorous vagina just wanted to climb onto his magic stick and not leave the hotel room until we got a noise complaint.

Micah and Alistair inhaled deeply and groaned. "You smell so good. There's nothing more potent for Lycans than the smell of their mate's desire," Alistair sighed heavily. "Unfortunately, our meeting with the Alpha of Nîso is set for this afternoon and we don't have time."

As the elevator doors opened, Micah picked me up

and carried me out into the hallway. He passed an elderly couple who gave us dirty looks and I practiced my smug look. Alistair scanned the key and the door opened.

"I say we send Alistair by himself and we'll stay in. Well and truly sully this bed until they have to burn the sheets," Micah growled.

I couldn't help the laughter that bubbled across my lips. Happy laughter. I was happy. The very idea shocked me into stillness. I reached down and found none of my former misery remained, completely burned away by these two and Locke. And I had friends in Pea and Ramer.

I was where I was supposed to be. Argh, I was going to cry. Instead, I wiggled out of Micah's arms. "One, ew. Be nice to the housekeeping staff." I lifted my arms and sniffed my pits. "Two, I need a shower asap. And three, we cannot send Alistair anywhere by himself. We're a team. A family."

Micah looked down at me, his face filled with emotion. "You're right, Little Red. We're a Pack. We go together." He kissed me softly, his hands sliding down my back to my ass. Then he pulled back his hand and slapped it hard. "But I get the first shower."

Alistair's face was filled with such raw emotion it was hard to look at. "Are we?"

"What? A Pack?"

"No, a family."

I walked over, wrapping my arms around his waist and snuggling into his chest. "You bet your furry ass."

My phone rang, breaking the moment. It was a video call. I answered and Locke's smiling face filled the screen. "Hey Baby Girl, how was the trip?"

I couldn't help but grin back. I could hear the sounds of the common room in the background. "Long, but, umm, good."

I flushed bright red as Alistair's gaze heated up. Yeah, we were both remembering the same thing.

Locke quirked an eyebrow. "Are the hairballs there with you?" I nodded and pointed the camera at Alistair, who just rolled his eyes.

"How's Eden?" He asked like a worried mother hen.

"It's surviving without you, you ancient control freak. Terrance, put down the acid! Caroline, do not make your sister walk out into traffic! Ramer, control yourself and stop having sex with Anastasia in the rafters," he shouted as he looked out into the common room.

Alistair narrowed his eyes. "Not funny, Locke."

Locke just grinned back. "Stop stressing. I've got this, you just work on getting us a place to move these delinquents. Speaking of which, I have some news. Some really good news."

Alistair sat down on the bed, pulling me into his lap so we could both see the screen. "I got a call from an old friend today, a bear Alpha from down near

Black Mountain. Same place that lion Alpha, Axel is from. Life's funny, considering that I haven't heard from either in a decade, yet I've spoken to both in the space of a week. Karmic, right?"

"Kismet," I whispered back. He winked.

"Anyway, he wanted me to meet with a guy, a human. This guy has mated with a snow leopard shifter, and she'd been taken by bounty hunters who'd dosed her too much with those tranqs they like to use." He frowned, his eyes pulling down in sadness. "Real sad story, but we hear it too much. On the streets, on the run the whole of her life. It's stories like hers that let me know that we're doing the right thing, you know, having Eden?"

I swallowed hard, my heart constricting for the poor kid. Well, woman now. My life was hard, but always running, never being able to settle, always on the streets and searching for safety? That shit was heartbreaking.

"They were after a number for the Witch Council, so I gave them the number for Wilde."

Alistair snorted. "You gave them the number for the Convocation Representative for the Witches? He's going to hate that. Pompous asshole." I raised my eyebrows. Nice, polite Alistair throwing shade at a witch? The dude must really be a jackass.

Locke sucked his teeth. "I don't give a shit. He owes me one, and if I can save this kid's mate and unborn cub, then it's a favor well spent. Anyway, here's the interesting part. This human is Reese Townsend." I whistled. I'd even heard of Reese Townsend. Richest man under thirty, tech genius. "I was telling him about Eden, about the Academy, and he wants to fund the whole thing."

Alistair went stiff with surprise, and I didn't blame him. It was like fate had dropped the perfect solution in our lap. "What does he want in return?"

"A place for his Pack to live, there's three human mates, the snow leopard shifter and their cub. He wants to be able to put a house on the Academy grounds and have the protection of our wards. But he's happy to supply all the security tech and pay for the building of the compound."

Holy shit. That was millions of dollars worth. It was the answer to everything. Alistair wrapped his arms around my waist, his fingers splaying across my stomach as I wiggled against his crotch. Whoops. "Did you tell them that we'd protect them regardless? They don't have to feel obligated to buy their safety."

Locke rolled his eyes. "Of course I did. But he believes in what we are doing, Alistair. He wants to help."

I couldn't help the smile that spread across my face. We had a benefactor. Now all we needed was land.

Eden was about to live up to its name.

. . .

WE WERE MET on the borderlands of Nîso by a tall, beautiful Indigenous woman with hard eyes and the presence of an apex predator. She scared the shit out of me.

"I'm Kelly. Come, the Alpha and the Elders are waiting for you." She tilted her head. "You'll have to walk from the boundary. The wards won't allow your car to pass."

We followed along behind her, and the guys were on high alert. Their eyes took in everything; every shadow, every person. I didn't doubt that there was more security on us than Kelly, but they were very good. I couldn't spot them among the trees and houses, both of which seemed to coexist in this settlement.

It was like they'd interspersed the town among the trees and I loved it. "We should do something like this with Eden, don't you think?"

Alistair nodded, his hand tightening on mine.

It was late, so the streets were mostly empty. We were having this meeting at night to accommodate the vampire representative from Dark River. The guys had me protectively between them, and I knew they would wolf out in seconds if they sensed a threat. Honestly, on the way to meet a vampire and a shapeshifter, and I'd never felt safer in my life.

I wanted to make conversation, to ask questions about the town, but Kelly didn't seem like the talkative type. She led us to a well-lit building in the middle of the town which could have been a church with its pitched roof. There were quite a few people roaming around considering how late it was, but maybe that was just how they operated up here. Kelly led us up the front stairs and the eyes of the crowd followed us.

Walking through the heavy wooden doors, I noticed that the collective age of the people in here was older. They looked physically older, but if being at Eden had taught me anything, is that you can't judge a person's age from their appearance.

An elderly woman walked up to us, her smile tight and regal. "I am the Matriarch of Nîso. We welcome you to our lands. The Alpha and the Alpha Mate will be here shortly."

Micah dipped his head. "Thank you, ma'am."

She smiled politely again, and then there was a murmur from the front of the room. "Excuse me," the Matriarch said, and when she looked toward the door, her smile was genuine. Her stride was spritely, which made me rethink her age.

The group that walked in made Micah tense beside me. A tall man strode in first, with a power so potent that even my puny human brain sensed it. It was earthy, and almost magical.

But his power was nothing like the young guy beside him. He was covered in light blue tattoos that swirled over his skin. When he looked toward me, I knew that his youthful face was just his facade. His eyes were ancient and the weight of them was crushing. I wanted to run away and hide beneath my blankets. Micah leaned toward me. "Vampire," he breathed. But this guy wasn't like Anastasia at all. He was far scarier. It was like an alley cat compared to a tiger.

The vampire kissed the Matriarch's hand, saying something that made her laugh and blush. Between them was a woman with ombre red hair. She was pretty in a way that was hard to pin down to one thing. Her smile lit up the room, and you only had to see the awestruck look on the mens' faces to know they were completely head over heels for her. She was curvy and confident and I envied the hell out of her.

They strode to the back of the room, and the woman smiled at me and I couldn't help but return it. I held out my hand and she shook it. She was cool to the touch, but her expression was warm. I shook the hand of the two men beside her as well. Alistair and Micah did the same.

"Thank you for meeting with us on such short notice," Alistair murmured. He held the other man's gaze, the Alpha I guessed, and they had this weird staring match. Alistair didn't drop eye contact until the man nodded.

"I am Brody, Alpha of the North Western Pack and Nîso. This is the Matriarch, Nell," he introduced us again to the regal, elderly lady. "This is my Alpha Mate, Raine." He gently touched the back of the girl with the fire engine red hair, before pointing to the powerful vampire. "And this is the founder of Dark River, Nico."

Raine smiled, and I noticed two pointed fangs. "Your Alpha Mate is a vampire?" I gasped, and Alistair shot me a warning look. *Danger, Will Robinson, danger!* "Uh, sorry. Hi, I'm Layla and high pressure situations make me lose track of my tongue. This is Alistair and Micah. My, uh, boyfriends?"

"Mates," Micah corrected gruffly.

Alistair rested his hand on my lower back in a manner that was distinctly proprietary. "We thank you for meeting with us on such short notice, but when word came back of your location, we thought it would be perfect for what we want to create." He took a deep breath. "You see, we run a sanctuary down in Boston called Eden. But it's no longer as secure as we'd like, especially for the young ones, so we wish to start an Academy for preternatural beings. More than that, we want to create a refuge for them." He gave the Alpha and the Vampire a sheepish grin. "And sandwiched between a powerful shapeshifter pack and the only non-predatory vampire colony in North America seemed almost too good to be true. It was like fate placed you in our lap as a solution to an issue that is very quickly spiralling out of control. We did think of a place in Minnesota, but anywhere in the US is too close to the... threat."

Raine asked what the difference between preternatural and supernatural was, and I was happy to be able to contribute. I explained that preternatural people included humans with extra abilities, and she gave me the most blindingly bright smile that I almost missed her fangs.

The guys discussed the specifics while I took in the rest of the room. It was rustic, but still warm and inviting. My eyes stilled on a man in the shadows, and he blended so well that I almost missed him. I didn't know how though, his hair perfectly white and his eyes a weird shade of blue. I smiled and gave him a small wave, and though his demeanor didn't change, he gave me a finger wave back.

The vampire, Nico, asked a question, and my skin prickled. I frowned, tuning back into the conversation.

Alistair's face lost color, as he stuttered over his words. "Bounty hunters. They hunt down supernaturals, selling most on the black market, but more unique beings they keep for themselves."

I held my breath, waiting for their response. There was a chance we'd be bringing trouble with us, and in their position, with towns and people of their own to protect, I didn't think I'd be so generous.

Raine cocked her head to the side, as if she was weighing us up. "What would you need from us?"

I breathed a deep sigh of relief and relaxed. They hadn't said yes, but they hadn't straight up said no either.

"Just land between your two townships, but probably closer to Nîso. We have a lot of shifters in our group," Alistair said softly, like he was worried they'd spook.

"And your offer of support if we are ever raided by The Hounds." And Micah had the tact of a raging bull.

The Matriarch spoke for the first time. "I speak for us all when I say we aren't likely to let children be persecuted if we can offer them a haven, so it is best if you tell us everything."

My body wanted to sag with relief.

We'd rehearsed this bit, making sure we could provide all the information in a succinct manner. "We have about a hundred full time charges in our care, and moreover, we offer a safety net to those who have integrated into human society. At the moment, we are funding the whole operation ourselves, which leaves us little to spare now that we need to run."

Brody waved to the chairs at the front of the room. "Let's grab a seat. So how do you plan to build this Academy without funds? The North Western Pack owns much of the land around this area, and I am sure we can come to some agreement about transferring you a portion. Unfortunately, we have no spare money to fund the construction of a compound of the size that you're suggesting."

Nico the Vampire tucked Raine close to his body, and I wasn't even sure he realized he did it. "We have lived a long time, and most of us live fairly simple lives. We can donate to your cause if you need it."

I felt like crying. These complete strangers were willing to help people they didn't know, didn't care about, just because we asked?

Alistair gave him a warm smile. "We have a human benefactor, with a shifter mate, who is willing to fund the construction of the Academy. If you have any construction crews that can undertake the work, we'd appreciate not having to take it out of the area. The less humans involved the better."

Nico nodded. "We agree. We have tradesmen who can aid as well."

"As do we," Brody laughed, leaning across him to kiss Raine's cheek. "Look what you've done, Rainey Day. As X would say, you've brought two warring factions together with the power of your v-"

Raine slapped her hand over his mouth. "No."

His laughter was muffled but his eyes were sparkling.

I don't know if they were just showing off or what, but both Micah and Alistair transformed as we left Nîso. Maybe it was a display of power, maybe it was just to hear Raine's gasp of surprise, but as we crossed over the border of Nîso and strolled back to our car, they both shifted. I hadn't seen them often enough in this form, and I'd forgotten how beautiful they were.

Alistair's coat was paler than Micah's even in the darkness, but they were similar heights. I knew I should logically be scared but I was fairly sure there was some part of me that also knew that these guys were my mates, especially Micah, who constantly poured love down the bond since 'the fuck-up', as Locke liked to call it.

"I don't think you guys are going to fit in the car like that."

"Want to go for a run, Little Red?" Micah growled beside me, and I'm not sure what it said about me that it turned me on. Even big and furry, I was still so attracted to the man inside. And kind of wondering what he could do with his tongue.

Oh shit, did I think that out loud?

When no one pounced on me and gave me a monster style tongue lashing, I breathed a somewhat disappointed sigh of relief. I'm complicated, okay?

"I don't think I can keep up."

Alistair laughed, and the pitch was even lower than his normal voice. "That's the point, Love. We'll give you a headstart."

Now I was thankful I wore my Converse. I grinned and took off.

Firstly, let me say that I am not athletic. In the event of a zombie apocalypse, I will lay down my life first so no one truly realizes how out of shape I am. Secondly, judging by the looks of pure lust on both Micah's and Alistair's faces, I really, really wanted to be caught.

I raced along a trail that I could see by the light of the full moon, and the frosty air made my breath fog before me. All of a sudden, there was a monster in front of me, and I skidded to a stop. I knew his shape in the moonlight, and instead of scaring me, I felt like the safest person in the forest.

I should definitely have had a phobia of the woods, or the dark, or wolves, just something after the accident, but I didn't. I'd been more traumatized by the town's response rather than the event itself. I wondered if it was because of Micah. I don't know. The human brain is a weird organ.

"We caught you, we caught you and now we're going to eat you," Alistair whispered in my ear, and now I knew I was deranged because while that should have been disturbing as hell, I was turned on. Desperately, crazily, turned on. I spun and Alistair was back in his human form, thank god, and I launched myself into his arms. He caught me easily and kissed me. He spun me into the nearest tree, and my jacket protected my back from the harsh scrape of bark. I was wearing thigh high tights under my skirt, with cat faces at the top. So there was nothing stopping Alistair from sliding his hand between our bodies and inside my underwear.

"She liked the chase, Micah. She's so wet," he growled, and I turned my head to the side to see Micah standing so close I could lean over and capture his lips. Alisiair's chest rumbled beneath my palms and I ground my pussy against his hand. He slid two fingers inside me and I broke the kiss, letting my head fall back against the tree. It snagged my hair, tugging, and I moaned at the pressure.

Micah's chuckle was dark. "God, you're perfect."

He captured my lips again, but this time he edged the kiss with pain. He bit my bottom lip until it swelled beneath his assault.

A throat clearing behind me had Micah tearing his lips from mine and Alistair dropping me to my feet, my body pressed between him and the tree protectively.

"Sorry to interrupt, and normally I am all for group sex in the woods, but there's vampires roaming these woods and not all of us are the Patron Saints of Dark River." The big vampire had a smile, but it was dark and twisty. "Normally I'd just watch, because hooboy that was about to get hot. But Lucius will have a snack out of the three of you, and your girl there smells delicious."

Micah shifted, and the vampire, completely covered in tattoos and scars, looked vaguely impressed. "Lycan-thropes? Shit, I thought you were all dead." Micah snarled and he held up his hands. "Don't get your furry dick in a knot. If I wanted to eat you, I would have done it while you were otherwise occupied." He waggled his eyebrows. "Actually, back in the old days I would have asked to join in and then I would have eaten you. I love a good orgy. Unfortunately, I only have a thing for fiery redheads and assholes now." He winked at me. "Pun intended, Love."

He cocked his head to the side. "Oop, here they come. I suggest you get out of here while you can."

Then he was gone so fast, I wondered if I imagined him.

Alistair tugged me out from behind his back and lifted me into his arms. "I say we take the crazy vampire's advice."

And then he sprinted from the clearing back to the car, Micah following along beside us still in his Lycanthrope form. I breathed a sigh of relief when we reached the SUV. Alistair placed me in the back seat, kissing me softly.

"To be continued, Love."

Micah shifted back to human, and I was kind of impressed that they kept their pants in both forms. Sure, when they grew seven feet they stretched to their capacity and looked like they were capris, but still, they covered their dicks. Definitely handy.

The whole thing was kind of exhausting. I walked like a zombie out of the car and past the concierge of the hotel. My hair stuck up at all angles, and my eyes were sunken in my head from lack of sleep. I probably looked even less worthy of being in a ménage with these two, who still looked amazing despite the fact they'd been awake longer than me.

Once we got into the elevator, Micah scooped me into his arms, and I nuzzled my face into his neck. He smelled like home and everything good.

"Love you," I whispered, and he squeezed me harder.

"Love you too, Little Red." Alistair opened the hotel room door, and Micah walked me to the bed. Sitting me on the side, he helped me undress and then tucked me beneath the blankets in my tank top and underwear. He kissed my head and stood.

I pouted a little, but I was slow blinking because my eyes felt like lead. "Aren't you guys hopping in too?"

Alistair kissed me softly. "Later. We need to talk over some of the details from tonight, but Micah will be beside you before you know it."

I grabbed his shirt and pulled him down for a longer kiss. "You too. I want to be snuggled between you both."

Micah huffed out a laugh. "That's going to be a tight squeeze, but we'll make it happen for you, Sweetheart. Now sleep."

They wandered over to sit at the small table in the corner of the room, their voices low, and I fell into a deep, dreamless sleep.

LYCANS WERE HOT. I mean, duh, Micah and Alistair were smokin', but apparently they were also physically hot because I was pretty sure I was melting. I wiggled out from between them, but it was only a queen size bed. I watched as Alistair rolled away onto nothing, and I reached out to try and grab him. But he was huge and I wasn't that strong, so we both ended up on the floor.

Alistair let out an 'oof' when I landed on his gut with my elbow.

"Shit, I'm sorry!" I squeaked out, trying to scramble off him. But he just wrapped an arm around my waist and held me closer.

"Waking up with a beautiful woman on top of me is my idea of a perfect morning." He squirmed a bit. "Except I think I landed on Micah's shoe."

I couldn't help the giggle that bubbled out of me as I reached around, tugging the jammed shoe from under his back. He leaned up and kissed me, a gentle caress that set my blood to slow a boil.

His morning hard-on was trapped between us, and now that I knew it was there, I couldn't help grinding on it. It was a compulsion.

He wasn't wearing a shirt, just his boxers, and he was beautiful. His skin was pale and smooth, which was funny considering he turned completely furry when he shifted. He wasn't as broad as Micah, but his chest tapered down into trim hips and those abs. I wanted to lick every single groove of them.

I shifted on his lap as my core clenched. His groan was loud enough to wake up the dead. "Hell, Layla," he breathed, and the smug grin that came over my face was pure sexual power. I had this strong, smart, gorgeous man beneath me. In my control. That was just as heady a feeling as his eyes roaming my body like he was trying to catalogue me for his spank bank.

"We're taking it slow, remember?" he groaned, his hands sliding to my hips to keep them still.

I sat up on his hips, looking down at him all mussed from sleep. Would time change my mind?

"Do you want to wait? Are you not sure?"

His fingers pressed into my hips. "I've never been more sure of anything in my very long life."

I leaned forward, and kissed his jaw. "Then I don't want to take it slow."

His whole body shuddered and he rolled me onto my back. He kissed along my shoulder, across my collarbone, nipping and sucking at my skin like he was tasting me. He pushed my tank top up and his pupils widened at the sight of my boobs. He bent forward and kissed them, first the undersides, then along the curve until he reached my nipple. He swirled his tongue around the hard bud, and my core clenched in anticipation. "Alistair," I groaned. "Don't tease."

He raised an eyebrow at me. "Oh, Love, I intend to tease and taste and take this so slow you'll be begging me by the end."

I groaned, arching my back. "Torture me next time. This time I want it hard and fast. I want to be yours."

He groaned again. "I'm not sure I can deny you a single thing." Then he sucked my nipple into his mouth and I bucked against him. He ground his hips into my core and the friction was delicious. He moved onto the other nipple, sucking it, swirling his tongue around the bud then sucking it hard. He followed it up with a scrape of his teeth and I swear my body lit up like it was electrified.

He hummed contentedly around my nipple. "So responsive." He gripped my underwear, peeling them down my legs and watching its progress with rapt attention. I squirmed under his laser focus, and his eyes snapped back to me. "Beautiful," he breathed, as he leaned down, capturing my lips again.

The hard length of his cock was still covered by his boxers, giving me a delicious friction when he slid it along my wet core. I dug my nails into his back and made a pathetic mewling noise that I was pretty sure I'd be embarrassed about later. "Alistair," I whispered.

There was nothing dry about our humping right now, and he was blinding shoving at his boxers, unwilling to break our kiss for even a second. I felt the head of his dick slide against me, and I moaned. He dragged his mouth away. "Are you sure?"

"Fuck me already, Alistair."

He slammed into me in one thrust, burying himself to the hilt. He was girthy and it stretched so deliciously I almost came on the first thrust. He slid back and then slammed home again, and I couldn't help the shout that escaped my throat.

"Hush, Love. We don't want to wake Micah," he murmured, kissing my cheeks, my jaw, my throat as he slid in and out of me deliciously, torturously slow. He grabbed my thigh, pulling my leg back until it hooked over his shoulder and then thrust again. I saw stars. And then I saw fucking meteors and fuck, was that Neil Armstrong? I came so hard that my toes cramped where my foot was hooked behind his hips.

Alistair stilled, riding out my orgasm, the arm beside my head tense. "Jesus, you're milking my cock right now." He deep breathed through his teeth as my orgasm subsided. "Aw, baby, we aren't nearly done yet."

He grabbed my other thigh, hooking the other leg over his shoulder and then he moved. Oh fuck. The pleasure was like being shocked with a cattle prod as the angle hit my g-spot like he knew the female anatomy better than his own. Which, maybe he freaking did? Seemed unfair but I wasn't even close to complaining. He slammed in and out of me, and I don't know when one orgasm turned to two as the intense pleasure just rolled over my body in constant waves. He pulled back, fucking me shallowly, slamming into my g-spot over and over.

"Oh god, it's too much," I moaned in a voice I didn't even recognize.

"Come for me one more time, Love," Alistair grunted.

"Alistair!" I screeched as I honest to god squirted. I

thought it was a myth, something done by pornstars with ice cubes and good pelvic floor muscles. But when Alistair pulled out, his hands still holding my thighs, I came all over us both.

"Yes," he groaned, grabbing me up and flipping me onto my hands and knees. He maneuvered me easily into position and then he pounded into me again. My arms shook, my orgasm still rocking me even as he curled over my back, burying his face in the curve of my neck. I felt his teeth scrape my flesh and I knew what he wanted to do. He placed a kiss there, but I felt another orgasm creep up.

I don't know what came over me, but I wanted him to bite me there. The sense of rightness that washed over me chased the bliss of my orgasm and I knew.

"Bite me, Alistair."

He stopped dead, which was kind of fucking impressive considering he must have been so damn close himself.

"What? Are you sure? No Layla, you don't have-"

"I want it, please Alistair."

The noise he made was more wounded animal than man, but when he sank his teeth into my shoulder, I came again. He moved inside of me, and it felt so fucking right. I couldn't describe it. It was like my soul had an orgasm. A soulgasm?

His teeth stayed lodged in my shoulder as he continued to move, but I couldn't come any more. I was a wrung out, sweaty mess. When he came in me, buried balls deep, he unlatched his mouth so he could whisper my name. We both collapsed onto the floor, his body still connected to mine, and his arms protectively around me.

I could feel him, right next to where Micah was. He was so fucking happy I was going to cry.

"Thank you, Layla. Thank you," he whispered, planting kisses on the back of my neck.

I acted rashly but I didn't have any regrets. I wasn't known for doing shit the easy way. So I'd mate with a man before I fell in love with him, I didn't care. I knew his heart and if this was rushing, then consider me Usain Bolt because I was rushing to the finish line as fast as my heart could carry me.

I looked over my shoulder at his earnest face. How could I have any regrets?

I squeezed his fingers where they were twined in mine. He slipped from me, and climbed to his knees. "Come on, Love. Let's get you cleaned up."

A groan from the bed had us both looking over our shoulders. Micah looked over the edge of the bed, his golden eyes hooded and filled with lust. "We are all going to need a cold shower."

21

We stayed in Canada for a week. We met with Kelly and the Matriarch again, and they gifted us a portion of land between Nîso and Dark River for an acorn. Like, a literal acorn.

Best acorn I'd ever spent. They'd also made us promise to higher educate the children of Nîso if they wanted to attend, and Alistair had been only too happy to accommodate them. We'd stayed in Nîso for long enough for architectural plans and work crews to be arranged. We called in to Pea, Locke and Ramer to make sure we got their input, but now wasn't the time to mess around. We were banking hard on Reese Townsend coming through, but we had enough to ensure that the compound housing was built and we could move everyone to safety. If Reese Townsend flaked, we'd still be safe. We'd just have to find the money to build the Academy itself another way.

They were long days, and we met a lot of interesting characters, but it finally felt like we were making progress. Our architect was a vampire, and our construction crew was a burly set of shapeshifters. When the architect had mentioned that he knew a crew that could work on the site at night as well, the time frame for completion was unbelievable. Months instead of years. I could see the weight lift off Micah and Alistair's shoulders every time something went our way.

But I was eager to be back at Eden. I missed Locke, and I missed my pets. I missed my friends. Although I wasn't excited for the long drive back, I was ready to be in Locke's arms.

We drove all the way through to Minnesota. Back to Roseau. I needed to get my affairs in order, and say goodbye to the town one last time. And that was how I found myself standing inside the post office with literally the entire store staring at me. Well, more specifically, at the way Micah's hand was on my back and Alistair's twined with mine.

I smiled at Gloria, the post office teller. "Thanks for holding my mail. I appreciate it."

She looked between Alistair and Micah. "Layla, dear, what fairy did you say you prayed to? I'm going to need their name so I can get me a matching pair of those."

I snorted, making my eyes go crazy-wide. "Oh shit, you see them too? Are you sure?" I pinched Micah and he let out a huff. "That naked moon dance really worked," I said conspiratorially. I winked and strode out of the post office.

Alistair looked back at the staring faces. "Is anyone going to tell me what that was?"

I shook my head, grinning over my shoulder. "I'll explain later. We need to head to the bank and then to the realtor before they close. Then I'll take you home."

To say Mr. Staynes, the bank manager, was far less creepy with the guys beside me was an understatement. The first time he looked at my tits, Micah had snarled and Mr. Staynes had lost all the color in his cheeks. Apparently, he had no self control.

"I'm sure we could come to some arrangement when you return from the city, Layla." His eyes darted to my tits again like he was imagining that arrangement. "I wouldn't want you on the street if your new living arrangements in the city were to fall through, especially with your, er, mental issues."

There was no growl this time, but the level of threat in the bodies of the men beside me ratcheted up to eleven. Alistair stood, leaning over Staynes' desk ominously. "You're going to give Layla what she needs to sell her home, and the next time you even insinuate to her, actually to any woman, that you'll take sexual favors in lieu of payment, I will tear off your shrimp dick, jam it through your ear and into the space where your brain should be. Do I make myself clear?"

Mr. Staynes swallowed hard. "Yes," he said through gritted teeth and I smiled smugly. I didn't even make a flakey joke. I just glared at him and revelled in the fact that I didn't have to kowtow to him anymore because he literally could have destroyed my life with the click of a button.

It was quick work to get the paperwork I needed from him and my experience at the realtor was a lot more efficient. Denise was a single mother of five kids and she did not have time. She didn't have time for bullshit, showmanship, or fucking around of any variety. She was one of the few people I liked in town. She never raised an eyebrow at my outfits, or my mother's outbursts. She kept out of everyone else's business and made damn sure no one was in hers. She treated everyone equally, and everyone started out with the benefit of the doubt.

Piss her off though? She wouldn't take that shit lying down. Good luck trying to sell your house to anyone this century.

Everyone should strive to be Denise.

I also liked the fact she didn't ogle the guys. Denise's ex-husband had been a real piece of shit in a town filled with so many assholes it may as well have been a three-ringed circus. She was not swayed by a pretty face. She narrowed her eyes at them. "You aren't being coerced into this, right? Because all your contracts will be null and void, especially if they are taking advantage of you." She meant in case they were taking advantage of the poor crazy girl.

I smiled at her widely. "Can I tell you a secret? I'm not really crazy. It was just easier to give the town what they wanted to see rather than prove myself day after day."

Denise rolled her eyes. "Layla Lee, I have two teenage daughters, a precocious twelve year old, and twin toddlers. I can tell when someone is making fun of everyone around them. I've known you're completely sane for years. I meant the death of your mother. I know that would have affected you."

Could I hug someone who was basically a stranger? "I'm fine, Denise. Full mental and emotional faculties. I'm happier than I've ever been. But thank you for caring enough to check."

She searched my face. "Good. Let's get this stuff all drawn up so you can go back to the city and leave this place behind. You were always too good for what life handed you, Layla."

She was right, but I couldn't regret any of it, because look where I was now. So stupidly happy it hurt. I still had to sort out the farm animals, and say goodbye to Sue and Tony, but once that was done? I was going to say goodbye to Roseau and never look back.

LOCKE MET us in the garage of the apartment building like he couldn't wait the extra two minutes it would take for me to reach the second floor. I flew out of the SUV like I'd been gone a year instead of just over a week. I raced across the concrete and leapt into his arms and he caught me easily. He squeezed me tight to his chest, kissing my face noisily. "I've got a confession," he started, and I frowned. "I think I'm fully addicted to you. Honestly, I pined so bad that sweet Ramer threatened to test out how long it would take for me to grow back a tongue. Ramer!" His shocked outrage made me laugh harder until he stole the sound with a kiss

I'd missed him too. I searched my connection to Alistair and Micah for jealousy, but there was nothing but amusement coming from either of them. Locke looked over my shoulder, and whatever he saw on their faces had him raising his eyebrows. "Have you been conquering hearts as well as the Canadian wilderness?"

I wrapped my arms and legs around Locke's waist, and in that moment I wished I had a bond with him as well. It was like a cheat code or something. Instead, I had to communicate like a grown up. "I bonded with Alistair."

His huff of surprise warmed my cheek. "Sneaky bastard. Those coke bottle glasses make him look all sweet and nerdy, but that guy has some serious game." He looked me over. "Are you okay? He didn't rush you?" His words were light, but there was a seriousness in his expression that warmed my heart.

"No. If anyone pressured someone, it might have been me." Locke chuckled and buried his face in the crook of my neck.

"He was all but panting after you, I'm pretty sure he couldn't be happier right now." He kissed my pulse point. "I'm happy for both of you. A little bit jealous that I won't have that connection with you, but you showed me affection and now you're kind of stuck with me. Sorry, no take backs. No refunds." He nipped my throat playfully and the guys finally caught up, their arms laden with our stuff. He grinned smugly, moving his hands from my back to my ass. "Sorry guys, I'd offer to help, but my hands are full."

I groaned at his bad joke, but I couldn't keep the goofy grin off my face.

Micah rolled his eyes. "Good to see you too, asshole."

Alistair shook his head. "Remember when he used to be happy to see us too?"

Locke hefted me higher until I was hoisted over his

shoulder in a fireman's hold. "Good to see you ugly bastards but now I have to go and lick every inch of our girlfriend, 'kay? Bye."

He sprinted toward the stairs and I bounced on his shoulder. "Locke, let me go," I laughed, and he slipped me back until I was gripping him like a koala.

"Never, Butterfly."

22

Somehow, without a whole lot of discussion, we fell into a routine. During the day, there seemed to be a thousand things to do as each member packed up their life in preparation for the move. At night, we'd gather in Alistair's apartment, which was apparently halfway between Micah and Locke's apartments, and have dinner together. A lot of the time Ramer would be there, or Penelope. Sometimes Anastasia, or one member of Eden or another, and we'd eat and laugh. My favorite times though? It was when it was just the four of us. Me and my guys.

Not going to lie, it was a little weird at first, because every single one of them had seen me naked. Seen me orgasm. Knew what I *tasted* like. Let that sink in. Sitting in a room where they could compare you like a glass of cabernet.

It's weird.

But what I didn't really take into account was they weren't strangers. They were friends and had been so for decades. They knew each other's habits, how they drank their coffee, what movies made them cry those macho man tears, what their favorite foods were. In that way, I was the outsider to the relationship. Because they'd basically been cohabitating all this time, sharing me didn't seem to be weird to them.

I'd spend my time bed hopping, or sometimes we'd watch a movie on Alistair's large sectional and I'd wake up in the middle of the night cuddled into Alistair's side with my head on Micah's lap and my hand hanging over the side of the couch so it was resting on Locke's chest, because Locke preferred to watch TV on the floor.

That's what happened tonight, except that I woke up around one a.m. with the desperate need to pee and the inability to wiggle out of my hot guy prison without waking one up. Making the decision, I rolled off the side of the couch quietly, catching myself before I hit Locke's body, but not quick enough. His eyes snapped open, and he lifted his head to kiss me sleepily.

"Best dream ever."

This guy. This guy melted my heart in the best way. He looked at me like I'd saved him, and that was as heady as it was terrifying.

I leaned forward and kissed him again, pulling back only enough so that I could speak, but our lips still brushed. "I need to pee."

He loosened his arms. "Off you go. That has never been my kink," he whispered back, and I whacked him on the chest while trying not to laugh and wake up the guys.

Finishing up my business, I walked back into the living room and realized Locke was gone. A whistle from the hall had me turning in time to see Locke's smiling face in the doorway to the guest room. He curled a finger at me and I tiptoed toward him. Unlike Micah's loft, Alistair's apartment had a more traditional layout; master bedroom, guest bedroom, and a home office.

As soon as I was in touching distance, Locke grabbed me and pulled me against his body, hefting me into his arms like I weighed nothing. I no longer protested being hefted around. Locke's love language was touching, and when he was holding me in his arms, we couldn't be more together unless we were naked.

He walked me to the bedroom, kicking the door softly closed as he went. He placed me gently on the bed, pulling the blankets back so I could wiggle beneath them. He climbed in after me, curling his much larger body around mine. It was like being cocooned in love, and I pressed myself back into his arms even tighter.

"Are you happy, Locke?" His story about the lengths he went to end his loneliness still haunted me.

He pressed a kiss to the back of my head and held me tighter. He didn't answer right away, and I swallowed hard. Locke deserved happiness.

"I love you, Layla, and that makes me unbelievably happy but also soul-crushingly sad."

I rolled in his arms. I needed to see his face, even if it was dark. I reached up and cupped his cheek. "Because I'm human, right?"

He nodded, dipping down to kiss my eyelids. "You are a beautiful fleeting speck in my long, long life, and I'm not sure I can take the misery again." His voice sounded so uncertain, so fragile, that it was hard to believe he was the same person.

He kissed me on the lips, tender enough to break my heart. I kissed him back harder. "I promise I won't leave you, Locke. I'll find a way to stay with you guys forever, even if I have to beg Anastasia to turn me into a vampire or something. You'd still love me with pointy teeth, right?"

He huffed a laugh and it warmed my cheek. "I'd love you however I could have you, Layla. But you. Your humanity is part of who you are. I would never steal that from you with my selfishness." He bundled me closer so he could nestle his face in my hair. "No.

I'm going to cherish every single one of these moments and appreciate what it means to live as a Normal. To know that life is short and every moment counts."

His hand slid down my back, over my ass, until he gripped my thigh and pulled it over his hip.

"Starting with making love to you every chance I get," he whispered against my lips before he stole them with a punishing kiss. He rolled until I was sitting on top of him, the blankets falling to my waist, and the hardening length of his cock nestled against my core.

I continued to kiss him, before moving down his jaw, nipping his chin, and placing soft kisses across his chest. And boy, what a fucking chest. Broad, muscular, just a small smattering of hair to tickle my cheeks as I move down to his dusky pink nipples. I flicked my tongue over one of the hard peaks, his accompanying moan making me smirk. When I sucked it into my mouth, scraping my teeth along it, he gripped my hips and thrust his now solid cock against my core, hitting my clit and making me moan.

"Harder, Butterfly," he groaned and I bit down.

"Fuck," he barked, but his hips jutted upwards.

Ah, so Locke was a bit of a masochist? It kind of made sense that he liked his pleasure edged with pain. I moved down his body, scraping my nails down his sides until I got to his boxers. I freed his cock, and he lifted his ass so I could shimmy them the rest of the way down. His cock was long and thick, and honestly my jaw ached just looking at it. But I wasn't a quitter, that was for sure.

"Layla," he whispered, and I looked up into his gorgeous eyes as I lowered my mouth onto his cock. He threw back his head and moaned, as he hit the back of my throat and I gagged a little. Sliding back out, I sucked him deeper this time, my fingers banding around the base of his dick. I let my teeth scrape a little and he thrust up into my mouth in shallow movements, not overwhelming me but taking what he needed. Actually...

I let his dick out of my mouth with a pop, sliding my hand up over his saliva and precum slathered length, then moving my hand over his sack and down along his taint to his ass.

"What are you doing there, Butterfly?" he gasped out as I circled the tight ring of his asshole with my finger. Then I slid his cock back into my mouth at the same time as my finger breached his ass. He made an unholy noise between a moan and a grunt and I swallowed him back, taking him as deep into my throat as I could get him, as I slid another finger inside him. Was totally glad I wasn't the long fingernail type of girl.

"Jesus christ, fuck me, Layla." I wanted to make a smartass comment about the fact I was indeed fucking him, but I didn't want to stop what I was doing. I curled my fingers inside him, and he nearly rocketed off the bed.

"Fuck, fuck, fuck," he moaned, thrusting wildly inside my mouth.

Suddenly, his hands gripped my hair, pulling me to a stop. He was panting, his eyes wild with pleasure. "I want to be inside you," he groaned, reaching into his nightstand and pulling out a condom. Guess you could accidentally father a bunch of kids when you were immortal.

I still had my fingers in his ass, and I curled them again, making him moan again. He squeezed his dick hard, trying to get it back under control. "Get up here," he grunted, and I slid my fingers from his ass and climbed back up his body until I was straddling his hips.

He no longer gave me the illusion of control. He slid me further up his body, over his hard, latex wrapped dick, until I was poised over his face. Oh. Oh shit.

The wicked glint in his eye told me that this was going to be fast and dirty and I would love every second of it. "Ride my face," he grunted, before pulling me forward and sliding his tongue along my slit until his nose nudged my clit.

Oh damn. I braced my hands on the headboard and did what I was asked. I hoped he didn't need to breathe, because I ground myself against his face repeatedly, his hands moving my hips where he wanted them. He ate me like I was an icecream sundae and he'd forgotten a spoon.

I was coming way too fast, screaming his name, uncaring if anyone heard.

But Locke wasn't done, manhandling me off his face and back down his torso, and the delicious friction of his hard abs almost made me come again. He didn't go easy, instead he slammed me down on his cock, impaling me and making me scream.

It was so fucking good. His hands were crushing on my hips, and I'd definitely have his fingerprint bruises. He held me still for a moment, both of us breathing through the sudden wave of pleasure.

Then he began to move, sliding me up and down his dick, and I gripped his wrists to anchor myself because without them, I would have floated away on the pleasure. It was fast, rough and perfect, and in minutes, or hell maybe it was seconds or days, I was clenching around him as I came one more time.

Locke thrust raggedly, until he slammed me down on his hips, bucking shallowly as he unloaded inside me.

"Layla," he groaned, making me smirk. I collapsed onto his chest, both of us panting and sweaty.

"I love you, Locke," I breathed out, and he banded his arms around my waist.

He kissed my sweaty cheeks and pushed my hair out of my face. "I know, Butterfly."

I nuzzled his chest. "Do you think they heard?" I murmured.

When someone yelled "Yes!" from the living room, my face flushed and Locke laughed like it was the funniest thing ever.

See what I mean? Having three boyfriends was tough.

WE GOT a call two months after our visit to Canada to say the first of the housing was done. Apparently having an undead work crew really sped up construction. The mood here in Boston was electric, with both sadness and excitement clashing together to make everyone a little wired. There'd been three fights, countless arguments and the logistics were a nightmare, but when we sent the first set of teens and young adults off to Nîso with one of the older shifters, it was almost a relief. They all had fake passports, fake histories. We'd rented them a U-Haul, and that was as much as we could do. We would send them all out in small groups, each taking a different route to the same place.

Me and my guys, as well as Ramer and Pea all stood out on the front steps to watch the first group roll away.

"We did it," Alistair whispered, pulling me into his arms. He kissed the top of my head and I let myself melt into his body.

Micah tangled his fingers with mine. "There is still

a long way to go until we're safe."

Locke slapped him on the back. "Don't be such a downer, Micah. We know there is a long way to go, but those six people there? They're safe now. That's something worth celebrating." He looked over at me and waggled his eyebrows. "I say we celebrate with pizza and sex."

My stomach rumbled on cue, and Micah laughed.

Pea made a gagging noise and Ramer flushed so pink that I saw it through the hair on his cheeks. "You guys are disgusting. Honestly. Keep your lovey bullshit to yourselves," Pea huffed, but her eyes sparkled with mirth. "Come on Ramer. Let's go have beer and binge Netflix while these deviants have an orgy."

Ramer laughed and gave us a wave before following along behind Pea.

Locke's eyes lit up. "You know, an orgy doesn't sound bad."

Alistair rolled his eyes. "Come on. There's still work to be done, and our mate's hungry."

He was right. But now Locke had mentioned an orgy, I couldn't stop picturing it. Definitely a goal to work towards. I gave them all a bright grin. "I'm starved." I winked and led them inside, unable to resist the small smirk on my face.

Micah leaned down and nipped my earlobe. "I don't trust that look at all."

Smart man.

23

The attack came at night. On the top floor, the sound of the screams took a little while to drift into my consciousness. In fact, I wasn't completely awake until I felt Micah scramble out of bed, his ultra sensitive hearing picking up what mine missed. Before my eyes had even fully adjusted to the dark, he was in full Lycan form. I sat up in bed, the fear in Micah's mind making me instantly afraid.

"Micah, what's going on?" Stupid question. I already knew the answer. We were too slow and The Hounds were attacking.

"Stay here, Layla. Don't turn on the lights and remain very quiet. I'm going to send the kids up to you." He reached into the dresser and pulled out a gun and two clips. "I know you can use these." He paused, reaching down to touch his forehead to mine. "I love you."

I swallowed the lump in my throat. "I love you too." He snuffled my neck with his Lycan-transformed face then ran out the door. Climbing out of bed, I threw on yesterday's clothes and rested the gun against my thigh. I could still hear the sound of yelling and the soft pops of gun fire as I ran around behind the island counter for cover.

At least we'd cleared out most of the members. The Academy housing was all but complete, and we'd been slowly shipping people and things that direction. There were less than thirty members left in the building, mostly teens that needed to finish out their exams in public school, and adult members who were finishing up work contracts and tying up loose ends. We'd been too slow, but at least we'd gotten most of them out.

I sat there with my back against the oak cupboard doors, clinging tightly to the feeling of Micah and Alistair in my mind. Rage and fear were the two predominant emotions. I felt useless, just sitting here in the dark, listening to the yelling and the popping noises of gunshots. If anything happened to the guys... The fear swelled up in me until it threatened to choke me.

Someone banged at the door after fifteen or so agonizing minutes and I resisted a scream while chastising myself. Taking the safety off on the gun, I crept towards the door. Logically, I assumed that The Hounds would have just kicked it in, but I yelled for them to identify themselves just the same.

"It's Ramer." His voice sounded urgent. I pointed the gun down and opened the door. Ramer led a group of five members; Annabeth was there and so was a tiny shapeshifter who turned into a sparrow, along with three others whose faces I knew but not their abilities. I assumed they had non-defensive powers. I hoped this wasn't all that was left alive. I led them back into Micah's apartment, ushering them into the kitchen and behind the bench. I pulled Ramer aside.

"What is happening down there? I woke up to Micah in full Lycanthrope form handing me a gun and telling me to stay. All I can hear is gunshots."

Ramer looked dazed, shaking his head. "Not gunshots; tranquilizers. They're trying to capture us, not kill us. They just stormed through the doors and windows, dozens of them. Locke was the first to raise the alarm, being on the first floor. They tried to shoot him but it did nothing. By the time Alistair got there, they'd gotten onto the second floor and people were screaming and running everywhere. Then Penelope was shaking me awake and giving me the story and handing off these five. There will be more; I'm fairly sure the twins are coming with another five or so. It's just chaos." He was pale and shaky, and I realized I was shaking along with him.

"Why do they want to take prisoners?" I didn't know the answer, but I was sure it wasn't for altruistic reasons. To sell them was the most obvious reason.

There was another loud banging on the door and I pushed Annabeth to the floor in the kitchen and aimed the gun at the door. Ramer on my other side, we slowly moved towards the door.

"Layla!" One of the twins' voices was strangled on the other side of the door but I couldn't pick who it was, Lorelei or Caroline. I swung the door open quickly, and Carolines wild eyes made her face almost ghostly pale. Behind her was a small crowd of people, and I dragged them all inside before I bolted it again. With her was another six people, the only ones I knew were a young teleporter by the name of Sam, and Ricky, who was one of the youngest members and could turn invisible. Both had amazing abilities but not very useful in a fight.

A sudden searing pain stole my breath like I'd been stabbed in the heart, dropping me to my knees. I knew what the pain was; one of the guys was hurt. I clung to the bonds to Micah and Alistair, and Alistair was a thrumming connection of rage, but not pain.

Micah. I touched the spot he held in my mind. I gasped as the agony reverberated through my head and down my arms.

"Layla?" Ramer sounded panicked.

"It's Micah. He's hurt. I have to go, I have to help

him." I grabbed Ramer's hand and he dragged me to my feet.

Caroline reached out and touched my cheek, and her fingers came away red. "Layla, you're bleeding."

From my eyes? What the hell was happening to me? "Stay here. Watch these guys." I looked at the shifters. "There's a skylight over the bath. Smash it and get on the roof if you can. Run; you know where to go. Run and don't look back." I swallowed hard. "If the worst happens, go to Dark River in Canada. Talk to the owner of The Immortal Cupcake. Her name is Raine. She'll help you."

I tried to hand Ramer my gun but he shook his head. "I'm coming with you."

Caroline crossed her arms over her chest. "Me too."

Another wave of pain rolled over my skin. I could only imagine the physical pain I would feel if Micah died; it would be like ripping my soul in two. I composed myself and addressed the group.

"Annabeth, I need you to protect the group." I handed her the gun and she looked at it like it was a snake. She was the oldest and the kids needed her. "Sam, if they make it to the floor below us, you need to teleport who you can out of here."

I knew I was being an idiot. I was a human, going to fight a battle with trained soldiers. Without a weapon. But I couldn't sit here and let my heart be torn out.

With one last look over my shoulder which I hoped was reassuring, I raced out the door.

Caroline, Ramer and I rushed down the spiral stairs, and I breathed a sigh of relief when I realized The Hounds hadn't made it this far yet. There was still time.

I looked over my shoulder at Ramer. "Do you think that, if you had to, you could speed up someone's life so that they died in seconds? Only if you have to, I know how you feel about taking lives." Ramer looked horrified at the suggestion but nodded. I continued running until I was at the top of the next stairwell.

I turned to Caroline. "I need you to confuse anyone who comes up these stairs, instantly and to the full extent of your abilities, okay?"

"Yes." Her face was set in a hard mask, but her hands shook. I'd put too much on the shoulders of a girl so young. What was she? Sixteen? But what choice did I have?

"Thank you so much for this." My voice broke on the last word but I steeled myself again. Somehow, because I was sleeping with the majority of Eden's leadership, I'd defaulted into this authoritative role, when really I was just as terrified as Caroline. Ramer shook his head.

"Micah is our brother." He left it at that but my eyes had begun to well up. If anything happened to Micah... I shuddered as the thought repeated itself over and over in my mind. I could feel his pain so he was still alive. That's what I needed to focus on.

More gunshots, this time closer, had me tensing. The noise was so much louder down here, people yelling and the crashing of furniture and walls as we fought back in hand to hand combat. It sounded closer and I hoped that I hadn't run straight into the front line.

Ricky, the invisible kid that I was fairly sure I'd left upstairs in the apartment, appeared in front of us. "I found Micah! He's injured in front of Ramer's apartment."

I frowned at him. "You need to be upstairs. It isn't safe for you down here."

"Did you see any other injured members?" Ramer asked at the same time.

Ricky nodded, choosing to pretend I hadn't said anything. Damn kids. "I saw a few injured but there are captives too, on the ground floor, locked under the stairs. We can't leave them there!" His eyes welled with tears, and I grabbed him into a hug.

"We aren't leaving anyone anywhere. I need you to get back upstairs though, okay? Now, Ricky!" I used my most authoritative voice, and it seemed to work as I watched him take off toward the stairs, turning invisible in just a few steps.

I turned to Ramer. "I need you to get Micah to safety. I'll get the prisoners." Ramer opened his mouth to protest, and I grabbed handfuls of his shirt. "Please. If anything happens to him… "

Ramer frowned, but finally nodded. "If you die, Layla, I swear, I'll find a way to reverse my power, resurrect you, and kick your ass."

I smiled, even though I still had blood stained tears running down my face. I kissed Ramer on the cheek. "Please be careful, I couldn't stand losing you either."

He nodded, sprinting away, staying low and sticking to the shadows.

I looked over at Caroline. "Do you want to go back upstairs? This is a lot. I won't blame you for a second."

The girl snorted. "As if I'm going to leave you helpless." She was all sixteen year old bravado. No wonder those YA novels always had teen girls as protagonists. They were fearless.

I stepped out in front of her, her hand clasped tightly in mine. Edging around the corner, I saw that the hall was clear. Staying close to the wall, we crept closer to the stairs. When we got to the edge of the stairway, I saw Spiros, who controlled lightning with his fingertips, electrocuting soldiers as they tried to ascend. They thought he was part Djinn or something, because apparently one of their races controlled lightning, and as electricity flowed from his fingertips into the bodies of the oncoming bounty hunters, I didn't care what he was. I didn't think the charge he was using was enough to kill them, but it knocked them unconscious and sent them rolling back down the stairs.

The soldiers were dressed in camouflage fatigues with a vertical and horizontal white stripe crossing on the left hand side. It created a single luminescent cross on their bodies; kind of like camouflage wrapped Christmas presents. They were wearing night vision goggles with reflective red lenses. However, the bursts of light coming from Spiro's electric flashes silhouetted them against the stairway easily. I had to find a way down those stairs. I turned to Caroline.

"Do you think you could confuse them all so that they could no longer shoot or even walk?"

Caroline nodded and smiled eagerly. "It's easy. Though all of them at once might be a problem, I can't hold them very long." She closed her eyes and the line of troops ascending the stairs came to a sudden stop, although some still toppled backwards from Spiros' bolts of electricity. Spiro turned to us, and he looked relieved.

"Oh god, I'm so glad you two are okay. They're keeping prisoners beneath the stairs."

"We know. Caroline has them stunned, but she can't hold it forever." I looked at the girl and her face had turned pale with the force of holding so many people against their wills.

"I say you've probably got about thirty seconds before they are fully functioning again so make your zaps count." Caroline and I started to edge past the soldiers.

They looked at us, their eyes darting wildly back and forth between us, confused why they couldn't move. More than one had fear in their eyes at being so defenceless.

We walked straight past them, but being so close to them made me feel ill. I wanted this whole thing to be over, but I still had work to do.

This close, I could pull that one guy's knife and end them all before they could even begin to process how to defend themselves. But that wasn't me. At least, it wasn't yet. Still, I grabbed a metal tube thing that I was fairly sure was a flashbang. I'd seen one in the police chief's gear, though why he'd need a flashbang in Roseau was beyond me.

When we reached the landing, the first floor was chaos.

No, it wasn't chaos. It was war.

Bodies lay around on the floor like abandoned toy soldiers, as well as some faces I recognized but tried not to see. There was blood and torn throats, the air thick with gun powder and death. I pushed Caroline closer to the wall, edging us around the outside of the fighting. I could see Alistair in his Lycan form, and I suddenly understood why people in the Dark Ages had feared them so much. He was the perfect killing machine. Fast, smart, and with jaws that could snap your neck.

His head whipped toward me and I held my breath as he growled so loudly that it made my knees weak. There were other members fighting, and I saw Anastasia right beside him, a long sword in one hand and her face coated in blood. He waded through the mass of bodies, and I could tell they were the true defensive line, stopping The Hounds from getting further up.

When he reached me, he grabbed me up in his very much not-human arms and pulled me close to his chest. Caroline had created enough compulsion that people got confused when they looked in our direction, creating a pocket of almost invisibility.

"Layla, what are you doing down here?" Alistair growled, and I clung to the soft honey fur of his shoulders.

"Micah's hurt. They've taken captives. I'm taking care of it."

He held me tighter, like he was trying to shelter me with his will alone. "But who's taking care of you?"

I wriggled from his arms, grabbing his hand. "Me and Caroline have got this, Alistair. You guys just make sure they don't make it any further up. We'll only be a second, I promise."

I pressed a kiss to his knuckle, wishing he was human for a second so I could kiss his lips. But while he was strong as a human, he was formidable as a Lycan. "Go, they need you."

I pushed him back toward the line holding the stairs. Alistair looked torn, and I shoved him again. "You have five minutes, Layla, and then I'm coming to get you myself."

I crossed my heart and dragged myself away. One more flight of stairs and we would be on the ground floor. We couldn't rely on backup to distract the enemy from us this time. Creeping softly down the stairs, I was thankful for the noise muffling our steps. Reaching the landing, I peeked around the corner.

There were possibly fifteen or more soldiers down there, probably more unseen in the darkness. There was no fighting down here, just the heavy footfalls of reinforcements coming in, and the injured coming out. How had no one noticed this? We were inner city, goddammit. This was an all out tactical assault and there were no human cops in the vicinity? Smelled like corruption to me. They had the cops on the books.

The Hounds seemed to have a never ending stream of willing bodies, ready to throw themselves on the teeth of monsters.

I hadn't seen Locke or Penelope yet, and I was beginning to worry. Caroline and I ducked back up the stairs. I doubted we could just march into them like we had the others. Caroline had figured the same.

"What do we do now? I can't confuse that many

people and still ensure I get the ones I can't see," she whispered furiously.

I didn't know if any of the members being held captive would be helpful. There could be anyone in there, but they would most likely be tranquilized and no help in a fight. I was starting to panic; I couldn't think of a way to get them out.

Caroline hesitated. "If I could get a better look at them, I can do this thing that I was told I wasn't ever allowed to do but it would work."

"What's that?" I whispered back, but my heart sank. This was going to be bad.

"When I was a little kid, before I came to live at Eden, I accidentally destroyed my hamster's higher brain functions. It was like he forgot how to do anything other than primal reflexes, like breathing. So I can, like, I can burn out neural pathways or some-thing? If I try really hard. And you say it's okay."

Holy fuck, was that okay? That was more than a moral grey area. This was the kind of thing that black-ened your soul. Was I really going to ask this teen to make vegetables out of these men, these soldiers? Was it different than giving her a gun?

Slowly, I nodded, giving her a reassuring smile that probably didn't reach my eyes. That was a terrifying power to be in the hands of anyone, let alone a teenage girl. I'd assumed she could warp your cognitive abili-ties, but to such an extent of making a person a reflexive vegetable? That was a terrifying prospect. But this was war, and I was pretty sure that whatever they had planned for the captives under the stairs wasn't going to adhere to the Geneva Convention.

"I think it's okay. I don't want you to do anything you are uncomfortable with, Caroline. We are going to survive this, as will our friends, and if we have to do it another way, we will. I don't want you to feel pressured. But if you think you can, and that you can do it within a short timeframe... "

Caroline gave me a small smile. "Only you would worry about peer pressuring me at a time of life and death." She squared her jaw. "I can do it."

I nodded, pulling her into a tight hug so she didn't see the sadness on my face. I stepped away, and we crept back down the stairs. Every instinct in my body screamed for me to run, to go as fast as I could.

"Close your eyes and cover your ears. 3...2...1... NOW!" I threw the flashbang and slammed my eyes closed. My ears immediately began to ring, but when I opened my eyes, it was like watching dominoes fall. The soldier closest to us dropped to the floor, landing awkwardly and hitting his head.

I kinda hoped he was dead. Soon they all started to drop, their legs just giving way as they forgot how to stand.

I didn't look down, pushing Caroline in front of me so she didn't have time to stare at the chaos she'd created. We moved quickly, crossing the floor to the closet under the stairs. It was just for cleaning supplies normally but it made an efficient prison. The door was locked but not very thick, and our combined body weight should be enough to kick it in.

"Hello? It's Layla. We are going to kick down the door. Move away!" I yelled through the door. On the count of three, both Caroline and I kicked as hard as we could at the bottom of the door and it swung open.

They were crammed in like sardines. Locke was tied in the corner, his bulk taking up the majority of the room, even hogtied as he was. There were three unconscious women lying next to him, haphazardly piled on top of each other like dead bodies.

"Layla." It came out of Locke's mouth in a sigh of relief. "You're bleeding. Is Micah with you? Alistair?"

I swallowed hard, shaking my head. His face shuttered. "Is he dead? Is that why you're crying the mortal tears?" His voice was neutral but his eyes were pained.

"Mortal tears?" I shook my head, swiping at my cheeks. "He's injured but he'll be fine. Ramer is with him now and I can feel him in my mind. He's in pain but he'll live, which is more than I can say for us if we don't hurry up."

"It's the blood tears you cry when your bonded mate is mortally injured. It's like a red flag so you can help them before they die, or so I've read in Alistair's journals."

I untied him, and I kissed his cheek. "They're okay, I promise. I need you to carry the women back upstairs to Micah's apartment. Anastasia and Alistair are on the second floor holding them back with a few other people, but I don't think they can hold them forever." He stood, heaving two of the unconscious women onto his shoulders in a fireman hold. His legs were shaking and he swayed from side to side. "Whatever they shot me with wasn't really effective, but it's making me feel like my drinks have been spiked at a frat house."

I laughed, leaning up to kiss him softly. "I'm so fucking glad you're okay," I whispered against his mouth.

"Me too. Let's go. I don't like being down here like sitting ducks."

Yeah, I didn't either. Solange, one of the shifters, was slowly waking up and I dragged her to her feet. "You're okay," I whispered. "We're going to get out of here."

I pushed her gently toward Caroline.

"We'll go back up the same way we came down." Making sure everyone was secure, I stuck my head out of the room. The soldiers were still on the floor, staring listlessly, and I could hear someone on the radio signalling for backup. That was good. Maybe we were gaining some ground on the second floor. Signalling for the others to come out, I leaned down and scooped up the AK that was just lying on the floor, having slipped from a soldier's hand. I'd take this, and hope to god I didn't have to shoot anyone.

"Don't stop on the first floor, just keep going. Make yourself known before you reach the second floor landing so Spiros doesn't zap you. Go, I'm right behind you!" I was glad for the almost darkness so I didn't have to see the stark brutality of the floor. Blood had dried on the ground, making the floor tacky, like running on fly paper.

I made it up the first three steps before I felt something sharp hit me in the thigh and suddenly running anywhere seemed impossible.

My legs felt like cement as I slowed down to a stop. I reached around and pulled out a pointed dart, its clear glass vial empty of all except a few tiny drops. I tried to yell for help, but even my vocal chords seemed disabled. I watched them get smaller and smaller as they reached the top of the stairs.

I spun around to find the source of the dart. I couldn't see anyone, the encroaching darkness making the world fuzzy.

Suddenly, a man filled my vision, the whites of his eyes almost luminescent in the darkness. He looked insane. Terrifyingly insane. He sniffed me, a little bit of saliva trickling from the corner of his mouth.

"Offspring! They will be happy with me for this!" His speech was loose and lazy, like his tongue was lolling around in his mouth, making his speech thick.

My vision began to cloud and my eyelids started to close. No.

No.

I had to stay.

Awake.

I stretched my eyebrows up in an effort to keep them open. The slobbering man was talking gibberish, slinging me over his shoulder and sniffing my leg deeply. He ran back down the stairs, towards the entrance of the apartment building. Where was my gun? I realized I couldn't lift my arms or legs to fight. There were soldiers bustling around me and I was as helpless as a lamb.

"Etienne, this is the one that released the rest but she's an offspring!" He bounced on his toes with excitement, his shoulder digging into my solar plexus, chasing the air from my lungs.

A man appeared, and even though he was upside down in my vision because I was slung over the crazy guy's shoulder, I could tell he was distinguished. He was greying, with short cut military style hair and small round spectacles. He looked like someone's grandfather.

"An offspring. Well done, Trey." He slapped the crazy man on the back. "You, my little lamb, are worth far more than all the others combined." He was interrupted by a soldier appearing at his side.

"Sir, the vampires are coming. Their arrival is imminent."

He moved away, shouting orders to pull back. He looked over at me again, his eyes filled with greed and something almost lustful. I didn't think it was for my body though. "Retreat. We've got our prize."

Trey, the crazy fucker, ran out of the apartment doors and I screamed silently, my mouth only managing muffled moans. Then I blacked out.

24

I woke up to Trey sniffing my cheek. I pulled away, a long line of drool forming between my cheek and his lips. I wanted to throw up.

A voice cleared from across the van. "You burned through the tranquilizers fast. Definitely an offspring." He smiled congenially. "Hello, my dear. My name is Etienne. What's yours?" I just glared, my eyes channeling all the hatred in my heart. "Not in the mood to talk? That's okay. I understand it may be difficult in the circumstances. You were quite a find, you know. In my forty years as a Hound, I've only ever caught one other of your kind. Then to find two in one night? Amazing. Though, the females do sell better. For breeding and... other purposes. No, I'm not mad at you at all."

I didn't know what the man was talking about. What the hell was an offspring?

"Trey here is a specialist at finding your kind, he can smell it in your blood. It smells different to everything else, unique. At least, that's what he tells me. If he wasn't so well trained, he would have torn you apart by now just to satisfy the hunger for your blood. Sometimes he gives over to his more...animalistic nature." I struggled to speak, my tongue felt swollen, like it was too big for my mouth.

"I don't know what you are talking about. I'm nothing... a normal."

Etienne didn't seem concerned; in fact he looked smug. I hated him even more in that moment. I reached out to Micah, taking calming breaths so our link didn't scare him. He was still there, I could feel the lingering physical pain, his worry and his anger. I knew Locke and Caroline would have realized by now that I was missing, and the vampires would have decimated the remainder of The Hounds. I felt fleetingly satisfied. Other than my capture, the battle had been a victory for us.

Etienne had turned back towards the salivating Trey. The man was gaunt and pathetic, his brown hair stringy and greasy, and his long limbs pale. He looked like a mangy dog that someone had starved and kicked around.

"Ah, so you can speak. What's your name? Who is your sire?"

Who the fuck used words like sire?

"Fuck you," I sneered at him and he backhanded me across the face, splitting my lip.

Blood trickled down my chin, and my eyes watered. At least my tears aren't pink anymore. If what Locke had said was correct, both my mates were safe and well. I was going to make Etienne pay for hitting me though, or if I wasn't around, the guys would make him pay when they avenged me. I knew they wouldn't rest until every last one of The Hounds was dead. Etienne raised his hand again and I flinched involuntarily.

My mother always said pick your battles, and I decided this wasn't the line in the sand I wanted to draw.

"Layla, my name is Layla." The man nodded in approval, petting my head as if I were a puppy.

"And your sire?"

I shook my head. "No idea?"

Etienne gave me a smirk. "See? There was nothing hard about that. Besides, I am trying to tell you something that you'd desperately want to know. So Layla, tell me, what *do* you know of your father? Was he around much when you were a baby or did your mother raise you by herself?" What did my father have to do with this? I shook my head, indicating that I had no father. "Ah. Not to worry, I'm sure your mother did a fine job by herself. Single mothers aren't so frowned upon these days." He shook his head, like society's issues with single mothers was appalling. But kidnapping and murdering? Totally fine. This guy was officially insane too.

He looked like a sociopathic Santa Claus.

"Well Layla, you are very special because your father was the rarest of being, even amongst the supernatural. In your blood runs the elixir of life, the pure embodiment of our life force itself flows through those veins. With a vial of your blood, the sick can become well. The weak can become strong. In the olden days, your blood could make someone so powerful, plebeians would worship at their feet like they were gods." His eyes basically flashed with dollar signs. "This makes you a very marketable commodity. Buyers all over the world will want you, to harvest your blood, or study it and try to replicate it. You will make me millions of dollars alone, and that is just in commission for your capture. If only I could have gotten the other one. A mating pair would have been a king's ransom in riches. Next time, I guess, now that I know where he is." He tapped his chin. "I wonder which you belong to? The Greeks? Surely. We won't know without the proper tests, I guess," he said offhandedly to Crazy-Eyed Trey, who nodded vigorously, making spit fly everywhere before going back to staring at me.

"The hell are you talking about? Elixir? Greeks? I think you guys have been drinking the Kool-Aid for a little too long."

Etienne rolled his eyes. "You must be young. You

have no idea what your blood hides. You are a demi-god. A deity. Descended from the original creators of the world."

"You are fucking crazy." He backhanded me again, but I don't think his heart was in it this time, because my head just bounced off the side of the van.

"Soon, my little immortal, we will be back at the labs and who knows, maybe the The Hounds will decide to keep you for their own. After all, you are an extremely valuable commodity."

My face felt cold and sweat beaded on my brow. An immortal? And there was another demi-god like me, or apparently me, at Eden?

Then it came to me, and I blamed the drugs for being a little slow to connect the dots.

Locke. He was the other demi-god. The other... whatever the fuck these guys called us. Offspring?

Etienne was still talking to himself, just out loud, and a little like a Bond villain. "Maybe we could sell you to the Russians, they are always looking for the upper hand in world politics and you would give even the most inconsequential country the upper hand. Yes indeed, maybe we could break the billion dollar mark for you..." I blocked out the sound of his voice, my brain threatening to crash under the avalanche of the situation. This guy thought I was some kind of deity?

I wanted to dismiss it. I had no real abilities. No

ageless, immortal beauty. I was the epitome of what everyone at Eden had called me. I was normal.

But then I thought about my mother, about her insanity.

In her last two months, I had thought she was delusional, making no sense to me. But what if she wasn't delusional at all, but actually trying to tell me that my father was some mythical god? I wasn't going to delude myself into thinking she was sane; she would yell and scream that the soap company was putting arsenic in the soap dispensers in attempt to murder her. But in her more lucid moments, when she spoke and I had dismissed her mutterings as delusions and barely listened, had she actually been confessing? I racked my brains for her references to my father. She had been pretty graphic in some conversations, describing how they made love and I had blocked those parts out. But when she gushed that he was god, well, now that statement didn't seem nearly as crazy as it did back then.

I'd thought she had meant it in an adoring sense, putting the memory of him up on a pedestal, as most heartbroken people do. I didn't think she could possibly mean it in the literal sense. Other things she had said over the years, when I thought she was just making excuses for his absence, like it was too dangerous for him to stay and he was just passing through and didn't mean to fall in love with her, suddenly made a sickening amount of sense. I had thought she was trying to convince herself that she wasn't merely a one night stand.

My heart broke and I sent out a silent apology to my mother. She was trying to tell me her darkest secrets and I had written her off as a crazy person.

"We're here."

Where Trey was salivating before, the idea of presenting his conquest to his masters had him panting with eagerness, his mouth open so you could see his tongue hanging loosely as he breathed heavily. The doors swung open and a nameless soldier stood there. Trey went to haul me over his shoulder but I pulled away in disgust.

Etienne laughed. "I think Layla can walk herself, Trey."

The human bloodhound looked crestfallen and trudged ahead. I gave an audible sigh of relief. I looked around what appeared to be a massive factory complex, with a row of hanger-sized buildings marked with roman numerals I-V. There was a large fence around the perimeter topped with razor wire and all the gates were guarded by armed soldiers. It looked exactly how I imagined Area 51 would. A rescue was going to be difficult. People would die trying to save me.

For the first time, I felt hopelessness grow into a burning lead weight in my chest. I pushed it down, but tears pricked at my eyes.

No. I wouldn't give them the satisfaction of my tears.

I was marched across a gravel yard, Etienne on one side and Trey on the other. Entering the building marked IV, soldiers saluted as he passed.

I gasped when I took in the contents of the building. On one side there were a row of glass fronted cells, the people inside them lying on beds and staring at the ceiling as if they were corpses already. On the other side of the room, there were lab technicians and doctors, as well as a varying array of familiar and unfamiliar equipment.

I was frogmarched past the horrifying spectacle of cells to a set of large oak doors, guarded by more soldiers. Etienne stopped in front of a stern looking man, whose eyes were hard and cold. A real military man, or perhaps a mercenary?

"I want to see Theiss. The raid did not go so well but I brought a consolation prize."

The man turned and entered the room, without so much as blinking, shutting the door in our faces. By now, Trey was whining, pacing back and forth. The military man returned and ushered us in.

There was a long glass table with five men seated around it in high back chairs. A man, in what appeared to be his late forties, sat at the head. This must be Theiss then.

His gold eyes gave him away immediately. "You're a

Lycan!" My gasp rang around the room, and the man gave a smirk, showing off sharp teeth.

"Etienne, it appears you have failed to crush the demon organization. Failure is not something I encourage, as you are well aware. Why should you avoid punishment at the hands of your comrades?"

Etienne cleared his throat and it was the first time I had seen him uncomfortable.

"The vampires interfered, even after we had good intelligence that they would not. There wasn't any choice but to pull back, otherwise our forces would have been sandwiched between the demons and the vampires, which would have resulted in an unacceptable amount of casualties. We intend to take a larger force in as soon as we are able to deploy, so we can capture what we can and eradicate what remains." Etienne shoved me forward. "But I have captured you a rare prize. I brought you an offspring and located another that I plan to capture in our next offense. I know his kind. He'll fight in every battle." Theiss' eyes lit up.

"An offspring? Well, this is a partial redress for your failure. Trey, I am going to assume she was your discovery?" Trey nodded eagerly, and I thought he was going to piss himself with excitement. "We haven't captured an offspring in a long time. There'll be a lot of interest in this one." There were pleased murmurs around the table as they looked at me like an animal at auction.

"You better take her to a containment room and inform Porter of our recent addition. I have calls to make." His smile was broad and predatory, and a cold shiver ran down my spine.

I gritted my teeth as Etienne grabbed my arm and dragged me back towards the doors. Still staring at Theiss, I spat on the ground and turned regally away, straight into the oncoming backhand of Etienne, which made stars appear in my vision. Theiss just smiled at me and laughed, motioning us away.

25

T he walls of my prison were stark white. Not eggshell white or off-white, a hard white that hurt your eyes if you stared at it for too long. The observation window was mirrored so I couldn't see outside the cell. I'd been here for countless hours now, clinging tightly to the feel of Micah and Alistair in my head like a child would cling to a teddy bear.

The rooms contained a single hard bed and a toilet that was embedded in the wall behind a sliding door. I'd laid on the bed, sat on the floor, laid on the floor and sat on the bed, but nothing eased my discomfort. Despair started to creep into my mind as I went over and over the specifications of the compound that I had observed.

I'd seen a dozen soldiers on my walk to Thiess, and

they'd all been in pairs. There were ten other containment rooms that would contain ten other people like
me. The idea that I was immortal, in the same way
that Locke was, was like a dream. I tried to think if I'd
ever seriously hurt myself. I mean, after the wolf
attack, but then I'd healed back up within twenty-four
hours, except for the bite on my neck which I now
knew had more to do with the mate bond than my
physiology. Alistair's bite hadn't healed all the way up
either.. That was probably weird, I guess. I never got
sick.

Could it really be true?

A voice suddenly reverberated in my head, scaring
me into a sitting position. It was Annabeth's voice.

"We're here Layla, we will get you out. Stay strong.
Your mates love you."

The relief was so overwhelming, I cried. Tears
streamed down my cheeks, all the terror I'd been
trying to keep pressed down, finally broke free.

They wouldn't quit until I was free. I channeled all
my love into our connection and felt it flood right back.
Tears welled in my eyes. I wondered if Penelope was
there, whether they were close enough for her to
hear me.

"Penelope, you must keep Locke away. They will
attack the apartments again soon so make sure
everyone is gone. Ten others here who need saving
also. Keep Locke away, it is really important, explain

later. Love you all." I chanted the message over and over again. Annabeth's voice returned to me.

"The connection is fuzzy. Copy on Locke. He's not happy about it though." I laughed through my tears, because I could imagine. He'd want to be the first to charge in here, and take me back by force. But I couldn't run the risk.

Happier, I began to plan how I could help Eden and punish Etienne and Theiss in the process. It should be easier to plan now that I didn't have to worry about dying.

I was lying on my bed when the door to my cell swung open and hope surged through me. It quickly faded however, when a man in his mid-thirties entered. He was attractive in an academic way, definitely not in the same league as Alistair though. He had a long oval face, black rimmed glasses, and a big smile plastered on his face. His white lab coat and stethoscope labelled him a doctor or scientist. He looked pleasant and I resented him all the more for it.

"Hi Layla, my name is Porter. I'm a doctor here. I just thought I'd come and introduce myself and take a few observations, maybe have a chat." His voice was even pleasant and it would be easy to imagine he was my local family doctor.

I gave him a hard stare. I hated him even more because he was trying to be nice while I sat in a cage.

"I don't blame you for not wanting to talk. In your

position, I would have clawed my eyes out as soon as I walked through the door." He sat down next to me on the bed. "I don't really approve of the conditions they keep you in. But I'm just a doctor, completely replaceable. I like to think by staying around to study you, I can at least personally offer you a little bit of dignity."

I gave him a stony look, but I felt my hatred drain away. He was just so inoffensive, damn him.

"They gave me a brief rundown of your situation. You're an offspring, and from what I can gather, it means one or more of your parents were what humans would consider gods. I understand that the idea of gods and goddesses being real is as new to you as it is to me. Maybe we can learn about your immortality together?" Just past the door, the steely eyed merc who guarded Theiss' office was watching. I had no doubt in my mind he was here to make sure I complied, despite Porter's gentle approach.

"We'll start easy, just taking a little bit of blood. Would that be okay?"

I nodded, because it was safe to assume that they'd get their blood, one way or another. He put a tourniquet around my arm, and I held still. He drew vial after vial of blood until I felt myself go pale. When he pulled out the tourniquet, the hole in my arm healed up almost immediately. How had I never noticed that? Was my rapid healing a new thing?

"Amazing," he breathed. "I want to pretend this is

all altruistic, but this is also why I stay. Where else could I study real life miracles of nature?"

I finally turned to look at him dead in the eye. "You mean, where else could you study us against our will, until we are sold off to the highest bidder as a captive for life? You're right, I can't think of anywhere else." I turned away again and Porter sighed as he stood.

"I know you're right. I can't sleep at night thinking about it. But tell me what should I do? If it wasn't me, it would be someone else. And I have my reasons to stay..." He trailed off, casting a quick glance at Robo-Soldier. He sighed and turned to leave. "I'll see you tomorrow, Layla. Try to sleep. Actually," he murmured as he fished in his white coat pocket, pulling out a paperback. "I brought you a book, in case you get bored." He handed me a copy of 'The Once and Future King' and left.

The doctor confused me. He wasn't the impersonal monster that I assumed he had to be. I wanted to hate everyone involved in my incarceration. I wonder if he even realized that he was as much of a prisoner as I was here? There would be no way that Theiss would just let him walk away from the job when he had seen so much, knew so much.

I couldn't save him too. He'd made his choice.

I rolled over, wrapping my arms around my body, pretending that I was safe in the arms of my men before I fell into an exhausted sleep.

. . .

I WAS LISTLESS the next morning. Mostly, I was bored and worried, but the thought of never seeing the guys again made me feel sick to my stomach. I was actually happy to see Porter when he came to do more observations and take more blood.

I was definitely getting Stockholm already. My apologies to daytime TV; it is possible to get institutionalized this fast. I was irrationally angry at myself, and as soon as Porter was finished, I rolled over on my bed and stared at the wall, pretending he didn't exist. That this whole institution didn't exist. Hell, that I didn't exist.

"Wait here, I have something I'd like to show you."

He said that as if going anywhere was a choice I could make. The connection with Micah held pain and anger, no doubt in response to mine, and stress and fear poured back at me from Alistair's. I wished that I had a connection to Locke, but on the other hand, I was glad that no part of him was in this place. I took the time to calm myself and told Penelope I was okay. I repeated it several times to ensure she would get the message.

Porter returned, pushing open the door and reappearing holding the hands of two tiny children, a boy and a girl. They looked like they were only three and four.

"Guys, this is Layla. She's a little sad and I think playing with you might make her feel better. Layla, this is Daniel and Stacey." The boy, Daniel, was the older of the two. His sweats were slightly too big for his waif-like body. They had to be siblings because they both had identical big brown doe eyes framed with thick lashes.

The little girl was dressed in pink sweats and held both Porter and Daniel's hands. She moved towards me, letting go of Porter but dragging Daniel behind her. She stopped in front of me, putting her little hand on mine.

"Why are you sad? I know for certain that Porter wouldn't have done anything to hurt you, Porter wouldn't hurt anyone. He's an exceptional doctor who adheres to a code of ethics."

I gasped, her perfect diction and extensive vocabulary were at odds with her baby face, and the combination was shocking.

The little girl giggled. "First impressions are my favorite. The looks people give me are always so funny."

Daniel still looked solemn, but Porter was smiling. He walked over and ruffled the little girl's dark wavy hair. The pair looked Latino, even if there was a sallowness to their complexion from being stuck inside so long.

"That's because you are always a surprise, Sweetheart. Stacey can speak seven languages, has an IQ that is 183 already but is increasing steadily. She has the ability to learn at astounding rates and has perfect retention. Her accelerated learning ability is a gift. She'll know as much about medicine and science as I do by the time she's five."

Stacey giggled again, and it was high and musical. The kind of childish laugh that made you smile as well. "I'm as knowledgeable as you now, Porter, and you know it."

Porter stuck his tongue out at her, and she giggled harder. They were cute together, like father and prodigal daughter. I turned to Daniel, who still looked solemn.

"It's nice to meet you too, Daniel. Do you have abilities?"

The little boy just continued to look at me with those big sad eyes and didn't say a word. Instead, the book Porter had given me last night floated across the room and landed in my lap as I gaped. His solemn face turned up into a barely perceptible smile.

"Daniel doesn't speak. We can talk to each other through ESP though. But he has telekinesis; he can move things with his mind," Stacey said nonchalantly. "He hasn't spoken since our parents died. I don't remember much about it, but bounty hunters killed them when they fought to protect us. Daniel has night-mares about it," she said conversationally.

Daniel glared at his sister. She just shrugged. Apparently, they were doing that ESP thing now.

My tears threatened to reappear. These poor little babies, seeing their parents murdered. It would be traumatic for anyone, let alone a small boy. I was reminded of Ramer, I was sure the two would get along.

"That's okay Daniel. You don't need to talk; we can be friends anyway. We could use our hands and play charades to communicate. Or I'm sure Stacey will help. You know what, I have a friend you would like. His name is Ramer and he is completely covered in hair, from the tip of his nose," I brushed Stacey's nose, "to the ends of his fingers." I held Daniel's hands and gently squeezed the tips of his fingers. "He lost his parents when he was little too. But now, he grows things really fast. He could make you two inches taller in minutes, Daniel, and make your hair really long in seconds. He grows hundreds of pretty flowers and they fill his room." I looked up to see that Porter was just as in awe of the story as the children.

"So the hair on his body is due to the personal accelerated growth? What other effects does it have? Is it involuntary or voluntary?" He was as eager as any boy who was shown something shiny and new. I smiled, but I wasn't going to tell him. It wasn't my place and quite frankly, the less spoken in these rooms the better. I had no doubt that they were bugged.

"You would have to ask him, and quite frankly, I hope you two never meet." I dropped my voice low. "Unless you want to help me escape, along with Stacey and Daniel. They would be happy and safe within my family, my organization. None of us are safe here." Porter looked pensive, his eyes downcast. I gave him a long look and turned to the little girl sitting on the bed beside me. "So Stacey, what are your favorite subjects?" I was still holding Daniel's hand and he sat on my other side.

"I like biology, especially that of animals. One day, I'd like to be a vet and help sick and injured animals, or maybe a marine biologist..." Her high pitch voice echoed around the room as she talked about her favorite kind of animal, the dolphin, and her favourite language, Icelandic. She told me that her and Daniel had been with The Hounds for over two years and that Daniel was six and she was three.

I would never have guessed that Daniel was six, because they were both small and elfin for their ages. They told me that Porter had looked after them since they first arrived and snuck them in treats and toys that they kept hidden in their room.

I looked up to find that Porter had snuck out at some point, probably to continue his rounds. Stacey didn't stop talking however, and I think some of it was coming from Daniel too. He wanted to be a fireman, he told me through Stacey, so he could help save people and get kittens out of trees. I wondered how much of his desire to save people stemmed from his inability to save his parents. They told me all about them too, their mother was a clairvoyant in a travelling carnival and their father could talk to animals, which probably explained Stacey's desire to be a vet.

In turn, I told them about Micah, about the farm I used to live on, about Monster the horse and Pip and Fred. I told them how Micah and Alistair turned into a half man, half wolf creature on full moons. The smile slipped from their faces at this. Stacey turned towards Daniel, who was obviously telling her to ask something.

"Like the bad man that killed my parents?" So Theiss did field work? I wondered where he was when they were attacking the apartments. I kissed the top of Daniel's head.

"No sweetie, not like Theiss at all. Micah and Alistair fight those men to save people, like superheroes. Lycans are like people. There are good ones like Porter, but there are bad ones too. Micah and Alistair, they are the good ones. Theiss is a bad man. In fact, Micah saved my life once..." I told them the story about the wolves in the forest and how Micah had saved me and taken me back to safety. I showed them my scar, which was fainter every time I looked at it. I told them about Alistair, who helped people like us and made them safe and happy so they could come and go whenever they pleased. They took all the things I said in like little sponges.

When I finally fell quiet and they had no more questions, Stacey had a determined look on her face. "We want to go to Eden."

"I swear it."

Even if I had to burn this place down around us to get us there.

Porter returned in the afternoon to take the children away. I didn't want them to leave and was just seconds away from throwing a tantrum until Porter let them stay.

I decided against it; I didn't want to act more immature than the three year old in the room, but I hated them being out of my sight. I couldn't protect them if they weren't with me.

I hugged them both and Daniel hugged me back even tighter. They were amazing kids, and as the day went on, Daniel had come more and more out of his shell until half of what came out of Stacey's mouth had been Daniel's words. He'd rearranged my room for me, picking up the bed with Stacey and I still on it and moving it to the other side of the room. We'd laughed so hard as we floated across the room, even Daniel was giggling, though he didn't say a word.

His powers of telekinesis seemed to have no limits;

he could move objects that were incredibly heavy with little outward effort. I was sure he could bring this whole building down around our ears if he wanted to. I briefly thought how useful he would be if a rescue was mounted but I swiftly chastised myself for the thought. I promised myself after Caroline that I would no longer look at children as weapons, no matter their abilities.

Porter returned an hour later, after he had returned the children to the room they shared. I was so glad that The Hounds weren't so inhumane as to separate them, or maybe it was just they knew that if they split them up, Daniel would demolish the building to get to Stacey. He was extremely protective of his sister. Even in the confines of my cell, he never turned so that she was out of his sight, even for a moment.

Porter sat on the bed next to me. "Do you see why I can't leave? Those two mean so damn much to me now, that the thought of leaving them here, alone... " He shuddered and dropped his voice low. "If I thought I could get them out without endangering them or anyone around us, I would have done it years ago."

I put my hand on his arm, trying to soothe his frustration

He turned and gave me a sad smile. "You should have seen them when I first arrived. They were these tiny little things, Daniel too small for his age and Stacey was barely toddling around. But when I walked through the door in their cell, Daniel stepped in front of Stacey and threw the bed at me. It only missed me because I stepped back through the doorway. It took me three days of sitting outside their door, talking to them, to convince Stacey that I meant them no harm. Her vocabulary wasn't as good as it is now but she had the learning of a ten year old. Daniel was nonverbal already, and she argued with him that I was a safe person, though how she could know was beyond me." He rested his hands on his knees. "I love those two kids as if they were my own."

I grabbed his hand and held it tightly. "Then help us escape. They will be safe at Eden and you can study us willingly. Alistair would love to share his research. Not that you could release any of your findings to the world or this would happen to all of us." I indicated the white walls around me. "When I'm rescued, I'm taking Stacey and Daniel with me. I like you, Porter, and I know your intentions are good but this is a war and you *must* choose a side. And those two innocent kids do not need to be collateral damage."

Porter just nodded. Even the gentlest guy could be hard when it came to the people they loved. "Whatever side leads to Daniel and Stacey being happy, that's the side I'm choosing. I'll do whatever it takes to keep them safe, and you too, if I can." Porter sounded defeated and I felt slightly guilty about making him feel like a monster, but it was a means to an end.

26

From all accounts, the rescue efforts were not going well. Annabeth was very careful not to put it in those exact words, but it could be inferred by the severity of her news. The vampires had gone. Fucking vampires.

"Without the vampires, we need to reconsider how to rescue you, as overwhelming them is no longer an option. Is it just me or are the vampires never actually around when they're needed?" Annabeth huffed, and it was an odd sound to hear inside your head. "We'll have to be stealthier now, I think. Reconnaissance tells us that there are about two hundred armed soldiers on the base, an arsenal that would rival the Israeli army and a security system that detects heat and motion. On top of that, it has armed guards and is, by all accounts, impenetrable. This means we can't just send Sam in to teleport you out, even if we did consider it safe enough. We'll have to wait until they launch another attack against the apartments, so our numbers are more even. Our contacts say that their follow up attack will probably be in the next two months. Everyone hates leaving you there for so long and I'm fairly sure we will have to physically restrain your Mates, but this is the only way to ensure no one gets hurt. I'm so sorry, Layla."

I couldn't talk back anymore, they'd moved further away so Penelope couldn't hear my thoughts. I was kind of glad for it at the moment because I couldn't muster up any reassuring platitudes about how fine I would be here. In all honesty, the thought of spending any time at all in these four walls was enough to send me a little insane.

A red light flashed near the door and the slot in the door opened up and bared my midday meal. I would give The Hounds one thing, they fed their captives well. I acknowledged that it was probably to keep us plump and healthy until we were sold at auction and not for any humanitarian reasons. Today, I was having rib eye steak with mashed potatoes and steamed greens. Normally I relished this part of my day, breaking up the monotony of my captivity, but not today. The food tasted like dirt in my mouth, but with my rescue in mind, I ate every mouthful on my plate. Swallowing became a monumental effort in itself.

Pushing my empty plate back in the airtight chamber, I paced around the room, letting myself contemplate two more months of living in this isolation without Micah, Alistair or Locke. Two months of plotting and planning, and hoping that Porter didn't get executed behind some building for his treasonous activities. The food I'd just eaten threatened to reappear, and I didn't mean back through the airlock chamber.

When my door opened, I resisted the urge to run up to it like a pound dog, but my mood did lift when Stacey and Daniel skipped into the room in front of Porter.

"Layla, Layla! It's an outside day!" The meaning was obvious but I raised my eyebrows. They let us outside, all together? It sounded like a stupid idea to me, letting the supernatural's mingle, but I wasn't about to complain. It would give me the opportunity to meet the other captives.

"Will all your other patients be out there?"

Porter shook his head. Fuck. I knew it would be too good to be true.

"At the moment, you three are my only patients. They usually take the patients out in pairs, but I managed to convince them that taking you and the kids out together wouldn't be a great risk. Stacey is so small that in their minds, she is hardly a threat, so they readily agreed. Are you ready?"

I nodded eagerly. I needed to be outside these

white walls almost as much as I needed to be free. I stepped out in front of him, all but racing for the door.

"Whoa Layla, I need to look like I have you under control and that won't work if you race out of here ahead of me. Here, take Stacey." Stacey happily launched herself into my arms, her little hands hanging onto my neck as she snuggled in.

Porter led us through the lab area, and I slowed my steps to take in as much as I could. There were windows around the top of twelve foot high walls, covered in bars. Guards blocked the only two exits to the building and also guarded the double oak doors that led to Theiss' office. I wouldn't call it impenetrable, but it was very close. I shifted Stacey to the other hip and did a rough count of the lab technicians. Twelve in total. I hoped they wouldn't be hurt during the rescue, after all, they weren't benefiting from our capture. They were just victims of their scientific curiosity, like Porter. I grimaced. No. I couldn't think of them all like Porter, because there was a likelihood some were here for the money, and didn't care if they were selling us off.

Eden weren't a murderous rabble, but they would eliminate who they had to, to get me and the other captives out safely.

Porter led us past Theiss' office to the rear exit. The dead-eyed soldier with incredibly wide shoulders blocked our path.

"Midday exercise party," Porter said in an authoritative voice. The soldier nodded, his eyes running over me appraisingly, but he let us pass. Through the doors was a long hallway which led to more doors and more guards. Once Porter had repeated that we were the midday exercise group several more times, the final guards moved back and swung open the double doors.

A park stretched out in front of me, lush and green, with lots of trees and flowers. It looked like any other park, except that it was contained in a giant cage. Wire covered all four sides of the cage and also along the roof. It looked kind of like an aviary you'd see at your local zoo.

As soon as we stepped out of the antechamber and onto the grass, Stacey was wriggling out of my arms and she hit the ground running, giggling in delight as Daniel gave chase. There were stone benches, and a cement chess table with marble inlays. A sandbox and tire swing kept the kids entertained, and all in all it had a homely feel about it.

But then I wondered how many kids they'd had through here to justify a sandbox and swing. And it was hard to ignore the armed guys on all sides.

The watch towers on every corner were big enough to house one soldier, and guards walked the perimeter of the enclosure. I hoped that their angry looking weapons only held tranquilizers.

I sat down as elegantly as I could on one of the

stone benches, trying very hard to appear regal and untouched by my situation in front of the soldiers. Porter sat down next to me.

"This is almost nice. I'm glad the kids could experience grass and playing outside. How often are we allowed out?"

Porter leaned over and plucked a four leaf clover from the patch beside the bench and handed it to me. I was amazed that it was so easy for him to find them. Maybe he had the luck of the Irish.

"We are allowed to bring the captives outside once a week for two hours. Just long enough for you to get the vitamin D needed to keep you guys looking glowing and healthy."

"You mean, for when we're sold, right?" He nodded towards the guards, who eyed me and the children as if we were time bombs that may explode at any minute.

I'd taken off my slippers and I curled the grass in my toes. I'd appreciate these two hours and then pray that I wouldn't be here in a week to have to experience it again. I walked across the lawn to where Daniel was pushing Stacey in the tire swing.

"Why don't you squeeze in there too, Daniel, and I'll push you both?" The little boy scrambled in next to his sister and I spun the swing around and around before letting it go, the children squealing as it whipped them in tight circles.

Before I knew it, I was laughing, the heavy shackles

of darkness and depression easing. It was replaced by the first hint of happiness I'd felt since I'd arrived. We played hide and seek, catch with a ball that Porter had brought along and made sandcastles with twigs and leaves as flags. If I closed my eyes for a second, I could almost make myself believe that I was just at the park playing with my children, and The Hounds and the confinement were all just a nightmare.

But then I saw him, on the edge of the woods, and my calm shattered. Micah was here, watching and waiting. I should have known that he wouldn't go far, that none of them could bear the distance when I was in so much danger. I channeled my anxiety and fear into the connection, screaming the word danger over and over in my head even though I knew he wouldn't hear. My quick indrawn breath had alerted the children that something was wrong as I played with them in the sandpit, however after a quick check, Porter was still oblivious on the benches.

"Layla, what's wrong?" Both children had stopped now and were staring at me in wide-eyed terror. I hushed them both, stroking their hair and going back to playing in the sand.

"It's okay, guys, let's keep playing. I just thought I saw something, that's all." I snuck a quick look at the guards to see if they noticed anything was amiss, but they seemed oblivious to the mood of their captives. I quickly darted a look back to the woods. I could feel his golden eyes on me, feel his frustration in my head.

I wanted to curse at him almost as much as I wanted to scream at him that I loved him. Why would he stay here, where he could be caught by the very people who would happily skin him alive, in human or Lycan form? But at the same time, just seeing him was comforting.

Stacey and Daniel had continued to play, although their carefree mood had evaporated. Stacey came over and sat on my lap, a smile on her pretty round face.

"You saw him too, didn't you? Was it one of your mates? Daniel saw him as well, but werewolves make him scared and angry, so he didn't say anything. I told him that we should tell you but he was being stubborn." Her little lower lip jutted out and I glanced across at Daniel, his face devoid of all expression, and smiled reassuringly. I stroked Stacey's little chocolate curls, my voice dropping to a low murmur.

"It's okay sweetie, I saw him anyway. You have to give Daniel a little leeway though, he has a good reason to fear Lycans. When the time comes, we will introduce him to Micah and Alistair slowly, so they can get to know each other without being uncomfortable. But it is very important you don't tell anyone else that you saw him," I said in a low voice. Stacey nodded, and slid off my lap.

I sent Micah a wave of love down our bond as

Porter came over to usher us back inside. The guards surrounded us but I couldn't help looking back at the woods one last time and my eyes began to sting when I realized he was no longer there.

As we were led into the anteroom, we passed another group on their way to the exercise area. There was an elderly male doctor, his white lab coat crisp. He nodded respectfully at Porter but his eyes slid over us as if we didn't exist.

With the doctor were two men; one tall and dark with liquid brown eyes that danced even in the lowlights of the anteroom, and the other was a short, round man, with ruddy cheeks and cloudy blue eyes, maybe in his late fifties? The short man patted Daniel on the head as we passed but didn't say anything and Daniel just blinked after him. I leaned down to Daniel as we were led back to the cells.

"Who were they?" I'd addressed Daniel but of course it was Stacey who answered.

"Caio and Tomas. They were in the carnival with my parents. They were captured on the same night as us, one of the first. Tomas makes ghosts, like in the haunted house and stuff, and he can just make anything you want appear in front of your eyes. Caio is a fire breather and he has scales and everything, like a dragon. But he's not a dragon, he said so. His girlfriend was a giant snake. She was taken too but we don't see her. They don't let her outside."

They were Daniel's words coming out of Stacey's mouth, and I could tell the difference from their styles of speech. Stacey didn't adlib for her brother. A fire breather I could believe, and a man who could conjure apparitions, which I was sure went down well in the haunted house, but a man-dragon? I shook my head. I didn't understand why the impossible still shocked me but it did. Man or dragon, they would both be useful, very useful. And where was his girlfriend? This giant snake shifter?

The mysteries of this place kept getting more intricate, and I was beginning to wonder if it was a web that was going to suck me down until I died here too.

27

The icy coldness of the slab table had begun to chill my bones. I resisted the urge to shiver. The cold managed to reach every limb of my body except my left leg, which was comfortably numb from the local anaesthetic.

Porter hovered above me, looking uncertain and decidedly uncomfortable about the procedure. But there was still a glimmer of excitement in his eyes, like that of a little boy with a firefly in a jar. He was, after all, a man of science and I was the most delicious experiment he'd ever seen, so no matter how much repulsion he felt at cutting open my body unnecessarily just to watch it repair itself, he was first and foremost a scientist.

"Okay, Layla, you are going to feel a slight pressure on your calf..." I tuned out his voice. I didn't want to know exactly what was happening because what it eventually boiled down to is that Porter was slicing and dicing me, so as to not raise suspicion among the other doctors. It's not every day a doctor gets an immortal patient and if he didn't do procedures that other doctors would expect to be done, well, it would mean trouble for all of us.

Porter had pumped my leg full of anaesthetic and now it felt swollen and bloated, like it was part of an already decaying body, and I couldn't feel anything from my hip down. But as the scalpel pierced my flesh, I was positive that I could hear it, like a dull popping sound, as it pushed through my unwilling skin. I glanced at Porter's face, but he'd gone to work in full professional mode, concentration knitting his face as he sliced through the layers of skin and muscle as cleanly as possible.

The purpose of the experiment was to record the process of my calf muscle repairing itself using my immortal blood. The idea seemed barbaric, but I understood that it was a ruse we had to maintain.

After seven weeks in captivity, people were starting to ask questions about Porter's commitment, when all he had done were some lousy blood tests. The last thing I wanted was for Porter to lose my case and another doctor take over my 'care', so I consented to a few procedures to protect us all.

"I'm done making the incision in your muscle. I'll

just clean up the wound and stem the bleeding and then we will wheel you back to your room."

I wasn't sure if he wanted my approval for this course of action or not. I may have been a willing participant in agreeing to the surgery, but that didn't mean I had to be an active participant.

"So, I've just put some butterfly sutures on the ends of the incision to stop the skin from tearing more if you stretch or move in a particular way. But you will have to be immobile for a little while." He leaned over and picked me up as if I was a porcelain doll, placing me in the wheelchair with my leg propped on a board. "Silver lining is that I have to record the progress on an hour by hour basis, so I'll be at your beck and call to fetch things and fluff pillows as much as you want." He smiled warmly and I managed to give him a tepid look back. An actual smile was beyond me at the moment. He looked worried, so I forced a small smile.

"Good. What are your baking skills like? Because I could really savage a bagel."

As I was wheeled back through the lab, I was given appraising looks by the other doctors. I scowled back, resisting the urge to bare my teeth at them like a wild animal.

"Unfortunately, not good. They say that baking is a science, but I only manage to burn things."

I only let go of the breath I was holding when we finally entered my room. I'd started to see it as a refuge instead of a prison cell these days, because my trips outside its four walls ultimately ended in some kind of physical discomfort. So far, in the last few days, Porter had tested my pain tolerance using electroshock, taken a biopsy of my bone marrow from my hip and countless pints of blood to give to sick and injured lab rats.

Let me tell you, there were now some seriously buff lab rats rolling around in their little wheels. Apparently, my blood had created some kind of super rats that were at peak physical fitness.

I shook my head and picked up the thread of the conversation as Porter lifted me from the wheelchair, taking special care not to bump my leg and tear open the wound further.

"Well, you can't have it all, Doc. Brains, looks and cooking ability? Unfair to the human race."

Lying me gently on the bed, he pulled the wheelchair up next to me and sat in it himself. He checked my blood pressure and heart rate, then checked out my leg, even though it had only been like ten minutes.

Prying apart the two layers of flesh, he drew back in surprise.

"Amazing, it's knitting back together already." He wrote enthusiastically on his clipboard, his eyebrows raised high on his forehead in amazement.

The local anaesthetic had started to wear off and I could feel the hum of pain starting to reverberate up and down my leg.

Porter was still murmuring to himself, gently nudging at the flesh that desperately wanted to meld back together.

"This is going to heal quicker than I had originally thought. My estimated time, based on our experiments of injecting your blood into lab animals, had indicated that it would take upwards of a week, or even two. But this will heal perhaps in two days at this rate, less if I don't keep the top layers from bonding back together. Do you know if this is the same with the other offspring? Your acquaintance Locke, that is?"

I'd been completely tight-lipped about Locke, not mentioning him to Porter, although I had mentioned him to Stacey and Daniel when I told them stories about Eden. Not about him being an offspring, just that he was big and exceptionally strong.

"I'm not sure." Lie. Locke was better than exceptional at healing. He was a miracle. Porter looked like he wanted to ask more questions but I shut my eyes and turned my face away. The pain was getting worse by the second. I breathed deeply and Porter handed me two more yellow tablets. I had to take my mind off the pain somehow.

"Tell me more about you, Porter. Where'd you do your residency?" He sat back down in the wheelchair, rolling gently back and forth.

"I did my residency in St. Vincent's in Manhattan. I graduated Magna Cum Laude. I have my diploma on the wall of my cubicle if you'd like to see my credentials?" I could hear the smile in his voice.

"I think I can take your word for it. It's not like I'm about to sue you for malpractice. What about your family? Do they approve of your chosen profession?" I couldn't help the disapproval leaking into my voice. He stopped rocking backwards and forwards on the chair and sat perfectly still.

"They're all dead. My parents both died by the time I was in my last year of med school. I had a younger brother as well. My parents had us fairly late in life. They were career doctors, and they realized when they reached forty that they had forgotten to start a family. My mother died of breast cancer when I was in high school and my father died later of heart failure. It goes to show that being a doctor is no guarantee of a long life." I waited for him to continue but he just remained silent, not mentioning his brother. The local anaesthetic had completely worn off now and the meds I'd just taken hadn't kicked in.

"What about your brother?" I asked the question, and when he flinched, I didn't take the question back like I might have done in any other situation. In a twisted way, I wanted him to feel the pain I was feeling, even if it wasn't in the same way. I opened my left eye wide enough to see the raw look of anguish that briefly crossed his face and guilt washed over me.

"Paul was involved in a single vehicle accident

when he was twenty-five. It's every doctor's worst nightmare when someone they know or love is being wheeled through the double doors of their emergency room. I was still in my residency and I was on the graveyard shift. When he came in, he had extensive abdominal and chest trauma, brain injuries and broken bones and cuts everywhere. The police told me later that he wasn't wearing a seatbelt, and swerved to miss a vehicle that suddenly braked. He ran into the barrier on the freeway doing eighty and flew out of the windscreen onto the oncoming lanes. He was hit once before the traffic could come to a stop. It was amazing he was even still breathing.

"He went into arrest before anyone could relieve me. I wouldn't stop until his heart was beating again, and by the time I moved away I was shaking so hard that I could barely stand. I was a doctor. I knew the odds were about a five percent chance of survival. They rushed him into surgery and managed to piece him back together but the brain damage was irreversible. The neurosurgeon told me it looked like someone had put it in a blender; it was swollen and bleeding, and there was nothing anyone could do apart from relieving the pressure."

I reached out and grabbed his hand, wrapping it in mine, guilt riding me for making him relive all this. What kind of jerk was I?

"He was in a coma for weeks. He would never

speak again, let alone walk or even be a shadow of the Paul I knew, so I made the decision to turn off his life support. But then he started breathing on his own. It was a goddamn miracle." He shook his head like he still couldn't believe it after all this time.

"But that was it. Months went by, and he never did more than breathe on his own. He didn't wake up. His brain didn't heal itself. It took me a month to work up the nerve, but one day I walked into his hospital room with an empty syringe and injected air into his blood stream, causing an air embolism. He died within minutes. The autopsy revealed it, but it was ruled accidental death caused by air in the IV. I'm fairly sure the hospital covered it up. I might have escaped criminal charges, but the hospital still fired me. No one else would hire me, and honestly, I didn't try that hard. I'd broken that golden rule to do no harm. I went to South America, drank myself into liver failure, then I was approached by a recruiter for The Hounds, and the rest is history."

"I'm sorry." What a fucking useless statement. It was a goddamn tragedy, and that deserved more than a paltry apology. I just didn't know what.

I thought about the soldiers that Caroline had used her powers on during the battle. They would have been like his Paul, vegetative.

"Porter, did they bring any soldiers back from the apartment raids? Wounded ones, I mean."

Porter nodded. "There is a whole ward of them one building over. It's horrible." He visibly shuddered and I knew he was referring to the men that Caroline had fried.

"Those men will never recover either." I looked him dead in the eye as I said it, accepting the blame for destroying all those lives.

"I know." He reached out and moved a stray lock of hair from my face. The tenderness on his face was raw, and made me swallow hard. I missed my mates, and this artificial world was screwing with my head, because I kind of wanted him to kiss me. To feel something again.

He dragged his eyes from my face. "It's time you got some rest, Layla. I'll be back to monitor you throughout the day. Try to sleep."

With that, he was gone. I watched the space where he'd sat and wondered if this weird feeling in my chest was pity, or some kind of deranged Stockholm syndrome.

28

Eden was back in town. Annabeth's voice had woken me from my sleep, and for a moment I thought it was a dream.

"We're ready. When The Hounds attack our apartment complex within the next few days, we'll just stroll in and take you back. The only thing waiting for The Hounds at the apartments is explosives."

I wanted to bounce around my room, but I quickly got myself under control in case anyone was watching me from the outside. It was going to be a good day. As it was, today was the first time the kids would be allowed to see me since the surgery. Both Porter and I had agreed that it was for the best if the children didn't see me incapacitated. Stacey may have an incredible intellect, but emotionally she was still a three year old girl, and probably wouldn't understand the necessity of Porter, her hero, intentionally cutting up her newest friend. Porter had stopped tearing open the wound to see the muscle reform after two days, no longer able to bear the pain that it inflicted on me. Three days after that there was nothing left of the wound but a faint scar.

Within days, we'd all be safe. Porter, Stacey, Daniel, and me. I would be back with my mates and safely tucked away in Canada.

The door opened and Stacey flew into the room, her arms going around my neck. "Layla! I missed you. Porter said you felt sick, but you look okay now. Maybe I should get Porter to give me your charts just in case?"

Daniel had moved back to stand next to Porter, which was strange and for the first time I switched my attention from the children to Porter. He looked like death, pale and sweating, anxiety written all over his face.

"What's wrong?"

Daniel's face matched Porter's almost exactly and my heart sank. There was definitely something wrong.

"Layla, we passed Theiss on the way down here. He's coming to see you. There's word they have a buyer." There was no time left to wait for a rescue. The lies we told and the secrets we kept were about to be found out. The rescue had to be now.

I sent out a plea to Penelope and prayed she was in hearing distance.

"They're coming, Porter. It's time to pick a side." Before I could even finish the demand, the door handle to my cell jiggled. The noose was around all our necks and the executioner was about to kick the block out from under us all.

Porter stepped toward me and kissed me hard on the lips. I reared back, shocked, and his eyes blazed. I didn't get time to say anything, do anything, because the door was sliding open.

Porter instinctively stood in front of me, blocking the view of anyone who entered. I had tucked Stacey and Daniel close to my sides but I couldn't stop Daniel from standing a little in front of me too, a big brave protector at the age of six. I held my breath as someone entered, wishing and hoping with every last ounce of my being that it wasn't him. I was disappointed.

Theiss' smirking face came into view and the hairs on the back of my neck stood up as hatred rose up in my throat like bile. I felt Daniel tense in front of me. I knew the little boy would be having flashbacks of the night his parents were murdered. I ran a soothing hand over his back but it didn't release his tension.

I wished the children were anywhere but here at this moment and I wracked my mind for ways I could get them out safely without them seeing any more violence in their short lives. I came up empty yet again. The monster spoke, ignoring me completely and addressing Porter.

"Hello Porter, I'm glad to see you are taking such good care of my most prized possession. I see she has made some friends among the other demons. These two don't cause much difficulty. In fact, the only difficulty has been that they're impossible to sell. Too young for war and not particularly unique in their abilities. But it's okay, The Hounds have been around for millennia, we can wait for these two to mature. Maybe I should put them in the cellar, like a good wine." He guffawed at his own joke.

I gritted my teeth to stop me from throwing a swing at Theiss' nose. It would only make matters so much more deadly. I looked past Theiss, out the open door. There were four guards I could see, including the hard faced military man who guarded Theiss' door on the day I arrived. He spotted me summing him up and stared back. His eyes were slightly too big for his face, giving him an innocent look that didn't sit well with the deadness they held. He shifted the semi-automatic weapon on his shoulder in a barely veiled threat and I looked away.

Theiss was moving further into the room, closer to me, and I had to fight the instinct to run away. It was not as if there was anywhere to run anyway. I saw Porter's hand clenching and unclenching, sweat starting to trickle down the back of his neck. I willed him to be calm, we needed just a little longer until Eden could make their move.

"Porter, give me a full report on your investigations. How far have you tested her immortality?" He pushed his arm, but Porter didn't budge. "Move out of the way before I have you removed permanently!" Theiss was standing directly in front of Porter now, the only remaining barrier between me and my jailer.

Porter shook his head and kept moving to block Theiss' attempts to go around him. Theiss' face screwed up in rage, he obviously wasn't used to his requests being denied, and with paranormal swiftness he had unholstered the gun that was hidden under his safari jacket and pistol whipped Porter. He went sprawling across the room, landing with a thud against the edge of the bed.

"Have you bewitched him, Demoness? He had so much promise too. Sloane, take him to the barracks and show him what we do to traitors in The Hounds."

Sloane advanced into the room towards Porter and I flung myself in his path. I stood there, toe to toe with the dead-eyed man, staring him directly in the eye defiantly. For a moment, a warm amusement lit up his blank eyes, and he looked more human than machine. But as quickly as it appeared, it was gone again and all that remained was an emotionless face. He moved me to the side, lifting me out of the way more than shoving me, and picked Porter up by the scruff of his dress shirt. I weighed the possibilities of overpowering

Sloane and quickly dismissed the idea. I turned to Theiss. I was going to have to bargain for Porter's life.

"It wasn't the doctor's fault, I had him confused. You know the ward of soldiers you have from your last raid on Eden headquarters? I did that. Porter didn't stand a chance. Your precious bloodhound obviously could only pick up the ability I inherited from my father and not the gift I got from my mother." I mentally apologized to Caroline for hijacking her power for a little bit. I gave Porter a meaningful look which basically told him to shut up and play along. "I kept him so confused, he didn't even know what day it was most of the time. I played with him like he was a puppet." I let out a cold laugh, sounding exactly like the demon that Theiss kept calling me. "My plan was to make him love me, and then get him to break me out of this shit hole."

A sudden loud siren threatened to burst my eardrums and Sloane dropped Porter like a sack of potatoes.

"It's the breach alarm, sir!"

Theiss was already striding towards the door. "I know that, you idiot. I designed the damn security system. Find Etienne. I want whatever got past the security line dead in front of me within fifteen minutes. Lock down the cells. Leave Porter in here, we'll deal with that little problem later. Don't want to damage the merchandise that is going to make us all very, very rich."

Sloane watched his retreating back with absolute hatred.

Hang on, what?

But in an instant it was gone and I was pretty sure I imagined it. He turned and left, following behind Theiss like a faithful lapdog. I looked at the closed door for a second before rushing to Porter.

His eye socket had swollen up so much that it looked like a mouse had tunneled under his skin, but other than that he was conscious and okay.

"Well, that could have gone worse." I helped him sit up, and he climbed to his feet. "Are you okay?" Porter was nodding and grabbing hold of Daniel's hand and lifting Stacey into my arms.

"We'll get Daniel to blow open the door with his telekinesis..." He was positioning the scared boy in front of the door and I could see the tremble in his hands at the pressure.

"Wait."

Something niggled at the back of my mind. I put out a hand to stop him and walked over to the door. I pulled down the handle and the heavy door just swung open.

Sloane hadn't locked it! I highly doubted that a man like Sloane would legitimately forget to do anything, and that only left one equally unbelievable possibility. Sloane had left the door open so we could escape. I didn't have time to analyze why the mercenary would do that. While Sloane may have grown a conscience about me for some unfathomable reason, I doubted it had extended to leaving all the other cells open too.

I swung Stacey onto my back and glanced out into the lab room. White faced lab technicians were running around senselessly, like ants that just discovered some kid had just stomped on their nest. They'd obviously been ordered to evacuate, but some were trying to save the most valuable documents and equipment from being destroyed in the fighting. I asked Porter where they were all going.

"There's a panic room where they put all the laboratory and non-military staff in emergency situations. It's where Theiss and the other board members go too."

Theiss and those other monsters weren't going to get away with this, even if I had to come back and kill them myself.

We ran to the cell next to mine and shook the door, but it was locked. I guess relying on Sloane turning into a complete marshmallow was too much to ask.

I looked down at a pale face Daniel. "Do you think you can force it open?" I kept my voice light, like this was some kind of game rather than life or death.

But Daniel had seen too much death to ever believe

the illusion. He just nodded solemnly, staring at the door intently and blinking several times, until the door just clicked open. I had expected it to at least fly off the hinges but I'd obviously underestimated Daniel's control over his gifts.

I quickly gave the woman inside the cell instructions. She was to run to the rear of the compound as fast but as stealthily as she could. If she came across anyone who wasn't a soldier, she was to tell them that Layla had sent her and they would take her back to the camp. She was more than welcome to join the other members in the encampment or to go her own way.

"You can make a run for it now, or wait until we release some more captives."

"I will wait until I have someone to watch my back. We will be much harder to take down in a group." I nodded and moved to the next cell, and Daniel preemptively popped open the airlock on the door. A man charged out, his hands raised ready to fight. I recognized him as Tomas, the man that Stacey had said came from the same carnival as her parents. Daniel ran to the man, who dropped to his knees and hugged the boy.

"*Chico*, I was worried when the sirens went off that something had happened to you and the little one." The squat little man looked like he was about to cry. I put my hand on his shoulder and nodded.

I gave him the same instructions as I had the

woman, but he indicated he wouldn't leave without Caio, the other man from the carnival.

We freed three more captives before we got to Caio at the very end of the row. He, too, almost burst into tears at the sight of Daniel and Stacey. There was one more room, and when Daniel busted it open, a pale woman with hair so dark it seemed to suck in the light stood in the middle of the room. Caio went to her, whispering to her in what I think was Portuguese but I couldn't really decide. He grabbed her in his arms and kissed her face, and she kissed him back. Then he was dragging her out, but no one introduced us.

Four captives left in a small group to head towards the safety of Eden's encampment, leaving only Caio and his girlfriend, Tomas, Porter, the children and I.

We had to get out through the exercise yard, as it was the only rear exit to the building, but we also had to go through the antechamber. "That's the direct route to the panic room, and if anyone comes across us…" Porter didn't finish but I knew what it meant.

Slowly pushing open the doors, we crept through before stopping dead in our tracks. Theiss had beaten us to the punch yet again.

Sloane stood at his side, military man down to the last fiber of his being. They had their hand guns pointed at us and Theiss waved for Caio to shut and lock the doors.

"Do you really think I would just let you walk out

of here? You are smarter than that. However, the rest of these animals I couldn't care less about," he sneered at me. "I'm actually quite insulted that you thought this attack of yours is anything more than an annoyance. My troops are destroying this little uprising as we speak. The bodies of your saviors litter the grounds of my compound like the trash they are. As will these demons." He pointed the gun at Porter and slowly started to squeeze the trigger. I wanted to move, to scream, to save him, but I froze. I hated myself for it but I couldn't move.

My eyes closed involuntarily as the sound of the gunshot bounced off the walls of the room and I could feel Stacey whimpering, her face pushed painfully into my neck. I opened my eyes and gasped. Lying on the ground at my feet was not the body of Porter, but that of Theiss, his blood starting to puddle around my feet. A slither of smoke drifted skywards from the barrel of Sloane's gun. I shook my head, looking at Porter, who had turned a sickening shade of grey. I ran to him, my hands patting down his body looking for bullet holes.

"Layla, I'm okay." Porter's voice was shaky and Stacey leapt from my back into his arms at the sound of his voice. Porter stumbled backwards but caught her in an enveloping hug. I turned back to Sloane, asking the question that I had wondered about since leaving my room.

"Why? I don't understand." He just shook his head.

"He got what he deserved. Now, just go!" His gravelly voice was deep and raspy, but it was as forceful as a jackhammer. His eyes flicked to the woman in Caio's arms, and I frowned. "Go!"

He opened the door and I quickly herded everyone through. I turned back to Sloane. "Thank you."

He nodded and shut the door in my face.

The exercise area had always been my retreat from the harshness of my imprisonment, but now I saw it for the cage it was. There were no exits or doors except those we just entered through, it was just one solid structure.

"We need bolt cutters or something to cut a hole in the wire." I knew that if I asked Daniel to try and blow out one wall out of the fence, the entire structure would come tumbling down around our heads.

Caio stepped forward, taking off his shirt. "No need to worry 'bout fence cutters, I can make the hole, no worries." His English was heavily accented and my eyes drifted to his torso. My mistake had been assuming that the children would have exaggerated Caio's physical similarities to a dragon. Because starting from just at his chest, shimmering red-gold scales danced in the light. They were sparse on his chest but as they travelled lower down his body, they thickened and overlapped, until they turned into a perfectly symmetrical scale pattern just above the waistband of his sweatpants. Caio took a deep breath, his chest expanding until it barrelled out so round that I thought he might pop like an over inflated balloon. Just as I started to fear for his safety, a red hot flame spewed from his mouth at the chain link fence. The metal melted away like hot wax, leaving a large opening, the edges still glowing red.

"Well now, that's handy, isn't it?" I smiled at Caio and walked through the gap, careful that Stacey didn't get caught on any of the protruding red hot wires.

As the others joined me on the other side of the fence, I took in the five hundred feet or so of concrete battlefield that stood between us and salvation. There weren't as many soldiers on it as I originally had estimated, and they huddled behind an overturned SUV and trucks. A few would occasionally pop their heads around the sides of their shields and fire their automatic weapons at the wave of oncoming paranormals and supernaturals. They were fairly evenly matched man for man, but with the added benefits of immortality and abilities, Eden seemed to be slowly driving The Hounds soldiers back towards the warehouses.

There were faces I recognized amongst the attacking numbers, mostly Eden members I had met at the conference. But there were others, beings that moved so fast my eyes could hardly keep up. The vampires had come back.

"*Dios Mio,*" Tomas exclaimed under his breath as he saw one of the vampires spring onto a soldier, like a cheetah on the plains of the Savannah pouncing on a gazelle. His speed and dexterity as he tore the throat from an advancing soldier made the spectacle grotesque yet beautiful and had us all mesmerized momentarily. I shielded Stacey, turning my body so that her view was blocked, but I wasn't quick enough to shelter Daniel from the gruesome sight, and he let out a small yelp of alarm. The male vampire heard the noise over the deafening roar of the battle and let the body of the soldier he'd been feasting on fall to the ground, drained of all its blood, and turned his head towards us. A smile spread across his blood-smeared face, his startling blue eyes warm as he acknowledged us. He was so achingly beautiful, like a golden haired angel, that the sight of the velvety red blood contrasting on his alabaster skin was almost painful to observe. He had swirling blue tattoos and crazy eyes. He scared the ever loving shit out of me, and his face tickled something in my memory. Nico? Of Dark River? He looked the same but different simultaneously. He nodded once in our direction, no recognition in his eyes, and then sprang onto the throat of his next victim with speed that made him invisible to the human eye. As the soldier tried to struggle and flee, I turned away, my stomach protesting at the sight.

"Layla!" A familiar voice behind me jerked me from my thoughts and made my heart lurch.

Locke.

Something broke inside me and the strength that I had steeled within my very veins for the last two months dissolved into a flood of tears. I spun around and launched myself into the familiarity of his big arms. He wrapped them around me gently, careful of Stacey on my back.

"Oh God Layla, I thought I'd never see you again. Here, let me carry the little one." Stacey's arms clung tighter around my neck. I turned my head so my cheek was touching hers.

"Stacey, you remember me telling you stories about Locke, the really strong man from my family? Well, this is the man in the flesh, and he could lift you like you were a feather and still run incredibly fast, something I can't do. Would it be okay if he carried you?" Locke was giving Stacey his most brilliant smile and she gave him a tiny one back.

"So this is your third mate? Well you weren't exaggerating, he is excessively big!" Locke's jaw dropped a little and he raised an eyebrow at me. I just smiled and helped Stacey as she gripped Locke around the neck and clung onto his side. There was no way she could have straddled the width of his back as she could mine.

"Layla really said I was excessively big? That may be so but I'm also very strong. Why, I bet I could carry you one handed. Let's make this a real challenge. How about I carry both you and your brother?" Daniel nodded eagerly, and swung up onto Locke's back like a monkey. "I've carried sacks of potatoes heavier than you two. Hold on tight though, and don't let go."

Locke took off at a jog towards the edge of the compound, down along the fence towards the rear of Eden's attacking lines, in what would have been The Hounds training grounds.

"We'll cut behind the lines and sneak down along the boundary fences without too much trouble."

The children looked like little koalas clinging to his back. As we weaved through the attacking members, I was thankful to see that Theiss was lying. From the dead faces staring lifelessly up from the ground, I couldn't see any that I recognized. We finally got to the back of Eden's offensive ranks, and our progress was slowed by the members who came to hug me and tell me how glad they were that I was alright. It was heartwarming, but there was only so much warmth I could feel as I stepped over the bodies of dead or dying soldiers. I was amazed at how hardened I'd become since I first found Micah broken on my front porch.

Now, as I glanced at the mutilated bodies of human beings with hard glazed eyes, I mourned for the innocent girl I was. I didn't even recognize that girl anymore, the one who couldn't trust anybody but herself, who had no friends or family and had no interest in acquiring any sort of attachment to anything. Now, I had mates who loved me more than life, and friends who were more like family, who loved me enough to risk their own lives to save me.

We were almost at the boundary fence when a Lycanthrope appeared in front of us, a piece of red cloth wrapped around his forearm. Stacey started to scream and Daniel buried his face in Locke's neck.

Alistair. My mate bond sang seeing him, and he was in front of me in seconds, barely skidding to a stop at the sound of a child's scream. Stacey was nearly hysterical at the sight of them and Daniel had started to shake violently.

Locke looked bewildered, sending me pleading looks. Porter grabbed Stacey off of Locke's back, and the little girl clung so hard to him I was worried she'd draw blood. I gently peeled Daniel away from Locke's shoulder.

"Daniel, baby, it's okay." I lifted him into my arms, getting a brief look at his white face before he nuzzled it into my neck. "They won't hurt you. This is Alistair, I told you about him, remember?"

Alistair was already morphing back to human, understanding that he was the cause of the kids' distress without me even saying a word. Damn, I loved that man. "Theiss killed their parents in front of them, in his Lycan form."

Alistair nodded. He leaned in to kiss me softly, but there was a world of emotion in that brief touch.

I looked down at the dark head of Daniel. "Hey,

look at me, kiddo." The little boy forced his head closer to my neck, and I knew that I would have a bruise in the shape of his nose later. I drew back until he had to look at me. "Daniel, Theiss is dead, he'll never hurt any of us ever again. Alistair and Micah aren't the same as he was, I promise you. He was a bad, evil man. They may look the same, but on the inside they couldn't be more different. Alistair is a good person, and he'll take care of us. He will never hurt you." Alistair peeked around my shoulder at Daniel's face.

"Hey, I hear you have been taking good care of both Layla and your little sister. You have my loyalty for life, just for that. If it helps, don't think of us as Lycans. Just think of us like really big, kinda ugly puppies." He stuck out his tongue in an imitation pant, letting out a few little yaps.

Daniel didn't smile but he had stopped shaking and loosened his grip on my neck. Stacey had stopped crying and was looking at Alistair with interest. I smiled, knowing that Alistair's reaction to the brilliance of Stacey was going to be amusing. She squirmed out of Porter's arms and flounced over to Alistair with a lightness that only children could achieve.

"So you're Alistair? I'm really interested in your research on immortality, especially any on the offspring if you have any. Maybe Locke's journals? Layla said you had them. I want to compare Porter's notes with yours to see if the sire makes a difference to their ability to regenerate."

Alistair nearly fell over as Stacey finished her request in her deceiving three year old form.

"Now I see why you like first impressions so much, Stacey," I said conspiratorially. "But now probably isn't the right time to talk science."

I was glad something had lightened the mood. Locke came back over and slipped Daniel back out of my arms, but left Stacey with Porter. "I don't want to hurry you, but I'd prefer to get these guys back to camp. If I lost Layla now, Micah would find a way to kill me, immortality or no immortality, and I would lay down and let him."

At the mention of Micah, I scrabbled around in my mind for the feel of him and let out a sigh when I found the connection I was looking for. He was fine, not injured at all, although he did have a burning anger in him. Alistair must have seen what I was doing because he gave me a reassuring smile.

"Micah is at the front, but not to worry. I'm fairly sure not even Satan himself could stop him from seeing you again. However, I better rejoin the fight and you should go back to the camp." He kissed me once more, and this one wasn't light and gentle. It was filled with fear and relief. Love.

If the battle looked like this when it was winding down, I shuddered to think what it was like during the heat of the battle. Caio stepped forward from some-where behind me.

"I'd like to fight too." He hadn't put his shirt back after melting the fence back at the exercise yard, and the sun glinted off his scales like diamond shaped mirrors. Staring directly at them made my eyes water. Alistair considered him carefully.

"I need to know what your abilities are, so I can place you in the most strategic position. I don't want you getting yourself killed either, so if beautiful skin is all you have, maybe it's better to go back to the camp with Locke." His friendly smile took any sting out of the words. But Caio just smiled in return, dropping his shirt on the ground, pursing his lips and blowing a small but strong flow of fire at it. The shirt turned to ash almost immediately, and Alistair's face lit up.

"Excellent. I have just the job for you."

Caio kissed the dark haired woman, and she looked back at him morosely, with eyes too blue to be real. He murmured something against her lips, and he jogged off with Alistair. We all picked up our pace, desperate to be out of this compound and free.

Our destination was in sight now, where the chain link fence had been peeled back far enough that four or five people could fit through it abreast. Sprinting the last ten yards, I heaved a sigh of relief as I passed through the temporary gateway into the dense forest that surrounded the compound. It must have been set back into rugged terrain, because the trees were so thick that they let very little light through. Freedom at last.

For the first time in months, I wasn't a captive. There were no bars or fences, glass or soldiers to hold me in now. I felt like the sun had finally come out after a long desolate winter.

That was, until an arm snaked out of the shadows and wrapped around my neck.

29

"Mine," a voice whispered hotly against my ear, and I shuddered.

I let out a choked off scream, but it was enough that everyone turned, whipping around to find me. I knew the voice immediately, with its distorted words and inability to pronounce vowels. It was Trey, the bloodhound that captured me. I hated him.

"And I smell another one. Come out, come out, wherever you are. You smell older than this one in my arms. Maybe I'll take you now, no one will know. They only want her." Locke took a menacing step forward. Trey was staring at Locke now, and I felt his drool running down my shoulders.

An explosion within the compound seemed to shift Trey's focus back to me. "You'll have to wait, offspring, my bosses want your little girlfriend back first. But I'll find you and then I'll drink your sweet elixir. Yes, I will. I know your scent. There is nowhere you can run that I can't track you. Nuh, uh, uh." Trey started to drag me away, his gun pressed to my head. "Now don't try anything funny or I'll shoot her."

I screamed, struggling against his restraining arm, but he just squeezed it tighter around my neck, pulling me along as I dug my heels into the dirt.

"No!" Daniel yelled. Then three things happened in a blur. I was lifted into the air and flung away as a large branch snapped from a tree above us, crushing Trey with a deafening thud. Another loud crack sounded, a gunshot, and I whirled around to find Daniel, fearing the worst. I saw Etienne emerge from the trees, the barrel of his gun pointed at our group.

Porter lay on the ground, blood blossoming on his shirt front.

"Porter!"

The ringing in my ears blocked out all sound but the thudding of my heart as I scrambled over to Porter's body.

Slowly, someone turned the sound back up and I could hear Stacey's screams. Locke and Tomas were struggling to hold the distressed children. Daniel pushed Locke with his powers, sending the big man flying across the ground like a shopping bag in the wind.

Before I knew it, he and Stacey were lying on top of Porter, sobbing. Stacey pushed Daniel off of him and checked his pulse and the bullet wound in his chest.

"The bullet missed his heart but hit a major artery. He needs help." Her voice was panicked and I could see she was bordering on hysteria. "He needs... he needs... I don't know what he needs. Help him, Layla."

"No one is getting help, runt. In fact, you are all going to join the good doctor." Etienne pointed the gun at Daniel. "Stand up, you little demon, I think we've underestimated your power for quite long enough. Best to take you out before you can cause any more damage." He pointed to Trey's body under the tree branch, only his feet were visible, like the Wicked Witch of the East.

"No!"

I jumped in front of Daniel as Etienne pulled the trigger. The bullet intended for him hit me square in the shoulder. Both Locke and Tomas were charging toward Etienne, but before they could reach him, a gray flash was there, tearing his throat out and tossing it away from his body.

Daniel was leaning over me sobbing. "Don't die, Layla. Please don't die too!" It hurt to speak but I murmured soothing words that he didn't seem to hear. Then a wolf head appeared in my vision.

"Micah," I whispered, relief making me feel light headed.

But before he could say anything, Daniel was on him, clawing at his fur, screaming.

"Leave her alone! Don't touch her! I won't let you hurt her too, I won't let you!" He was feral and Micah was momentarily taken aback. I saw Daniel narrow his eyes and I knew he was preparing to use his power to the full extent of his abilities, and I didn't want to think about what that would mean for Micah; he would probably tear him limb from limb and scatter him through the trees. I reached out for Daniel with my good arm.

"Daniel, stop. I'll be fine, it's just my shoulder. I can't die. It's okay." Daniel nodded and looked suspiciously at Micah, before his eyes tracked back to Stacey and Porter.

Stacey's tiny little body slumped over his stomach, and Locke was there, applying pressure to the wound. "We need to get him to someone back at camp, before he bleeds out." Her voice was barely more than a whisper and tears streamed down her face.

Micah went over to Porter and leaned over, sniffing. He was back in human form, but his sense of hearing was still exceptional. He looked at me and shook his head slightly.

No.

No, we couldn't have come so fucking close to freedom to lose him here. I wouldn't believe it. I felt a crushing misery right down to my soul. Porter was dead and it was my fault. I fell to my knees, leaning over searching for a pulse, but I could tell that he was dead. Tears streamed down my face, and I pulled Stacey toward me, her body was stiff and completely still. I wrapped her in my arms as I stood, my tears mixing with hers on my chest. I stroked her dark sable hair, and whispered soothing things that made no sense. Locke came over and picked up Porter's body.

"I'm so sorry," he murmured to us both.

Stacey hadn't said a word, I knew she was in shock, and my heart hurt for the girl who knew too much. Whispering platitudes about a better place would not help when she was a girl of science.

Micah was beside me, holding my hand. I soaked in his slightly too warm skin, hoping his light would chase away the darkness that was consuming me. Micah squeezed my hand tight, sharing my sadness through our bond, even if he didn't know Porter. Although he was overcome with grief for me, Micah was alert, gazing around the forest for any more nasty surprises. I knew that he would rather be in Lycanthrope form, with his hearing and eyesight more acute, but I could tell he didn't want to distress the children even more.

I looked at Porter's prone body in Locke's arms. I could only hope that my mates were ready to be fathers, because that was how I would make it up to Porter. To respect his memory. I would care for these two like they were mine by blood. Because I was the last certain thing in their lives, and I wouldn't give them up.

I squeezed Stacey tightly. I wished that I could prevent the pain they were feeling now. Kids were resilient. They would grieve and then move on and I vowed to Porter, on my immortal life, that I would make sure the rest of their lives were safe and happy. It was what Porter had wanted for them, and I was going to grant his wish if it took every ounce of strength I had left.

I tensed as I saw another flash of colour blur through the trees. I didn't know if I had anything left to face another confrontation, I was completely wrung out. But Micah just put his arm around my shoulders, briefly rubbing Stacey's back with his massive hand as she sat on my hip.

"We're here. We're safe. It's over now." I saw all the familiar faces as we got closer, and I thought I was just going to collapse onto the ground. Home, I was home. Among the family that loved me. Daniel, who hadn't left my side, grabbed hold of my leg tightly. I put Stacey on the ground and held both their hands. The people in the camp noticed the new arrivals and a cheer went up. Before I knew it, I was surrounded by smiling faces. My cheek was being kissed and so many questions and exclamations that it was just one long buzz. Penelope broke through the group, and tears poured from her eyes. "God, you're really here. You're safe." She pulled me into a hug and just held me. "I've been so worried and the guys have been basically useless, and I missed you so fucking much." She looked down at the kids clinging to me. "Oops. Um, who do we have here?" She leaned down to the children's eye level.

To my surprise, it was Daniel that spoke. "I'm Daniel, and this is my sister Stacey and that," he pointed to Porter's body on the edge of the camp where Locke had gently placed and covered it, "was our best friend."

Daniel's face was scrunched up in a fierce scowl, but his eyes were brimming with tears even as he fought them. I leaned over and kissed the top of his head. I wish I'd heard his voice for the first time in better circumstances.

Penelope nodded respectfully

"I am saddened by your loss, Daniel. From what I can hear, the battle is almost done. Let's bury your friend with the greatest honor we can muster." Penelope nodded over at Locke, who was grabbing shovels and Micah picked up Porter's body and led the sad procession into the darkness of the surrounding woods.

. . .

HALF AN HOUR LATER, we were gathered before a grave, six feet deep. Porter's body had been shrouded in bedding that Penelope had found somewhere and lowered into the hole by Micah and Locke.

We were standing around it, looking sadly at the body as it returned to the earth, when Ramer came hurrying up behind me. He grabbed hold of me and swung me around, quickly hugging and kissing my cheek before setting me down. The whole episode would have only lasted ten or so seconds, but it was such a rare sight for Ramer to voluntarily touch anybody, that everyone just stared. This was going to be one of the best things about being immortal, the ability to touch Ramer whenever I pleased.

No, not like that.

"I thought we'd never see you again, that you'd be sold off to the highest bidder or killed. Even when I was telling everyone to remain hopeful, I was starting to mourn you. I'm so glad you're home." He looked like he wanted to hug me again, but he held himself in check. It was only then he noticed us circling a grave, and his face went pale under all the hair. "Who died?" He frantically searched the faces in the ring of people, a panicked look on his face. "The twins? Alistair?"

It was Micah who answered. "It's no one from Eden, Ramer. It is the doctor who took care of Layla, helped her escape and was like a father to Eden's newest and youngest members." He indicated Daniel and Stacey, who were standing hand in hand, staring at Ramer. Stacey hadn't said a word since Porter was gunned down, but at least something was getting through to her, even if it was stunned disbelief over Ramer's appearance.

"I'm sorry I interrupted. Please continue." Ramer bowed his head. I figured it was my place to say a few words.

"Porter was my savior. He saved my sanity and eventually my life. He was a good man in a bad situation. He was a friend to those who needed it most and gave us dignity in the worst of situations. For that I will always be grateful." I threw some dirt into the depths of the grave and stepped back. There was silence within the group. Micah began shovelling dirt into the grave, but the image was blurred at the edges from the tears that flowed freely from my eyes. Regret mixed with happiness, mourning with rejoicing. It left me feeling confused and raw, and more than a little guilty about feeling joy only hours after Porter's murder. He should have been here with me, questioning people about their gifts and being in his scientific element.

Micah finished filling in the grave and wrapped his arms around my shoulders. Ramer reached down and put a hand on the soft swelling of fresh earth. Fresh green grass, slowly climbed over the mound, and tiny wild flowers bloomed in its wake. It was beautiful and a fitting tribute to Porter.

Stacey and Daniel each slid a hand in mine and I squeezed them tightly. "I wish I could say more than I'm sorry. He deserved better." So much fucking better. My heart hurt so bad for the man I'd come to respect and given more time, maybe something more.

Stacey just nodded and grabbed Micah's hand too. Micah looked taken aback, his big hand curled around her tiny one, but he gave it a soft squeeze and led us away.

EPILOGUE

I stepped out into the warm sunshine, tilted my head to the sky and just breathed. Well, for all of ten seconds before there was a knock on the car window.

"Layla, I gotta pee!"

I shook my head, opening the back car door and letting Stacey out. Pea had come out to meet us, her smile wide. She'd arrived two weeks earlier, and she looked more carefree than I'd ever seen her.

"Hey, Stace," she said, smiling widely.

"Can't talk now, Pea. I gotta pee." Then she stopped, grinning up at Penelope. "Pea, pee. Heh, get it?"

Yeah, even brilliant, she still had that childlike sense of humor. Penelope shook her head. "Through the door to the left. Ramer's inside if you get lost."

Daniel climbed out of the car at a slower pace, and

came to stand beside me, leaning into my hip. "What do you think, buddy?" Fred the dog was at his side. In fact, the two had been inseparable since they met. We'd sent Pip up with Pea, because two small children and a pissed off cat was just too much for one road trip.

We both took in the scene before us. It was paradise. It was still heavily treed, with a small village of houses interspersed around. There were no roads from house to house, more tracks and lanes. There were fifteen in total, and each one had the capability of holding six people, with their own bathroom and kitchen. There was a communal laundry in the south wing of the Academy building which everyone could use. I said wing, although so far, only the dorm section had been created of the Academy. While the outlying housing had been created, the main building was still under construction, and even now, there were shapeshifter work crews working.

Off in the far corner of the compound was a huge single story home that belonged to Reese Townsend and his family. We'd held up our end of the bargain, and Reese had fitted in all the state of the art security provisions.

Daniel looked up at me, his dark eyes shining with tears. "It's perfect, Layla."

Yeah, it really was.

I heard a childish shout, and Stacey was back, but

she wasn't alone. Locke held her in his arms, tossing her high into the air as she squealed.

"It's so good to see you, kid! I've missed you guys," he said as he caught her easily, putting her back on her feet.

"We missed you too, but Layla missed you the most. She had this look on her face all the time." She did a pouty face and then grinned. Honestly, I was never going to get tired of her laughter and jokes. They meant she was happy and I was doing alright at this whole parenting thing.

I poked my tongue out at her. "I did not!"

Locke looked at me, so much emotion in his eyes I swear it knocked me on my ass. "Hey, Butterfly. I missed you too."

Then I was running toward him and throwing myself in his arms. He'd only been gone two weeks, but it felt like I was missing a damn limb. He'd come up to settle the second to last group of people, and I'd been close to following him.

He met me halfway, kissing my face before he caught my lips in a kiss that made my toes curl.

"Ew," Daniel groaned, making Locke chuckle against my lips.

The car doors opened and closed again, and I felt a soft kiss behind my ear. "What are we, Love? Chopped liver?" Alistair whispered, and then pulled back, slapping Locke on the back. "I missed you too, brother."

Locke looked down at me, smiling. When I told him what I was, what we were, he'd cried. He'd held me for so long that my ass had gone numb, before pulling back.

"You're a gift. I can love you forever and nothing or no one can take you away from me. Not death, not old age. No one. Me, you, Alistair and Micah. A family until the end of time." He'd sniffed, lifting my hand to his rapidly thumping heart. "Feel this? This is goddamn happiness."

Argh, it made me tear up thinking about it weeks later. But whenever he looked at me, it was always with this look of awe like he didn't know how he'd gotten so lucky.

Locke pulled away, giving Alistair and Micah man hugs. He grabbed Daniel and hoisted him onto his shoulder. "Let's go and look at our new home, what do you say?"

Both kids screamed yes, and Stacey raced ahead. Every single one of us watched her like a hawk, even Daniel, making sure she was safe. Poor thing was going to be wildly sheltered with this many protective men in her life.

We stepped up to a normal looking house, exactly the same as the others in the row, and Locke opened the door, stepping aside. Shiny wooden floorboards were tempered by the light blue walls. Those walls were covered in artwork of butterflies, mostly in shades of blue. I gasped, looking up dumbfounded at Locke.

"It's beautiful."

"You're beautiful." He planted both hands on my cheeks and kissed me hard. "I'm so glad you're here, Butterfly." The way he said it, I didn't know if he meant in this house, or in the world.

The kids raced in, the dog hot on their heels even though his hip was acting up from the long car ride. Locke strode in after them, yelling at the kids that he was talking to the contractor about putting a slide from the first floor to the ground floor, which was meant with a chorus of ear piercing squeals.

I looked over at Alistair. "He's kidding, right?"

My beautiful, blond professor shrugged his shoulders. "Past experience would tell me that he is one hundred percent serious. I'll go and see if he has the plans already drawn up." He kissed my temple and then scooted around me into the house, his arms laden down with stuff. Kids came with a lot of stuff, I'd discovered, even kids as low maintenance as Daniel and Stacey.

Micah swept me up into his arms. He nuzzled his face into my hair as I rested my cheek into his chest. "It's probably too late to walk you across the threshold, and a mate bond is more serious than a human wedding, but I guess this isn't a bad substitute? Are you happy?"

I nodded, glad he couldn't see the pathetically gooey look on my face right now. "Beyond my wildest dreams. I got a happy ending with the sexy woodsman and got double the Big Bad Wolf. People wish they were me. This is heaven."

He laughed, kissing me sweetly then nipping my lower lip like a damn tease. "Welcome to paradise, Little Red."

ABOUT THE AUTHOR

Grace McGinty is eclectic. She has worked as a choco-latier, a librarian, a forensic accountant and finally a writer. Like her professional career, the genres she writes are also eclectic. She writes romance, reverse harem romance, fantasy, contemporary young adult and new adult books.

She lives in rural Australia with her crazy family, an entire menagerie of pets, and will one day be crushed by her giant piles of books that litter every room.

Head over to www.gracemcginty.com and join my mailing list for sneak previews into what I am working on and to stay up-to-date with new releases and giveaways!

Excited to dive into Eden Academy? You can preorder REBELS AND RUNAWAYS: EDEN ACADEMY BOOK ONE now!

www.books2read.com/eden1

Turn the page for a sneak peek at Serendipity (Damnation MC, Book 1)

SERENDIPITY

DAMNATION MC (BOOK ONE)

Prologue

He sat on his knees in the dirt as they lowered the coffin into the ground and we all stood around him, protecting his back, shielding him from prying eyes. He was crying silently like his heart was being shredded, but I knew what he was feeling was far, far worse. We were all heart broken, but his life had just been lowered six feet into the ground and guilt was eating him alive. It was eating us all alive. We had failed her. We had failed them.

When the sky opened up and rain poured down, it seemed fitting. It should rain when all the light in our lives was being buried beneath the dirt. I let a tear fall, hidden by the rain. I had to be stoic; I had to present a strong front despite the fact that I wanted to be in the dirt mourning her too.

People were drifting off, helped along by a few of our members, so the Pres could have some privacy. Two men stood off to the side, waiting to shift dirt back into the hole, sealing them away forever. We had insisted at gunpoint that they be buried together; Laura and the baby. She'd want them together, the little one forever cradled in her arms. We didn't care what the laws had said, what the undertaker had said, what anyone said. We were all wild in our grief, and anyone who stood in our way would have died too.

It rained even harder, the water rolling off my leather cut but soaking everything else. The dirt was turning to slush around our feet and the other two guys standing beside me, behind our President, sent me a look. It was time to go.

I knelt in the dirt next to him, putting my hand on his back. "We should go," I said in a low voice, not sure he'd hear me over his grief. "We have to go." I wanted to hug him, but I knew he wouldn't appreciate the gesture right now. I picked up a rose that was lying on the ground, and handed it to him. It was muddy and dirty now, but that seemed right too. Nothing we ever touched remained pure, not a flower, and not her. We were a plague on those around us, and no one was exempt, not even the most innocent. Someone handed down one of the red roses as well. I tucked it in his hand beside the white one and tried not to think about how much it looked like blood.

I got to my feet, uncaring that the knees of my black jeans were now caked in mud, and I pulled the Pres up with me. He stood on his feet, feeling insubstantial despite the fact he was two-hundred pounds of solid muscle. It was like all the life had leached out of him, leaving him just an empty shell.

His body shuddered, and he threw the two roses into the grave. One for his wife. One for his infant son who would never see his first birthday. A son who'd been killed by the sins of his father. Betrayed by his own blood.

I nodded to the grave diggers as they began to shovel dirt back into the grave. I grabbed his arm and pulled him away. Normally, I would have had a black eye for trying to drag him anywhere, and it worried me that he would never be the same President we had even a week ago.

However, if there was something that solidified the four of us, it was the need for revenge. We had all loved Laura. The need to avenge her death burned through my veins like acid.

When we turned, a man was standing behind us, and my gun was out and pointing at him in an instant. He didn't freak at having the barrel of my Desert Eagle in his face though. He didn't even look at me, he just stared at the Pres.

My Brothers had their guns out as well, searching the empty cemetery for an ambush. But there was no one else left. Just the grave diggers and this guy. He was dressed in black jeans and a t-shirt, completely out of place at a funeral. My heart was thumping like he had just pulled out an Uzi and my brain was screaming for me to run, but the man was just standing there, both hands in his pockets. He didn't have a gun, or any weapon that I could see.

"I know what it's like to have your love torn away from you," the man said in a smooth voice that sent chills down my spine. Who was this fucker?

The Pres just seemed numb. His hand hadn't even gone for his gun. It was like he was kind of hoping this dude was here to shoot him in the head.

I could understand the feeling.

"You wish for revenge? The most brutal kind of revenge. You want her pain and suffering to be avenged sevenfold?"

The Pres finally snapped out of it. He nodded slowly. We all wanted that, the entire Club. But especially the four of us.

The man in the t-shirt nodded. "I can give you that. I can give you the ability to exact revenge on all your enemies until they are buried so deep that no one will find them. And I will promise you that death will provide no relief for those you mark. You will be strong enough that they will all fear you and none will ever come for what you consider yours again."

Fire lit in the President's eyes, the first sign of life in them in days. Anger. I would take that over the god-awful blankness anyday.

"In return, you become mine for eternity. All four of you."

"What?" One of my Brothers whispered behind me.

The man didn't take his eyes off the President, and I didn't take my eyes off him. "I will give you power, money, whatever else it is that you desire. But more importantly, I will give you what you want most; the strength to never fail anyone again. Any of you."

"And you get what?" I asked, wanting what he was offering despite my gut churning. I wanted to be able to protect my Brothers-In-Arms. I wanted to be able to protect the Club Family. That was my job and so far, I had failed.

The man shrugged. "I get your souls." A chill swept through the air at his words. "You'll ride for me when I need you, but I can't see that happening in the near future. I have a lot to do before then."

"Yes," the Pres whispered.

"Yes," both of my Brothers behind me murmured into the fading light of the worst day of our lives.

Finally, the man looked at me, the depths of his gaze chilling me to my bones. But still I nodded. "Yes."

The man smiled. "Good. From today, you will no longer be who you were. You will no longer be the Punishers MC. You will no longer have your own names. You will be the beginning of the Damnation MC." I was mesmerized; I couldn't look away from him if I tried. My gun fell to the dirt as my hands went limp at my sides.

He reached past me so quickly I couldn't see his hands, placing his fingers on the chest of our Sergeant-In-Arms. "Goliath."

My Brother dropped to the ground like his bones were liquified, and I jumped away. My eyes whipped between them.

"Solomon." He did the same to the Captain, who went down in a heap. My eyes searched for signs of life and I let out the breath that had been caught in my throat when I saw their chests rise and fall.

He looked at me, and I stepped away. He didn't pursue me. I had a feeling I had to come into this willingly. "They aren't hurt. The swell of power just takes a while to settle into human bodies. Come forward, my Horseman." I stepped forward even though my feet tried to carry me away. He placed a hand on my chest. "Cain."

Something rolled through my body like a freight train, dropping me to my knees and then onto my back. I tried to stand, but it was like my body was paralyzed.

He stopped in front of the Pres, and I struggled to keep my eyes open. I needed to protect us.

"Judas. That is your name now. Own it. Revel in it. You will never feel weak again." Then the Pres was on the ground beside us, but awake like me. "Your sacrifice needs to be greater, Judas. It is always hardest being the leader." He leaned forward and pressed his thumb into the President's eye socket, popping out his eyeball like a grape. The Pres screamed and I roared as I struggled on the ground like a dying fish. The man waved a hand, and the Pres passed out.

"It's always an eye for an eye in these stories, no?" he said softly to me.

As my limbs came back online, I struggled to my knees. "Who?" I croaked out, but I already knew. I just needed to hear it before my mind shattered into a million pieces.

The man smiled, and it wasn't a pleasant expression. There was a flash of huge black wings splaying either side of his shoulders, gone so quickly that I wondered if I'd seen it at all. But when I drew my eyes back to his smiling face, I knew I had.

"You can call me Luc," he said softly, and then he disappeared.

Chapter One: Cain

Many years later

I couldn't help but look at the girl in the passenger seat, my hands flexing around the steering wheel as I drove down the freeway too fast. Judas was going to murder me; just put a gun to my head and paint my brains all over the Clubhouse walls. Wouldn't do much, but fuck it would hurt.

The girl, woman, whatever, slid her eyes to me, catching my gaze with her own violet ones. I swallowed hard and tried to ignore the bump of her stomach. Nah, Judas would take one look at her round belly and let me off the hook. He might be pissed that I'd agreed without consulting him or the rest of the guys, but he was a sucker for a woman in distress. We all were, after what happened to...

I snapped down my mental walls on that thought. This wasn't the past. We weren't who we were any longer. We were better able to protect the more vulnerable. Better able to close ourselves off to that emotional bullshit. I took the turnoff, pulling up behind a bar and strip club. On the other side of the lot was the Clubhouse. It had its own bar, with a bunch of rooms out back. That's where I'd take the woman. I'd get one of the Prospects to clean it something fierce, because let's face it, it had seen more bodily fluids than a fucking spank bank, but she'd be safe here.

A former customer had dropped her off like an abused puppy at Pestilence Tattoos, my shop in town. The redhead, Hope was her name, had come in once before looking like she'd been beaten half to death, and I'd wanted to rip the head off the pretty-boy she'd come in with, despite the fact that he had a real fucked up vibe that made the hair on my neck stand on end. But Hope apparently remembered, so when this woman, Serendipity, needed a place to stay, why not send her to your friendly local tattooist with a bad attitude? I don't know why she decided I was the safe option, considering I had so much blood on my hands that I could have painted the town red, but she'd taken one look at me and decided I was the good guy. She was wrong; I wasn't a good guy. But I'd never turn away a woman in trouble.

I couldn't fathom how Hope knew that, but she'd picked the right person.

I'd always been a sucker for a battered woman. Even before I'd joined the MC. Back when I was little and my father used to smack around Mom, it had broken something inside my head. Now, the idea of a man hitting a woman made me snap. I'd put my father in the ground, and joined my local chapter of the Punishers Outlaw MC. Then I'd loved a woman who'd had her life ripped away from her in the most brutal of ways, and my heart had died. Now, all that was left in my chest was the black lump that pumped with the near-demonic need for vengeance against those who would use women and children as pawns.

I wanted to punch myself in the head to chase away any thoughts of Laura. She was dead. A ghost. The only thing keeping her alive now was that guilt that infected my soul like the plague.

I got out, grabbing the woman's bag. *Serendipity. Not the woman*, I chastised myself. What kind of backwards, new age name was that anyway?

"Come on, we're gonna have to pass you staying here by the Pres, but I'm sure it'll be fine." I hope I sounded more self-assured than I felt.

Serendipity looked around, her eyes flicking between the strip club and the Clubhouse, and all the motorcycles in between.

"You're a biker?"

I raised an eyebrow as I passed her the tote bag with her stuff. "Will that be a problem?"

I desperately wanted to get on my bike and ride away from all the shit that seemed to be bubbling up inside me at the appearance of this chick, but I had to get her settled first.

"Cain, what the actual fuck, man?" Solomon appeared from nowhere, which was basically his superpower and his most annoying trait. I winced and turned, transforming my face into a menacing scowl.

It must have been a pretty good one because the woman backed up a step. "What the hell was I supposed to do? Some piece of ass came in, said this one was being stalked by some guy who knocked her up and what? I was just going to leave her there to be murdered by some psychotic asshole like–"

"I get it. Judas isn't going to be happy though."

Yeah, tell me something I didn't know. I nodded at Solomon, and he smiled at the woman. Serendipity. Shit, I had to start calling her by her name in my head. Solomon was a lady killer, and I was fairly sure he'd have her on her back with his face between her thighs before the night was through. He was tall, with golden hair like some kind of hair care model. Hell, he probably could have been a model if he wasn't such a cold blooded murderer. He had tattoo's up and down his arms, most of them compliments of me, and I was a badass fucking artist. He had a few scars, most from before our time at Damnation MC. "Hey, Sweet. I'm Solomon. And you are?" He gave her that Hollywood smile, but she didn't smile back.

"Sera," the woman said quietly, her eyes taking his measure. Not as a man, but as a threat. Whoever was stalking her had really done a number on her. "And Hope isn't a piece of ass. She's an angel and you won't speak of her that way." She was frowning, her eyes blazing intensely and I swear to fucking Satan, I got harder than a rock.

I looked over at Solomon, who had a shit eating grin on his face and a growing bulge in his pants, but I wasn't surprised. I liked my women feisty. Solomon just liked them breathing.

"No last name, Sera?" Solomon basically cooed. Geez. Women actually fell for this shit?

She shook her head. "Not for you."

I grinned, the expression reaching my eyes. Fuck yeah. Apparently, the woman was immune to Solomon's ability to charm a nun out of her panties. Solomon just grinned, smug bastard. Of course he'd see it as a challenge.

I thumped him on the arm. "Don't get excited, Douche. Still gotta pass it by Judas."

Solomon waived me away and grabbed Sera's tote bag. "Let me take that for you," he murmured. "Come this way. Judas is in his office. I'm not missing this for anything."

I rolled my eyes and waved Sera forward, following up the rear. Despite the fact she had to be three or four months pregnant, the woman was too thin. She had a big round baby belly, but I could see she was nothing more than skin and bones underneath her clothes. Her body was all but wasted.

Solomon pushed through the doors of the Clubhouse, and all conversation ground to an awkward halt. There were dozens of people in that bar, patched members and their old ladies, some sweet butts that were on their knees beneath tables. I placed my hand on Serendipity's lower back, trying to ignore the heat coming from her skin and the way her spine was beginning to curve into an amazing ass. She flinched but didn't step away, so I kept my hand there as I directed her past the bar to a long hallway down the back. At the very end of the hallway was the large room where we held Church. Just up from it was a heavily fortified door where Judas' office sat.

Solomon banged on the heavy door, and the grunted response from the other side had him pushing it open. Solomon threw me an amused look. "Hey Pres, your VP brought you a present." I was going to put my fist through his face next time I got the opportunity, just for being such a jackass. Still, I straightened my shoulders and pushed the girl into the room gently.

She froze in the doorway, the first sign of hesitancy I'd seen in her yet. So far, she's taken the whole thing in her stride with sass or stupidity, I wasn't sure which, but standing in front of the Pres was enough to make her quiver beneath my hand. Maybe she wasn't so stupid after all.

Judas was a scary man. After he'd had his eye plucked out, it had healed roughly and now he wore an eyepatch like a fucking pirate. Combined with the five o'clock shadow and his shaved head, the guy looked like a demon. The irony was real.

Amusingly enough, Judas looked just as stunned. I

didn't smile though. I liked my intestines where they were. Judas broke from his shock first, his stormy eye finding me and pinning me to the spot.

"What the hell is this? Get this bitch out of my office and back to wherever you picked her up from, Cain. We talked about this, no more strays."

He said that like I picked up women in desperate circumstances every day of the fucking week. I don't. Sometimes I offer the street kids a place to crash and get on their feet, but they work fucking hard for the Club. And never the girls. This was no place for a woman who wasn't an old lady or someone who wants to be passed around. But I made an exception for this woman. She needed us. I could feel it in my bones.

Apparently being called a bitch would knock the shock straight out of a person because Serendipity was no longer frozen. She was rigid with indignation. This was going to go south real quick. I put my hand around her forearm, shaking my head to deter her from whatever tirade she was about to launch to verbally shred our President. It wouldn't endear him any more to the idea of her staying. "You don't even want to hear me out?" I say softly, not keeping any of the disappointment from my voice. I loved Judas like a brother. Hell, he was my brother. More than that even. We were bound by something greater than blood or love or any other such existential bullshit.

Judas sighed, dropping his pen and standing up. As

he did so, I saw his whole body go rigid. He must have missed the rounded bulge of her stomach. I didn't blame him though, her face was pretty damn distracting. His one good eye shot to me, and there was a world of feeling in it for a moment before he shut it down. Yeah, bro. I'd been there. There had been a reason I couldn't say no despite the 'no more strays' mandate.

"Speak."

I rolled my eyes at his command, like I was a dog or something, but I let it slide. "Some piece–" Serendipity glared in my direction, "Uh, a customer from a few months ago brought her in. Real sweet kid. I told you about her and the blond guy who felt a little like someone from our past. Do you remember?" Judas nodded. "This customer, Hope, said that Serendipity needed our help."

The Pres switched his gaze to Serendipity. "So you decided to get in a car with a stranger who dragged you to a biker bar?" He raised his eyebrows. "Can't protect against stupid, Cain. Gotta have some self-preservation instincts to start with. Take her to a women's shelter somewhere."

Solomon's gaze was bouncing between the three of us like he was watching a train wreck, which he probably was. Serendipity growled. "I trust Hope's judgement and somehow she knows the giant has a good heart. She wouldn't have sent me with him otherwise. I trust that he doesn't hang around with the kind of person who rapes women and kills children." She lifted her chin, daring him to prove her wrong.

Judas' body was so rigid I worried he was going to snap. I edged a little closer to the girl, and noticed Solomon doing the same. Judas' jaw flexed as he got himself under control.

"Tell me."

She frowned, her nose screwing up in a way that was fucking adorable. "Tell you what?"

Judas crossed his arms over his chest and gave her a look that had made grown men piss themselves.

"Everything."

Want to read more? Available on Amazon and Kindle Unlimited: www.books2read.com/Dippy

www.ingramcontent.com/pod-product-compliance
Lightning Source LLC
Chambersburg PA
CBHW030234120726
47903CB00005B/1486